D1230597

Porcupine-Man

Other Books by *Sam Toperoff*

ALL THE ADVANTAGES
CRAZY OVER HORSES
PILGRIM OF THE SUN AND STARS

Porcupine-Man

SAM TOPEROFF

Saturday Review Press/E. P. Dutton & Co., Inc.
New York

Copyright © 1973 by Sam Toperoff

All rights reserved. No part of this work may be reproduced or transmitted in any form or by any means, electronic or mechanical, including photocopy, recording, or any information storage and retrieval system, without permission in writing from the publisher.

Published simultaneously in Canada by
Doubleday Canada Ltd., Toronto.

Library of Congress Catalog Card Number: 73–78916

ISBN: 0–8415–0285–4

PRINTED IN THE UNITED STATES OF AMERICA

To *Edgar Snow*—the man from Missouri who showed me

CONTENTS

PROLOGUE
Curtain Time

The Allies had won the war. The survivors wanted the peace they thought they deserved. There existed, unfortunately, the extremely unpleasant task of telling them that the Allies weren't really allies and that peace would not be quite the Peace for which most of those "supreme sacrifices" had been made.

Blame had to be assessed for the new hostilities; a new terminology was required to simplify and to make a rotten situation that had been denied for years crystal clear. Red had to be painted Black, convincingly. A marriage of convenience had to be publicly annulled without a scandal. Distinctions that didn't even exist a few years earlier had to be made into irresolvable antagonisms of the deepest sort. A new war that wasn't actually a war had to be announced to people tired and sick of the old one. Survival was again at stake so soon after survival had been won.

So it mattered terribly how to let the people know. Their misconceptions might prove fatal in the long struggle of wills. Proper words. Proper tone. Proper time. Proper place. Proper man. The future of Freedom as we have known it since Greece; nothing less was at stake.

Only one man for the task. Only one man great enough to pull it off. Roosevelt dead, and even some question if he would have seen the antagonistic forces clearly at the end. No, only one man for the task. Only one man with the words, the style, the reputation. Churchill would come to Missouri. He was seventy-two in 1946. Although at war's end, as he himself had written, "I was immediately dismissed by the British electorate from all further conduct of their affairs," he was still the only man of real moment.

Harry S Truman, the thirty-third President of the United States, was accepted as Vice-President on the ticket by F.D.R. at the '44 convention with more reluctance than historians generally recognize, but this is not the important fact. He *was* accepted and became President on April 12, 1945. On May 12 of that same year, the Prime Minister of England had sent a telegram to the new President in Washington using the phrase "Iron Curtain" for the first time. The two men agreed to meet inconspicuously on the world's stage; President Truman would introduce Churchill, and the former Prime Minister would, in turn, introduce the new hostilities.

We cannot know exactly how the announcement in Missouri was planned or who actually conceived it. Tactically and psychologically it was a touch of absolute genius. Winston Churchill had a face that reminded some of a brave bulldog and others of an uncomfortable infant, but he was regarded by all sane men as the last, best hope for freemankind. And in Missouri, of all places; certainly the Ruskies wouldn't miss the significance of that.

Westminster College, Fulton, Missouri: a small, Presbyterian liberal arts school with 481 undergraduates, sitting like a well-tended garden in a wheat field, renowned for nothing, but quite adequate in tennis, debate, and the humanities. One hundred and fifty miles east of Independence, and the education capital of Calloway County, population, 7,106.

The trustees of the college had been made to believe that if they invited the former Prime Minister of England to receive an honorary Doctor of Laws degree, he would not only accept but would even make a little speech. And bring his friend the President.

Unlike the Lieutenant Governor of Kansas, who had spoken at Westminster the previous year, Winston Churchill was not given a tour of the town or the college buildings, and he certainly did not request one. It was mutually understood that this was a business trip. Also, he was not in the best of health. The winter had taken its toll and what he called an old war wound in his leg began acting up on the flight over, in addition to which he had become increasingly dyspeptic as a result of the criticism of him that had appeared in English papers since the Second World War's apparent end.

He had composed his speech in his mind at the time when his public appearance had been confirmed. He worked as he always had; that is, by listing quite coldly all the forces that were at play, the favorable changes he wished to produce, and the objections that the average, sentient Englishman might have. Then he sought the precise tone that such a man would listen to, not be persuaded by but merely listen to. That tone was not easily achieved because it was always the resultant harmony of diverse and often dissonant chords. So his very best speeches really were nothing more than a searching for the harmony that eventually would emerge in the end. To achieve and maintain this incredibly fine line required that he become deeply, emotionally involved in the dissonance, so he was always irritable when trying to change the world for the better. The wonderful phrases that the world remembered were nothing more than the distillation of those evasive forces and the rendering of the harmony into words. The

Fulton, Missouri, speech would be replete with such phrases.

Two premises, though, and those two quite reasonable: first, the average, sentient Englishman had his counterparts the world over; second, such a man could take bad news constructively only if it were delivered with a stiff upper lip straight from the shoulder, *and* in the proper tone. Although we are waiting for a final determination of the validity of those premises, Winston Churchill never had a doubt.

The train carrying Mr. Churchill and the President from Washington arrived in Jefferson City, the state capital, shortly after midnight. In the company were some men from Whitehall, a few friends of long standing, Harry S Truman's secretary, and three State Department officials. None of the Englishmen brought their wives to Missouri. They had not been left home; rather, they chose not to make the train ride. Most of them opted for New York. Mrs. Churchill elected to remain at Chartwell. There would be an open limousine ride before Jefferson City's throng and a brief one through Fulton; there was a considerable bite in the early March wind.

After the initial agony of having to find a way to make the unpalatable acceptable and to make the enemy reconsider the cost of his strategy, after realizing once again in his heart that the course of history was not inevitable, and after reconfirming the value and worth of Anglo-Saxon enterprise (something his detractors would say was axiomatic in the man), after considerable effort and difficult self-appraisal, the tone came suddenly and the words served it willingly. It would be a speech that said, "We have been betrayed but no damage has been done yet so I am telling you to be careful and not expect the world we would have had if the betrayers hadn't deceived us." With overtones of, "We are all on to you fellows now so why don't you give it up."

The key phrases had been in that great head for years;

and other, harsher ones, too. But there was no need to say tough things right out—a bulldog had been flown to Missouri, U.S.A.; certainly those "fellows" would know the dog wasn't merely growling.

The finishing touches had been done on the flight over. One serious problem remained: whether or not to use the word "war." The newspapers would certainly pick it up. The fine line might be broken. He changed "cold war" to "cold conflict"; then he changed it back again. He thought about a "frozen armistice" and a "bellicose peace." Settling again on "cold war," he determined to make certain the phrase would not be dissected, that the "cold" would so modify the "war" that a new, a less frightening blend would hit those sentient minds.

Breakfast on the train was jovial. The President, after a long, intellectually exhausting discussion with Churchill into the wee hours, decided to forego it in favor of an extra hour's sleep. "A shame," Winston told the man from State, "that Herr Hitler is not around to see your haberdasher; God, what subject matter for that lewd mind." The voice was the one parodied by comedians when they croaked, "If I were any more British, I wouldn't be able to speak at all." The White House staff had not provided kippers, and the best the cook could do with poached eggs was a glutinous approximation. Churchill held forth. Still in control of his realm even though out of office, and his ungrateful children still enjoyed his protection. Unless one allowed oneself to think of a pink complexion as a physiognomical sign of a weak, carefree disposition, the expression of manly strength was unmistakable. But the mood was light, almost gay; no, not the nervous gaiety of a strong man full of doubts. Rather, the relief before the final, least difficult stage of an arduous task.

"The world, you see, assumes the largest, most profound explanations for things. So when at Yalta I am shown in photographs looking warily at Comrade Stalin, the world assumes a political motive when in fact the man had just expelled quite the most noxious odor ever to come from a head of state—of course, I take anatomical liberties." A good laugh all around. Too good a laugh, actually. There were many others throughout the day, as the former Prime Minister saw fit to tell anecdotes about the crises of his lifetime: Smuts and the Boer War; Gallipoli; Selassie in Ethiopia; his role in the General Strike; Munich and Teheran and his problems with de Gaulle. Everything, constantly. He had not smoked a cigar the entire day.

If you had not known that the man running on between spoonfuls of poached egg was the "Man of the Century," his physical presence would have been comic. White hair that fringed a large, asymmetrical skull was uneven in length and whimsical in direction. The eyes were surrounded by wrinkles and pouches of flesh; like a pool covered with lily pads, the liquid eyes seemed to come and go with changes of the breeze. The face was fleshy and cheerful. Tiny red capillaries, which spread like a spidery web from cheek to cheek on a path across his nose, seemed from a few paces away the dabs of an expert clown. Add to the appearance the animated manner of an excited boy, and you have one of Tolstoy's foolish cuckolds, not the Right Honorable Winston Leonard Spencer Churchill, P.C., C.H., T.D., M.P.

A huge bedsheet hung from the Science Building across from the Auditorium. Unfortunately, Churchill did not get to see its message, for the limousine deposited him and the President at the stage door in the rear. Its phraseology anticipated both his purpose and Mr. Truman's reelection campaign. It read: "GIVE 'EM HELL, WHINNY!" Its sentiment and quaint, colonial flavor would have pleased him without a doubt; the misspelling would not.

The afternoon had been overcast and now a sharper wind blew in from the western plains. Farmers expected a storm.

The limousine was met by the president, Dr. Franc Lewis McCluer, and the provost of Westminster College. Their wives wore clashing purple and blue coats. Winston got none of their names. Some faculty were introduced; some students. The custodian of the building, standing on a scaffold and dressed in a brown wool suit with the cuffs of his pants tucked in his overshoes, flashed Mr. Churchill a victory sign with his fingers, but it was not returned. The celebrated visitor was himself the apex of a "V," with the other officials, Harry S Truman included, trailing backward as the arms. At his request, he was shown to a small room in which he studied his speech one final time in silence. This quietude was broken only once, by the chairman of the Westminster Faculty—a Professor Levin or Blevin—who clumsily deposited Winston's robe and cap and then backed awkwardly through the doorway.

He read the speech through very quickly. And, then, impetuously, penned out all references to a "cold war." "The term will certainly be in use soon enough," he thought, "but I will not be the man to issue it." The deletions necessitated other changes—transitions, transpositions, emendations—and these he made with surety. The harmony seemed right; his speech was ready for delivery.

Harry S Truman entered shortly thereafter. The men discussed travel accommodations and the weather. The storm, it now seemed, would hold off for another day or two.

A knock on the door that Churchill did not answer, followed by a stronger one which he did. "Ee-ess?"

A cracked childish voice: "Procession starting very soon, your majesty. Help with your robes?"

"Come in, then."

He did not, at his own request, lead the processional. Trustees and Administrators and Faculty did that. He and the President of the United States were prominently inconspicuous about a fifth of the way along. He limped bravely through a reedy "Pomp and Circumstance" to the stage and looked at the wide-eyed, whispering assemblage of students and relatives. It was not the bright face of the young, well-educated and -bred, albeit somewhat cocky, back-bencher from Oldham that showed itself to the Missouri congregation.

The Westminster College Orchestra played "God Save the Queen" and "The Star Spangled Banner" as a medley, with a gliding shift from the former to the latter performed as smoothly as the organ music at any roller rink. Only trouble was the tempo, just a trifle slow, and Winston began to feel the strain just about the time "proof" was coming "through the night." He tried to distribute weight more evenly, but his legs wouldn't handle the adjustment. His discomfort showed clearly on his face, but it was generally taken for the deepest sort of patriotic reverence. The thoughts that enabled him to endure the ordeal were of Deauville and the tranquillity that would be his when the round of postwar honors was over.

The president of Westminster College introduced the President of the United States. A standing ovation. Harry S Truman wore the hood indicating the honorary Doctor of Laws conferred on him the previous summer by the University of Kansas City; Mr. Churchill wore a scarlet hood indicating an Oxford degree. The President of the United States introduced private citizen Churchill. He did it with that characteristic and peculiar combination of stiff informality that was his greatest asset as a politician. When he later called a music critic an s.o.b., most Americans knew it to be the paternal anger of a good, straight, God-fearing man. Never any harm intended, really.

In his brief introduction the President talked about something that both he and the former Prime Minister valued very highly; namely, freedom of speech. It was a pity that this great gift was not so highly valued by all people all over the world, but perhaps that would not always be the case. Perhaps someday all men would value what he and the former Prime Minister valued. He preferred, this afternoon, to let Mr. Churchill exercise that wonderful gift of ours, adding finally, "I know he will have a few constructive things to say."

Before Churchill stood up and came forward, the crowd was on its feet cheering. It was he, the newsreel and cartoon face, right here in Fulton. Even the reporter from the *Sun-Gazette* who had interviewed Alf Landon in 1936 lost his objectivity and his pencil in the rush of emotion. Winnie flashed some victory signs to the crowd, whose heritage, by the way, was primarily Germanic; and they responded with countersigns and shouts of "Bravo" and "Good Show." After almost two minutes, the speaker's eyes emerged clearly from the wrinkles; they requested silence, and it became silent. He placed a pair of spectacles far down his nose and touched his bow tie with both his hands.

In that red hood he looked like a bulky ex-prizefighter; the cherubic face might have seemed incongruous if one did not think of Michael, the warrior angel. "I am glad," he said slowly, so his audience could get used to his peculiar manner of speaking, "to come to Westminster College this afternoon, and am complimented that you should give me a degree." There, they could measure themselves on that sentence before he slowly began to pick up the cadence. Even in the rear of the balcony they could hear him quite clearly. They had been primed; now for the joke. "The name 'Westminster' is somehow familiar to me." The large head was thrust forward over the text and it did not move, but the eyes emerged slowly above the glasses, they focused on the rear ceiling. "I seem to have heard of it before." The laughter was accompanied by nods and smiles in most cases.

He said, "The Dark Ages may return. . . . Beware, I say! Time may be short . . ." and all the smiles came off. The sentence, "A shadow has fallen upon the scenes so lately lighted by the Allied victory," kept the smiles off. When he said, "There is deep sympathy and good will in Britain— and I doubt not here also—toward the peoples of all the Russias . . .," they all could sense who the betrayers were. When he said, "It is my duty, however, for I am sure you would wish me to state the facts as I see them to you, to place before you certain facts about the present postion in Europe," it was wartime Winnie giving the Sentient Everyman the bad news straight from the hip and shoulder.

Then he went right to the heart of the matter: "From Stettin in the Baltic to Trieste in the Adriatic, an iron curtain has descended across the Continent. Behind that line lie all the capitals of the ancient states of central and eastern Europe. Warsaw, Berlin, Prague, Vienna, Budapest, Bucharest, and Sophia, all these famous cities and the populations around them lie in what I must call the Soviet sphere, and all are subject in one form or another, not only to Soviet influence, but to a very high and, in many cases, increasing measure of control from Moscow. Athens alone —Greece with its immortal glories—is free to decide its future at an election under British, American, and French observation."

Twenty seconds later, the simple solution: "From what I have seen of our Russian friends and Allies during the war, I am convinced that there is nothing they admire so much as strength, and there is nothing for which they have less respect than weakness, especially military weakness. For that reason the old doctrine of a balance of power is unsound. We cannot afford, if we can help it, to work on narrow margins, offering temptations to a trial of strength."

There was a caveat to the people of Missouri and the Soviet leaders: "Let no man underrate the abiding power of the British Empire and Commonwealth." And a warning of what might happen if this speech, which Churchill had entitled "The Sinews of Peace," was not heeded: "Last

time I saw it all coming and cried aloud to my fellow countrymen and to the world, but no one paid any attention.
. . . There never was a war in all history easier to prevent by timely action than the one which has just desolated such great areas of the globe." This time he would be heard, damn it! Harry S Truman was all ears. Either men had become more sentient after a bloody decade, or Winston Churchill's voice carried better.

After Mr. Churchill had finished and received prolonged and grateful applause, Mr. Truman added a few words; the most meaningful, to most of our lives, turned out to be these: "It is your moral duty and mine to see that the Charter of the United Nations is implemented as the law of the land and the law of the world."

An epoch had formally begun. The President and the former Prime Minister embraced each other on the stage to the applause and cheers of the students, faculty, and friends of Westminster College.

This stupendous man still had to look forward to the completion of his six-volume history of the Second World War, reelection to the office of Prime Minister, knighthood, the Nobel Prize for Literature (and Oratory), and some quiet days on the beach at Deauville.

PART I

ROCK-BOTTOM

1

Years of the Stork

His strength was not the sort that might belong to an ox or a bull, and he did not even have the persistent tenacity of a hunting dog. He had the sudden violence of a large, enraged bird. Even in the pads and tight-fitting uniform, his sloping shoulders and stiff-jointed movements were unmistakable. "Stork" became his nickname.

"Stork" Collier did not start the first game of the year against Parkersburg; as a matter of pure fact, he was not then even called the Stork. He wasn't really called anything at all. Most of his teammates and Coach Crowder didn't even know his name; it was just a matter of "Hey, Ninety-seven, get in there for Pruitt, they're running through him like he was a pin-up girl's pussy." Then he smacked Eugene Collier, Jr., on the back of the leather helmet and propelled him on to the field. Pruitt was on his knees growling and swearing when Eugene arrived and pointed back over his shoulder toward the coach, who waved his starting tackle-turned-pussy off the field. The look of rage and hatred that Pruitt showed Eugene would have been unforgettable to anyone else, but when Eugene Collier, Jr., first became the Stork, he carried very few memories with him.

The transformation from Jr. to Stork began on the very first play that Parkersburg ran against Pleasants. Naturally it was a run at Eugene. Coach Crowder, with narrowed eyes and a hand over the bill of his green cap, conceived the play long before the Parkersburg quarterback saw it as the logical possibility. It was 97's job to get the competitive juices flowing in the peevish Pruitt, nothing more. As Eugene Collier, Jr., dug in, he thought of nothing. He was slow in reacting to the snap of the ball; the Parkersburg end missed his block, merely brushed Eugene's outside shoulder and fell with a grunt flat on his face. At this moment the Stork was born. Eugene rose up full, elbows and knees churning, stiff-striding toward the sidelines, a high-pitched screech coming involuntarily from his throat. Compact, muscular Parkersburg blockers struck him and dropped heavily, as though felled by an invisible weapon. The tackle he made five yards behind the line of scrimmage was a freakish thing, a monstrous act of genuine worth to football coaches. Stork Collier had shriveled momentarily only to explode in the path of the man-child in the orange jersey who was too confident to be surprised by the shock of such rapidly expanding limbs.

"Fumble. Fumble, get on it, Chrissakes," yelled Coach Crowder, his voice as shrill as his new tackle's had been moments before. Billy Ames rushed up and fell on it for Pleasants High.

"Son, you play that position like a wild old stork protecting her babies' nest," the coach said during his halftime visit with the player who had turned a tough game around, the one who could benefit most from his encouragement. The coach also knew full well the competitive effect on those he chose to overlook.

Pruitt, of course, was finished. After the Elizabeth City game he didn't suit up anymore; shortly after that no one noticed him in school. If anyone missed him, they were publicly silent in their sorrow. Eugene Collier, Jr., a tall sophomore from over in Hundley, previously friendless and unseen in every aspect of life at Pleasants High, became Stork Collier, visible around the gym and more often in Coach Crowder's trophy-filled office. Seen with packs of boys in green jackets, lettered in gold on the backs, "PLEASANTS HIGH—1946—FOOTBALL." Seen by his teachers behind the rear desk of classrooms with a vacant look on his long face, sleepiness reflected in the eyes, legs stretching far down each aisle. Seen perhaps eating a sandwich in the bathroom, or in other unlikely places. Always unseen by girls—even the ugly ones—because Billy Ames, Tater Tate, Timmy Clements, J. D. Bryan, and even Jimmy Arnold were the only fit objects for every coed's fantasies. Barely visible on the bus to and from Hundley; no other football players traveled on that one; all the activity, game-playing, and teasing taking place up front while the Stork sprawled across the rear seat.

Even though the championship game was a real event, and would be played at night, under the lights at Memorial Field in Charleston, the state capital, none of the other Colliers planned to see Eugene play.

"It's for the championship of the entire state of West Virginia," explained Crowder slowly and carefully so that the full importance of the statement would have a chance to root itself in this simple family. When he had driven up to the house on Mine Road No. 1, they were not quite as pleased by his friendliness as he had expected them to be. They were kind to him, of course; the soup was hot, if not thick, the stew was a display of gratefulness.

Ben Crowder had come to show the Colliers his concern for their Stork; to cement a winning relationship between himself and a potential football star; to reconfirm the fact that he himself had avoided working in the mines for another year. This last was his truest motivation. He needed these mine families, for it was from them that his players came. He required their existence, their toil, their misfortunes for his success and sense of well-being. This was the coach's third visit of the evening; he planned to work his way back toward Pleasants.

The small kitchen was crowded with heavy women and tall men. Ben Crowder was neither heavy nor tall. He was a spare man in his early forties with a finely shaped fringe of light brown hair that rounded the most perfectly shaped cranium in the mountains; because of it and his clean hands, his most commonly attributed characteristic was intelligence. The constantly narrowed eyes appeared to support the judgment of intelligence but also revealed an insatiable hunger to the seeker. That which Crowder could not feed on immediately was stored away in that cranium for future nourishment. This year he wanted to taste the State Championship, and soon after he would be offered something at the university. His reputation throughout the state as a football coach was good; only one criticism, and that from purists: His teams had never gone all the way. Perhaps some of those same careful observers of his eyes detected his real limitation: Pleasants High had winning teams not because Crowder produced cohesion or instituted a successful system; they won because he tapped a hunger in big, strong mountain boys and made them feed on each other. "He produces great players, not great teams," was how Ed Lambert, the reporter, put it in the *Speculator* last year. To give the coach his due, he had an unerring eye for talent. Tonight he was visiting with the Colliers.

Coach Crowder was in the place of honor at the head of the small table. Behind him and facing the window was a large, untidy old lady, Grandma Gossett, the Stork's mother's mother; she was stone deaf and occupied herself with mending most of the time. She was sewing heels on stockings. Her daughter, Hildy Gossett Collier, even taller, heavier, and more untidy than her mother, stood over the stove stirring what appeared to be a pudding, but the strong smell was more pungent than pleasant, causing Coach Crowder to say, "Ma'am, that sure is a sweet-smellin' concoction you're makin' there." She was not flattered and did not respond. The whispers and giggles of girl children were heard from other corners of the house.

Stork Collier was seated at the kitchen table with a book before him; its pages wanted to close from habitual disuse, but a knife and fork, placed on the margins, held them open. Gene Collier, the father, was seated in a small rocking chair near the hearth. He was a tall, awkward man, a good deal fuller in the chest and shoulders than his son, but also more stooped. If you looked carefully, you could see a pale young stork overgrown with flesh and a gray-dappled, leather skin. A knowing eye could discern that he had gone to the mines fairly late in his life, in fact, not until after his thirtieth year.

The scene was unusual only in one respect. Usually, it was Gene Collier who was reading at the head of the table and the son who was folded into the small rocker. And the father's books did not have to be coerced into being read.

Coach Crowder had declined a seat at first, believing that his announcement—"I want you all to be my guests at the championship game. And that means *everythin'*. Transportation both directions. My brother Charlie will be drivin' a busload down. Well stocked, if you know what I mean. And I'm invitin' you all personally"—would have been sufficient. After all, he did have some other stops to make. Then from out of nowhere he pulled that pint of rye whiskey, and what else had to be said?

"Young Gene can do whatever he wants to do, Mr. Crowder." The father's voice was very tired. "He's of age, as far as I'm concerned. If he makes wrong choices, well, there's always the mines, isn't there? He seems to have taken a fancy to football."

At precisely this moment the old lady lost the thread from the needle's eye. "Damn-ole-shit," she said all at once, and with an involuntary jab of her tongue took back the spittle that had fallen onto her chin. The laughter of little girls was heard clearly now from behind a door.

" . . . he's pretty good at it from what I've heard. But that's his business. We can't go truckin' all over watchin' him playin' at games."

It was at this moment Coach Crowder decided to stay for dinner: "Ma'am, that sure is a sweet-smellin' concoction you're makin' there."

The soup was tasteless, the thicker stew was better, and the hot pudding was thickest and best of all. No bread and no conversation. Blowing, sucking, and chewing. The re-pressed squeals of the girls—nine-year-old twins—and the shushing of their mother were the only irrelevant sounds. The small table and cramped quarters required that the diners alternate as they came forward to partake, almost like typewriter keys; occasionally they jammed. Supper over, the women cleared the table and disappeared—God knows where—leaving the kitchen and the rye whiskey to the men.

Coach Crowder opened the bottle and passed it to the senior Collier who swigged from it silently, eyes on the ceiling, and moved it in front of the coach. Crowder cleaned off the top with a fisted hand and began to bring it up to his mouth. All eyes were on the small bottle. Crowder leaned forward and put his elbow on the table edge; he deliberately placed the bottle down a long arm's length away. "I've got somethin' to confess to you two men." His eyelids fell. "I've come here with a secret motive, and I just can't go on a-foolin' you like I have. Truth is I'm askin' you to go to the game not only because it's Pleasants' chance to win the football championship of the state, or even because I want you to have the chance to see your wonderful son play the game. No, there's other reasons, more selfish reasons." At this moment a creaking sound was heard from another part of the house; Crowder's eyes darted toward it. The Collier men looked steadily at him. Then the coach continued: "You see, Mr. Collier, I believe your son is goin' to become a very fine, a *very*, very fine football player. Matter of fact, I predict that coaches will be comin' from colleges all over the South to *re*cruit that son of yours. If you think he's been a-wastin' his time in school, you had better just think again."

The Stork's eyes widened and flashed to the far corner of the room; his father squeezed his nostrils between darkened thumb and forefinger and blew out—mostly air. "It happens that I'm bein' considered for the head coachin' job at the West Virginia University, and I want you to remember me when I come back in a couple of years with a scholarship in my pocket askin' for your son."

Gene Collier asked two smart questions: "If you ain't got the job yet, how's come you're makin' all these plans? Who'll be payin' for this here trip?"

Ben Crowder gave brilliant answers: "I've got confidence we'll win the title, Mr. Collier. Your son has All-American written all over him already, and I'm tellin' you he'll never have to set foot down one of them mine shafts for the rest of his life. And maybe not you, either."

The coach took his leave quietly without having put lips to bottle and without further contact with the ladies. The Collier men eyed each other steadily across the table. Finally the Stork looked away.

What had happened was this: Eugene Collier, Sr., had been given a reason to reverse his already deep skepticism of men who had schemes to keep youngsters out of the mines. Eugene Collier, Jr., understood the value of knocking other boys down on a football field for the first time. The women had listened from behind doors with the respect due men's business. Ben Crowder had cast out his line, but he had other fish to catch this night.

Everything he had said was a coach's truth. The job at the university was his, the outcome of next week's game notwithstanding. The Stork did indeed have the ability to play football for the next ten or fifteen years of his life for fame and money and personal satisfaction.

Crowder was off to the home of Tater Tate, a boy with the arm, if not the brains, to bring West Virginia University and Coach Crowder to national prominence.

Before the women emerged from the other room, the father folded his large, blunted fingers on the table before him—the hands were those of a toiler. He said, "Son, if you really do believe that college story, I reckon I ought to see you begin to pick up a book around here once in a while."

"Okay, Paw."

It almost seemed like the reversal of some great natural force when the head of Ben Crowder with a pork-pie hat on it squeezed through the door again and announced: "Mr. Collier, I know you don't have no reason to believe all I've told you here tonight, but I'd like you to give me the benefit of the doubt as a Christian and a gentleman, least 'til I give you some actual reason for doubtin' me." As quickly as it had reentered, the head disappeared.

Collier, Sr., was a man who could think a thought and move a stone, but he realized that there were forces in life that did not yield to reason or exertion. They would take people wherever they wished; they would leave them when they were good and ready. And then there would be other forces to continue the process. He remembered two consecutive days and nights on the town in Paris, France, back in 1919. He remembered vividly the rainy day he opened an ice cream parlor over in Pleasants. And the sunny day he closed it down. And how lucky he was to get a job in the mines when no one was getting jobs anywhere—a favor of one of his father's friends. Forces which not only carried you along, picked you up and put you down, but also worked like some grinding machine, so that your body, especially your face, just wasn't the same when the grinding machine was through with you—hair or teeth or eyes or everything all at once. Yes, picked him up in an ice cream parlor over in Pleasants all white and clean and set him down dirty in the Hill and Guinan Bituminous Coal Company in Hundley, West Virginia. He guessed that someone could be lucky, somewhere, but never considered any of his offspring in that hypothetical possibility; and if ever the good word did happen to come, it wouldn't be from the likes of Ben Crowder with his fancy car and his darting, beady eyes.

The son's face was a freer version of the father's. The same trapezoid served for both, with the dark hair cut in the same stark, no-nonsense line by Mrs. Collier. Large ears stuck out prominently, not exactly jug-handles in either case, but closer to it in the father. Long thin lips turned down slightly on both. Noses that broke downward acutely enough to be considered beaks. And watery eyes, very dark, very large, and set wide apart. All the constituents the same, and yet on the father there was a settled quality that manifested itself in the jut of the jaw and the weary, almost mournful quality of the gaze. It was an immobile face. The son's lips suggested the glint of a smile, the eyes were usually rounded, and the hands of a child often ranged over the face absently creating new contours. There was no way to know if the tuft of hair that stuck up straight on the back of both heads was due to heredity or to Hildy's haircuts, but the point was purely academic—it was the same tuft on both heads.

"We're not goin' down to Charleston, and maybe we're wrong. If you believe there is a chance for you, well then, take it. But if you want me to believe it too, Gene, then I've got to ask you to prove it to me with them books."

"I said I would, Paw."

The men shared the same true shyness.

Pleasants High lost the championship game to Stenneton. Through no fault of Coach Crowder. Ahead by a point, 7–6, with one minute to play in the first half and under strict orders from the coach to run out the clock, Tater decided on his own to try a surprise pass. Well, J. D. fell down going out and one of Stenneton's little defensive backs picked the ball off and went right down the sideline without anyone coming within five yards of him. Except for Tater, who missed the tackle. Pleasants lost it 12–7.

The Stork remembered almost nothing of the game. He knew he had played well; there were indications—Stenneton didn't run a single play to his side of the field throughout the second half. Even though they all had whiskey breaths, the disgruntled men who had come down on the bus from Pleasants were sober enough to single Collier out for genuine praise after the game. It was the first time the Stork ever played on a losing team, and the truth was it didn't feel too bad. Mostly, the disappointment he wore was to meet his teammates' expectations. A lot of the guys were competitive in their grief: Tater was crying so hard he couldn't catch his breath; J. D. pounded the wall until his knuckles bled; Billy Ames tore the leather straps off his shoulder pads. Stork said, "Goddamn, goddamn" whenever someone came around who seemed to need his sense of loss confirmed.

But the memories of the evening—the success of forcing an early fumble, the strangeness of playing in artificial light with the grotesque faces in shadowed perspective—were all but forced out by Coach Crowder's behavior. Three things: his pregame talk, his half-time display, and his postgame reaction. "Boys," he had said in the cavernous locker room before the game, "no, let me start over again. Men, this is the most important day in the history of Pleasants High. But that don't matter. Everyone knows what the State

Championship means, so I don't have to get you all excited and aroused. In my opinion you're ready for this game. Matter of fact, I'd just like you all to calm down a bit, just go on out there and have fun, but play your game. That's the point, men, the real point. This is *your* game. *Yours.* I don't want you thinkin' about winnin' this football game for anyone other than yourselves. Not for me. Not for your girl friends. Not for the school or the town. Just go on out there and relax and play *your* ball game for *yourselves.* J. D., how about you sayin' the prayer tonight?" A tight circle of boys and men had formed beneath the bare light bulb; band music drifted through the concrete walls; and the Stork had become angry with himself for thinking, at the moment of deepest spirituality, of the lyrics, "Oh the monkey wrapped his tail around the flagpole."

At half-time everyone was averting his eyes, especially Tater. Guys just sprawled all over the floor. The assistant coach looking at a clipboard and mumbling. But no Crowder. Then a round of nervous coughs. Then some whispered questions. Then the earliest sensations of fear. Finally, in through the big metal door came the coach, flushed and as wild as a fighting cock. "Listen up, you bastards. For a while I was gonna just wash my hands of this team, if you call it a team. Let you stew in your own juices. Since you don't seem to know what the hell a coach is for anyway, I thought to myself, okay, then, let 'em get on without one. Don't matter what I tell you nohow." And then he smiled sarcastically and seemed about to give a few words of encouragement, but no. "Tater, what the hell you tryin' to do to me? Eh, boy? You tryin' to take that job at the university away from me all by yourself, that what's in that head of yours? Well, listen, you don't even have to wait. Here, take my wallet di-rect." He threw a black leather wallet at Tater; some cards fell out. "Here, take my money." Quarters, dimes, a half dollar, and a crumpled dollar bill were hurled against the locker above Tate's head. "My car? Here, Tater, take the goddamned keys to that; you're takin' everythin' else I ever worked for. Make me sick, all of you. I tell you, I don't care what the hell you do out there this half, I'm through with you." And he stomped off to the latrine and took a long piss in the silence. A long piss. No one had ever seen such a display. No one knew what to do. Everyone was searching for a lead. Stork thought it was sort of funny, but he was certain he was wrong. A knock on the door: "C'mon, Pleasants, second half. On the double." Ben Crowder faced the corner and breathed deeply. Genuine fear and confusion in the room. The leader whirled. "All right, you selfish bastards, let's get the hell out there and knock heads. A touchdown'll win it. Tater, goddamn your ass, you owe me one; now let's get it quick." A primitive whoop—the instant transformation of fear into hope—one of the few things that never left the Stork's memory. The second half was a complete stalemate played between thirty-five yard lines.

Coach Crowder was not seen after the game. Anywhere. By anyone. It was explained at school, first, that the coach needed a week or so to rest up . Then it was announced that he was taking the head coaching job at West Virginia University. But no farewell, no testimonial dinner. Some said there just wasn't enough true sentiment for one. Others said he didn't want anything. The Stork didn't think he'd ever see Ben Crowder again.

Stork Collier was at Pleasants High for two more years. Girls smiled at him occasionally but their smiles were unreturned, for the Stork assumed his ugliness and loneliness were permanent conditions of his life. It was many years before he learned that being ugly, or believing you were ugly, was very much subject to change.

In his free time he felled trees and sold firewood cheaply to anyone who could cart it away. He charged around three dollars a cord; if he could have delivered it, he'd have gotten almost double. A lot of boys chopped wood, but

Gene was the best; he had the best temperament for it, had the stroke and stroke and stroke mentality that brought down all trees, that produced more uniform stove-lengths than anyone. And a long, sinewy angular strength that met the trees on more equal terms than any of the boys and most of the men in the valley.

At the beginning of his senior year, Stork Collier had still not ever read a book through from cover to cover. His father pretty much wrote him off. Ben Crowder had moved on to Morgantown, and still the Stork's greatest success in the world had been knocking down other boys on a football field, which he continued to do with ever greater skill. In his junior year he was second-string All-State. Ed Lambert wrote in the *Speculator:* "Stork Collier, from over in Hundley, looks to be the best young lineman to come out of these hills since the late Earl Plumb, who was killed in Normandy in '44."

In 1949 Stork Collier, at the ripening age of eighteen, was two inches taller than his father (the boy was 6' 4"), a good deal less cynical, every bit as tight-lipped. He was just about as ignorant of the world beyond the valley—its past, its patterns, and its powers—as any other West Virginia mountain boy. The process that changed most of these conditions (his height being the only exception) and a great many others was begun by a small, red-haired woman who was the new senior English teacher at Pleasants High. Her name was Mrs. Phoebe Philpotts. She was just about five feet tall, freckled, finely boned, small-breasted, coldly efficient, and thirty-three years old; she was also bright-eyed, hot-tempered, worldly, and mysterious. In other words, she embodied for the first time in Stork's experience a range of diverse human possibilities. She was kinetic energy in an entropic system; the embodiment of potential set against a community of people being wrung out by forces they could not even recognize. Only because she had something the Stork wanted was she his temptress. Of course

Stork felt the temptation on many levels at once and understood none of them. The only thing he could possibly compare it to was when he first noticed a brown man up real close. He was four or five years old and was sitting right next to him on the steps of Mr. King's Notions Store. He remembered distinctly wanting to pet the wrinkled skin, to cuddle the whole head to him, and even wishing that he himself could be brown-skinned. When he told his folks, his father smiled and his mother blew some hair out of her eyes and said, "That's just about all I'd ever need."

Mrs. Philpotts was mysterious to anyone in Pleasants who had an eye for mystery. No one knew where she lived; she arrived at school in a shiny new Ford every morning. Or if she had a husband and kids. She was a Mrs. who didn't act like any of the other Mrs. at Pleasants. She had two great passions—Shakespeare and China—which she mentioned in every English class regardless of the assigned subject and topic. And you could just see that she never planned to bring them up; she'd be trying to make something clearer or to explain something or other and would take an example from Shakespeare or the way China used to be and a look would begin to come over her face, her eyes would get a far-away stare and her voice would grow husky and so quiet you'd have to lean forward to catch it all. Lots of times she would even walk over while she was looking that way and, still talking huskily, click the lights off in the room.

She would say how Shakespeare changed her life because he was a "Universal Genius." She uttered that phrase with a special reverence and her head tilted back; her eyes began to fall back too. Stork never knew what the phrase actually meant, but he understood the feeling by the way she showed it. Mrs. Philpotts never explained things exactly—she embodied. She didn't tell you about Macbeth's ambition; it was on that small face not ten feet away from you. Hamlet's indecision ran down her shoulders and into the hand that held the ruler that just could not be plunged into that rotten stepfather. Hers was the only class in which Eugene did not sit in the rear.

China was related to Shakespeare. Maybe. Mrs. Phoebe Philpotts had probably read an awful lot of Shakespeare when she was in China. If, indeed, she had ever been to China. But Stork Collier understood the connection much better; it had to do with what "Universal Genius" was all about. His English teacher spoke of China as though it were another planet that only she had been selected to visit, a planet inhabited not merely by very wise beings, but by a whole race of Universal Geniuses.

When it became clear that the Stork could not actually take what Mrs. Philpotts had earned for herself, and when she had sufficiently inspired him to find, if not those, then comparable, things within himself, conditions were right for the relationship to grow.

"Eugene, this is a book I would very much like you to read," she said one day after class, her hand resting lightly upon his broad forearm.

The Stork was almost overwhelmed with the smell of lavender and soap, but he had decided he would say something to make her notice him, damn it. "Well, Miz Philpotts, I'm awful busy playin' football. . . ."

"Eugene, how you decide to spend your time is entirely your business. However, I expect it to be read by next week." As her heels clicked out a mincing rhythm down the hall, Eugene looked at the cover—ARROWSMITH, Sinclair Lewis.

He read it. Not wanting to capitulate entirely, he tried not to let his father see him in the act. When he was found asleep over its opened pages on the kitchen table by Eugene, Sr., at 4:30 A.M., the older man resisted the strong temptation to wake his son and say, " 'Bout time."

"That guy sure was stubborn, Miz Philpotts," was how the Stork broke the considerable ice later that week.

She knew exactly his reference: "Stubborn is not quite

the word you want, Eugene. Say, perhaps, conscientious or even socially aware and then you'd have a bit more of the driving force of a man like Martin Arrowsmith." Her green eyes flashed in a way he'd never seen before. She touched the length of his left forearm lightly; her fingers were cold but the Stork felt a sensation of heat. "Eugene, it's sort of late for you. I could never teach you all you have to know. Maybe . . . maybe someone else." The Stork wasn't thinking at all, so close was this sweet-smelling, hot-touching woman. His next book was *Huckleberry Finn.* "Eugene, it will tell you everything about slavery you'll ever need to know."

In rapid order that senior year the Stork read *Tale of Two Cities, Dragon Seed, Giants in the Earth, Drums Along the Mohawk, The Hunchback of Notre Dame, Othello, Anthony Adverse, Les Miserables,* and the first twelve chapters of *Moby Dick.*

In football Stork Collier developed the subtlety and finesse to enable him to get maximum effect from his rage and strength and to master various new techniques, particularly as a blocker. He was so effortless that many people didn't notice him on the field as readily as before. He was a very complete high school football player, no longer a stork in his abrupt movements, but he remained a Stork in name.

In February Ben Crowder returned, like an old Jesuit coming back after a promising young theologian. Direct from two moderately successful seasons at the university, "rebuilding" years during which the team won a few more games than it lost. The big years seemed to lie just ahead —years of the Stork.

2

Why, Eugene, Imagine Meeting You Here

In the fall of 1949, Morgantown, West Virginia, was, in the words of the Stork's roommate, "a real wild place." "Fatty" Conklin was the leanest fullback in the conference, but what he lacked in size he made up for in speed and guile and treachery. A fake cast on his wrist, appropriately weighted and shaped as a weapon; the ability to provoke an opponent to throw a punch in front of a referee—these were some of the tactics that kept him off all-star teams but made him the only sophomore who played every minute of every game for Coach Crowder.

Conklin was a coal-mine kid with a difference: His father owned the company. So Fatty was not scratching and clawing to avoid a life of grime, time-payments, and black lung; he came to viciousness with the purest of motives. Ben Crowder's plan was to place Eugene Collier, Jr.—whose reputation as the wonderful Stork preceded him and was known by most serious football fans in the state—in a room with such a model. It promised to be an interesting exercise in cross-fertilization.

The Stork was just about the most impressionable fresh-man at Morgantown. The first day of classes he walked through the Student Union after breakfast and saw two guys playing chess. One sucked on a pipe while he studied the board; he began to move a piece two or three times and then reconsidered. Finally he moved a pawn on the far side of the board forward one square. He made the quiet, regu-lar lip-smacks of the contemplative pipe-smoker. Later that day the Stork bought a pipe and a package of Rum and Maple tobacco with a large chunk of his spending money.

"Industrial Management," said the narrow-eyed coach, "that's where the future is and it would be just perfect for a bright young man like you, Gene. Pretty good in math, natural leader of men; hell, it's made to order for you." The coach appeared to have come to Hundley at great personal inconvenience in order to save the Stork a trip down to Morgantown to register for classes; that sacrifice showed.

"What exactly does an Industrial Management do?"

"Do? Why they do all sorts of things. They, just for example, would go into a place, let's say a coal company, walk around for a while, stayin' in the background but all the time lookin' things over, writin' down every wasteful thing they see. (That's what we'll be trainin' you for.) Then you make up a report about all the things they're doin' wrong, all the ways they could be makin' more money."

"Who gets this report?"

"Why, the boss, of course."

"Won't I be costin' some poor guy his job?"

"Oh, no; actually you'll be helpin' him. The boss can go an' tell him all the things he's been doin' wrong so he can correc' them—probably be makin' his job a damn sight easier."

"Oh."

"Lemme just put 'Industrial Management' down on that

card. You're goin' to be bunkin' with another feller in 'Industrial Management'—ever heard of Conklin Coal?" In West Virginia, a rhetorical question. "Well, Fatty Conklin has asked to room with you. You're lucky. He can help you with your courses, your football, your—" A careless wave of his pen and a conscious squint suggested the word "career," but the suggestion was lost on the Stork.

It was not true that Fatty Conklin had asked to room with Gene. He did not, in fact, know who Stork Collier was. But about two weeks before the semester began Fatty received a personal letter from Ben Crowder on university stationery. After thanking the boy for his contribution to last season's "successful campaign" and hoping for an even more rewarding season ahead, "culminating perhaps in a bowl bid"; and after inquiring about the health and well-being of his progenitors and his younger brother (twenty pounds heavier and three inches taller) the coach got down to basics: "Edwin, I have selected as your roommate Eugene Collier, an interior lineman from Hundley. I would consider it a football setback if we were to lose Eugene, so your ability to make Eugene happy here will be considered a contribution to the team. Your unselfishness in the past has led to your starting every game." And there it ended. That abruptly. Edwin "Fatty" Conklin got the message.

He had intended to take an apartment downtown; now he had to entertain some hick from the hills. Conklin was a hell of a team man, but he was woefully ill-suited for this task. A loner and a devoted sybarite himself, he was constitutionally incapable of bringing pleasure to anyone else. This totally selfish and spoiled young man at least went through the motions of being helpful to Gene; though he didn't succeed. He was perceived as strange by the naïve freshman—in the way country folks had always heard city folks were strange.

Their room was in a quonset hut out by the football stadium, about a mile and a half from the main campus. No problem; Fatty had a Ford. (*"Undergraduates are not permitted motor vehicles,"* proclaimed a university bulletin.) No problem; Stork preferred to run the distance. Theirs was the choice room in the quonset. A hallway ran along one side of the building; nine small cubicles opened off it. The tenth room was at the far end, larger, with three windows and space for two separate beds. Stork lived out of his footlocker. Fatty's clothes occupied both poles in the room; his photographs and magazines and souvenirs from New Orleans, Atlantic City, and Miami Beach were all over the place.

The first handshake had been a hearty one. "Gene, welcome to West Virginia University. I look forward to playin' with you this year. Sure do. We'll have a real wild time out there. Yes, sir." Because he had had a few weeks to prepare and practice, this was Fatty's warmest moment.

Gene, sore, weary, and constipated from an overnight bus ride was happy. His face, which when weary tended to register a deep sense of sorrow, was instantly transformed. He smiled broadly and sighed; the eyes widened and he slapped himself behind his neck with his free hand. "Tough trip," he said. That was all. Fatty Conklin figured it wasn't going to be easy.

Edwin "Fatty" Conklin was a playboy—a term the Stork would have related to football if he had heard it—perhaps the most advanced (for his age) ladies' man in the entire state of West Virginia. The greatest hardship in his quonset existence was the fact that he had to share the telephone at the far end of the hall with nineteen bumpkins. The loss might be irreparable. Nevertheless, the coach's threat was sufficient to hold the balance in favor of football and against the high life he had already begun to win a reputation for. No, that last part is not fair to him; truth is that Conklin was becoming notorious precisely because he *combined* a football reputation as a cad with the amorous propensities of a beast. "A lot of wild pussy in this town," he told the Stork one night long after the lights were out, "and I'm gonna get me all of it before I'm through here." It was a statement preceded and followed by silence. The Stork thought it was a very strange thing for anyone to say.

Although Gene had never before perceived anyone he had met as funny-looking, that was his reaction to Fatty Conklin. Fatty's presence, or even the memory of it, always brought a smile to the Stork's usually thoughtful face. None of us sees anything in precisely the same way, and certainly most of the "wild pussy" in Morgantown did not see the incredibly weak chin, eyes that bulged more than slightly, and thick, untidy lips that slurred even the most careful pronunciations. Perhaps the world was too impressed with the valiant pompadour, the long dark sideburns, and the slick sweep of the hair into tail feather behind. Or perhaps, because of the movies, everyone just assumed that rich kids were good-looking, so they saw not Fatty Conklin but George Raft.

Football practice started a week before classes. It was very different from Pleasants High. Even in the number of coaches: there seemed to be an assistant coach to take care of every detail. The Stork was going to play tackle, and even though he had played the position for three seasons, now there was someone to coach him, almost like a private tutor. There were hours of drills for the guards and tackles on positioning, timing, and the proper steps to take at the snap of the ball. Other hours of simulated blocking techniques. These classes were punctuated by wind-sprints, laps, and calesthenics. The assistant coaches criticized everyone but the Stork at one time or another, although Gene knew that he had made comparable mistakes. Days were devoted to individual responsibilities on the basic running plays. On the fifth day the linemen, who had worked separately until then, came together and lined up. The line coach stood behind them and commanded them into their stance—Stork remained erect a half beat too long—then he called a play, a simple trap, and on the shout of "hike" his charges misfired. In all directions. Stork and the burly Army veteran next to him crossed legs and went down in a heap. "Goddamned Chinese fire drill," said the coach. "Next line!"

Ben Crowder was nowhere to be seen.

Two days later the Stork's line began to cohere. They fired perfectly at blocking dummies snap after snap, delayed counts and quick ones. Stork had mastered all his assignments on offense. On defense, he was a big, wild bird, making up in energy and combativeness whatever he lacked in finesse, but this lack, too, was met. Then the first two lines stood against each other and battered each other for hours in the hazy sun of a late southern summer. Two kids were carried off. On the ninth day men with footballs appeared for the first time; and the linemen were told these would be their centers. Then lithe young men were introduced—quarterbacks. Soon after, the missing parts were added and the human machines began to develop distinct personalities.

Conklin was the fullback on Gene's team, the blue team, so there was a strong indication that they were the starting eleven. However, it was clear to everyone that the red team had the better quarterback, so the matter remained doubtful. In the locker room after a particularly grueling evening practice one of the assistant coaches stood on a bench and announced, "Ten minutes early tomorrow. Fifty-yard line. Meeting with the coach."

The subject matters of Gene's courses were easily comprehensible. That in itself was something of a disappointment; he had expected college work to be so far beyond his grasp that only a supreme effort on his part could bring success, and felt a bit empty when this never materialized. In English class he easily mastered the form of composition the teacher required. In Math his answers usually matched those in the back of the book. History was reading, and he had begun to enjoy reading. Biology? Hell, that was nothing more than common sense and keeping all those funny names straight. If any course came close to interesting him, it was Economics; and it was indeed the course, not the teacher. For Dr. Richert was nothing to write home about. But the textbook was another matter, very provocative: It was called *Our System and Theirs* by two fellows with hyphenated names—Professor Pryce-Thompson and Mr. Bennett-Holmes. "The finest economists Great Britain has ever produced," said Dr. Richert when he held the book up before the class on the first day.

"Economics is the system of organizing the wealth of a nation. This semester we are going to compare the various economic systems in the world and try to determine which is the best. Ladies and gentlemen, let me remind you that you are at Morgantown—not in Eustace or Crawford, Clyde or South Forks—therefore be apprised of the fact that when a professor is lecturing, the appropriate response is to record his words." Immediately notebooks flew open and various approximations of the Richert definition of Economics were penned.

The textbook opened with a sentence Stork Collier always remembered. "To paraphrase the words of Winston Churchill, free-enterprise capitalism is far from the perfect economic system, but it has, over the course of time, proven superior to all the others." That's how they taught Economics in Morgantown, West Virginia, in September 1949.

The team had already formed a large circle around the small man standing on the fifty-yard line when Stork trotted out of the tunnel and onto the field. Ben Crowder stood bare-headed in the sun, dressed in sneakers, gray flannel pants, and a blue jacket that had the word "Mountaineers" written diagonally across the front. "So nice of you to join us, Mr. Collier," he said sarcastically. A number of players turned in the Stork's direction. There was more envy than pity in their feelings. Stork said nothing.

"Men. Men. Those of you who played for me last year

know who I am. Probably you wished you didn't." Crowder paused for a laugh, but it was much briefer than he expected. The laughers then filled up the allotted time before his second thought. "Some of you know me because I talked you into coming here to play for me, to play for the West Virginia University Mountaineers." He casually drew a finger over the word on his chest. "Probably you'll wish't you didn't, too." No pause, no laugh. "Some of you never even saw me before this minute. My name is Benjamin Aldridge Crowder, and I am the coach of next year's Orange Bowl Champions."

A cheer, begun by the assistant coaches and picked up after a beat by everyone else. "You ain't seen me around much, and that ain't very important; but I've been seein' every one of you in action, and that is. I like what I've seen. There is enough talent out here to kick the Japs all over the Pacific if they ever start up again."

"Damn straight, Coach," a kid yelled out.

"An' then turn around an' kick the Marines' ass too," said Crowder, and the kid yelled, "Don't mess with us!"

"All you got to do, men, is follow what you're told. For that you got to have something deeper than talent, or even toughness. You've got to have trust. Talent's here. Toughness, too. But what makes the winner when the goin' gets rough is T-R-U-S-T. Do you trust that man next to you? Do you really trust yourself? And most of all, do you trust the men that have the responsibility, the men who have the toughest decision of anyone—do you trust your coaches? No—don't answer now. It ain't a question you can answer with words. You answer it over the long pull with action."

He seemed finished. There was silence except for the distant buzz of a small, single-engine plane flying into the sun. Stork Collier shaded an eye to seek it out. He was the only one. All the others seemed to fall into prayerful thought.

"Light drill today," Crowder said. "Scrimmage on Satur-

day. Red team against blue team. Game conditions. We'll
separate the hens from the roosters."

The first two weeks with Conklin had been uneventful.
But after the Blues had smashed the Reds on Saturday by
four touchdowns and Stork made eleven unassisted tackles, Fatty decided it was time to celebrate downtown. He
was dogged in his persistence and, as a matter of fact, he
had talked about that "wild pussy" so excitedly and ap-
pealingly, the Stork became curious—nothing more. Two
other fellows, crewcut, blue-faced vets who had shared in
the Red annihilation, joined the tour. They were unique,
not only because they were about six years older than
most of their teammates, but because they continued to
wear their army boots and their pant-legs bloused. One
was Raymond; the other was Leroy. The Stork couldn't
keep them straight.

The drive downtown built to a raucous peak at just about
the moment Conklin's Ford cruised into Green Street. The
first five minutes had been quiet. Then Raymond or Leroy
slapped Gene on the back and said, "Boy, when you picked
that feller up and slammed him to the ground and that
smack echoed all around the place and his eyes went way
up in his head like he was dead, I tell you I like to shit. I
just knowed we wasn't goin' to lose. Maybe we wouldn'ta
won, but I knowed we wasn't goin' to lose." And then all
of them—Stork included—in progressively louder voices
began recounting each other's exploits, making up the details where necessary.

Green Street in Morgantown in 1949 was a narrow winding street on the far side of town along the freight tracks.
The college boys usually stayed away, but it was Fatty
Conklin's home away from home away from home. He
pulled his car over to the curb in front of a store whose
windows were painted dark green, all except for a thin strip
up near the top. Shadows flickered by constantly and in the
gloom Gene perceived a pair of eyes peering steadily out.

Fatty thrust his head clear out of his window and shouted up to the sky: "Serina, you up there? Serina!"

"Yeah," he turned to the Stork, "she's there and waitin'. Whyn't you go on up? Door right over there. She'll be top of the stairs."

"Go where?" said the Stork, understanding fully without knowing.

"Coach said to take good care of you, *Eu*-gene, welcome you to college life an' all. Whatsamatter, *Eu*-gene, you tryin' to tell us you ain't never had it before?" The eyes bulged out even further and Gene didn't find them the least bit funny now. "Well, ain't you?"

" 'Course I have," said the Stork.

"Well, the best lay in Morgantown's waitin' for you right at the top of those stairs there. So whateryou waitin' for?"

"Don't feel like it tonight."

"You kiddin'?" said Leroy or Raymond.

"The poor boy's scared," said Fatty over his shoulder.

"Ain't," said the Stork getting out of the car and striding water-legged to the door next to the shadow store. The door was open a crack. It fell all the way open at the Stork's probing. Darkness. A stairway. A pungent, urinous odor. Now with feeling coming back into his legs and only the irrational fear that a club or a fist was waiting to crash over his head or into his face, he started to climb the faint steps, one arm hooked over his head, the other held out before him, ready to ward off any blows.

A door clicked at the top of the stairs. A husky voice said, "Come on, honey." Just before he reached the landing, a small light flashed on alongside a charcoal-colored woman clad only in a white slip. She was large-lipped and her eyes seemed dead; her heavy body smelled deliciously of sweat and fresh perfume. The Stork hesitated two steps below her. "Come on, chile." She leaned down. "Don't be scared, I won't hurt you." Her arm reached out. Stork leaned perilously backward.

A frozen moment. The woman smiled, stood up, and flicked the shoulder straps of her slip. A slight wiggle brought down the top of her slip. Long, full breasts swung gently before the Stork's wide eyes. The woman placed her breasts in her palms and raised them so the dark, round nipples were aimed directly at the young man's head. She began to speak. "This is just my way of saying . . ." Her deep voice was audible as the Stork hurried down the stairs, but while his ears heard the sound, his mind jumbled the words. He slammed his shoulder into the opened door, but the blow hardly cost him a stride.

The car was empty. Gene was grateful to be spared an explanation. He sat in the back thinking of nothing but those breasts, the nipples, that voice. His eyes remained wide, the offering clearly before him.

After a while Raymond, Leroy, and Fatty emerged from the store with the painted green windows and the eyes. "Man, you're a fast one," said Conklin.

"Ain't no need to stay an' discuss the state of the world," he heard his voice say with surprising coolness.

They made a stop at a fraternity house. Girls in flowered dresses. Fellows in sweaters and ties. Dance music playing dreamily from some vague source. A few beers, and then a deep weariness came over Stork Collier. In him were two strong, contradictory urges: one, to go back up that staircase and do whatever she asked him to; the other, to get as far from that street, that woman, those . . . (no word came) as possible.

The Stork learned a number of important things that first semester. After some mistakes—the result of overanxiousness—in the Maryland game, he settled down and played very well, particularly on offense, a development which pleased his ever-greedy coach. "Not bad for a first game" was Crowder's casual comment. The score was a 20–6 victory over one of the teams that had beaten the Mountaineers badly the previous season. The following Saturday, the

Stork played perhaps the best football game of his life against Duke. The Mountaineers won big. Even Crowder couldn't resist tempting the gods: "Men, I just want to tell you to keep your strength up, an' the best way to do it is with—*oranges.*" And the players howled.

But the team did not go on to the Orange Bowl that season. The fact that Collier tore ligaments in his knee in the game with Tulane when he took a misstep in a divot was a factor, but not the major one. Again it was a combination of things that couldn't be helped. Some injuries. Bickering between key players, a general letdown.

While his leg was in the cast, the Stork came to rely on Fatty Conklin for transportation. Drifted into Green Street more than once, hoping Fatty would mention another visit to that woman at the top of the stair. He didn't.

What Fatty did do was to teach Gene techniques for cheating in class, including the diabolical scheme of preparing a miniature scroll tied loosely with a rubber band that could be rolled backward and forward quickly between the thumb and forefinger. "Ain't much good for a composition, but it's the ticket for dates in History or a formula in Math, an' it'll hold a hell of a lot of information if you write small. Some guys stick it in a watchcase an' roll it back and forth right in front of the teacher, but that ain't really necessary." The Stork used the technique quite successfully on a Biology test.

Gene's grades were usually in the "B" range. The grade on his first Economics paper had been an F. That was one of the important things that happened to the Stork. The paper came back with the grade and the comment, "Who are you to refute the major premise of two of the greatest living economists?" Gene had decided, perhaps on a whim, to challenge the topic of the essay, which was, quite predictably: "Discuss the following, ' . . . free-enterprise capitalism is far from the perfect economic system, but it has, over the course of time, proven superior to all others.' "

Gene's essay began: "If like you have told us Economics is a system for organizing the wealth of a nation, then the best system is the one that doesn't have any very rich men or very poor men. And it seems to me that you don't have to be perfect to find out how to do that, especially when we live in a world that has enough for everybody." It went on that way for a while; then there was a sentence that Richert had boxed in red pencil: "How come some man should have a million dollars, if he can only wear one hat and pair of pants at a time." Finally: "If free enterprise is our system, and we have only been a country for a short while and there are countries around lots older than ours, how come ours has already proven out to be the superior? Who says so? Why should my daddy be working in a mine and some other guy have a half a dozen pairs of pants?"

Some process unknown to Gene brought information of the F to Ben Crowder's notice. "How's the leg comin'?"

"Fine, Coach."

"How's Fatty been behavin'?"

"Fine. He's somethin', that Fatty."

"Sure is. Gene, got word you got an F in Economics." No response; a blushing shamefaced turn to the team photographs on the wall of Crowder's office. "Havin' trouble in that course?"

"No. Not exactly. I just wrote a bad paper, I guess, but I understand the stuff okay."

"How come the F?"

"Bad paper."

"Like a chance to write it over?"

"Sure, who wouldn't?"

"Take care of the leg now. How much longer in that cast?"

" 'Bout three more weeks."

"Fine."

"S'long."

Richert called Eugene to him after the next Economics

class. "Mr. Collier, no one benefits when a teacher gives a student a poor grade and the student doesn't have a chance to learn from his mistakes. I'd like you, therefore, to rewrite your paper, taking a somewhat different approach this time, and hand it to me on Friday. That will be all, Mr. Collier."

The Stork found an A approach. In his comment on the revised paper, Dr. Richert wrote: "If an F can bring out this sort of performance, then it, too, serves a function. This grade, however, replaces the first one."

Yes, the Stork learned some very important things at the university that semester. The momentous lesson, however, was taught, quite unconsciously, by Fatty Conklin or some force much greater. It came just before the Christmas recess. The lesson began at 2 A.M. Earlier in the day selections had been made for the Orange Bowl and two or three lesser bowls; the players, hoping desperately that the various selection committees would regard a seven-and-three record from the point of view of the Mountaineer coaching staff, were broken-hearted when the inevitable rejection came. A team meeting was called. All of the assistant coaches said a few words of thanks and of assurance for the 1950 season. One of the assistant coaches conveyed Ben Crowder's feelings: "The coach can't be here today—personal things," he said, "but he wants me to thank each an' every one of you for your unselfish contributions. We had everything we needed to go all the way, but I reckon the Good Lord saw fit to give someone else a chance this year. Next year will be our turn." Each word uttered with the same stress and intonation. "An' for you guys who won't be back, you've got nothin' to be ashamed of. What you did for us this year is goin' to make next year possible." And the football season was over.

At just about 2 A.M., Fatty Conklin pinched the relaxed cheek of the sleeping Stork. His eyes burned red and his breath was whiskey-hot. "Goin' downtown; you wanna come?" Instantly Stork thought of the dark woman. "Hurry up, then."

Fatty's car did not turn into Green Street but rolled directly toward the City Hall, where Fatty parked diagonally. "C'mon," he said while he exited and the Stork hung back. Fatty led the way around the rear to a low brick rectangle of a building that was, surprisingly, without doors or windows. When Fatty stopped abruptly before a small wooden outhouse ten yards behind the strange brick building, the Stork almost bumped him from behind. Conklin knocked three times on the rickety door. An eye, part of a nose and mouth appeared where a sliver of moon had been carved in the door. "We've come to vote," said Fatty.

"Sure," the partial mouth said, and the door swung open.

Down a dozen steps, along a tunnel that was shored up with raw timber, just as in a mineshaft. The termination point was a huge green double door that looked like the rear of an armed car. Fatty knocked slowly seven times with his high school ring.

At the moment the door sprang open a roar of music and shouting burst out into the tunnel. "Quick," said Fatty, and he pulled the Stork through by the arm.

Unpitying light bulbs, an oppressive haze of smoke, shrill laughter and outrageous screams, violent colors, sweaty fat faces and writhing bodies. Five black men in the corner produced dixieland tunes that attracted only two dancers, both chunky women. In the opposite corner a billiard game played by men in evening dress attracted a large crowd of bottle-swigging onlookers. The wallpaper was a bright red flock on a brilliant gold background; the ceiling and floor a precocious baby-blue. Fatty Conklin was whisked away by a very tall, deep-throated woman who had announced the arrival of "Mr. Very Big."

Most of the drinking was going on at small tables scattered randomly about. The Stork, stranded and frozen by the door, was of interest to no one. But everyone interested him. He watched the mostly tactile exercises going on at the tables, touching of a highly personal sort. He could not take his eyes off a girl in a low-cut dress who had her legs wide apart under the table as a guy, an old guy with gray hair and a cigar, was grabbing way up her thigh. When her wandering eyes met the Stork's, they locked for a few seconds. She narrowed her eyes, scrunched her nose, and stuck her tongue out further than he had ever seen before. He looked away, embarrassed.

The bar attracted the largest crowd. Stork would be safest there. He walked slowly toward it, trying to cover his remaining slight limp. Since the bar was crowded, the Stork waited patiently for a minute. Then he noticed that everyone had been served; they merely preferred to stand there, locked in, talking and drinking. He took a deep breath. " 'Scuse me," he said and began to wedge through the denizens, most of whom he towered over.

"Don't push," said a thin, angry voice ahead. When the face spun around and their eyes met, there was a long moment of physical disbelief. "Why, Eugene, imagine meeting you here." The Stork and his athletic mentor had met on peculiarly equal terms.

"Hi, Coach."

"What you drinkin'?"

"Beer, I guess." The coach bought.

They talked nervously, mostly about pieces of things: Tater Tate. The coach's car. The official weight of a football. Charleston. The longest winning streak in college history. The true meaning of Christmas. They had segued into the health-giving qualities of beer when a woman's voice from behind called, "Benny, where the hell are you?" And then, "*Ben*-ny," somewhat louder and closer.

"Listen, Eugene," said Ben Crowder, "I've got to get back to my cousin." Their eyes met during a long pause in which neither of them spoke. When Crowder said, bending toward Gene Collier's large ear, "You understand, Gene," the words were as much a request as they were a shared piece of worldliness.

"Sure, Coach."

3

Sade-ist

The girl's name was Mary Jane Bloxham, and when the
Stork called at her quonset the first time, he brought a Mary
Jane candy bar, which he broke in two, but because she still
wore braces he ate both pieces. She told him *he* was sweet
enough for her, but it was just something to say.

Mary Jane was very dignified. Her posture was perfect;
she walked tall and carried her head and large shoulders
squarely. She was also blond and the Stork had seen
enough technicolor movies by now to make him partial to
blondes with very red lips. Mary Jane's lips weren't that red,
but they had a rare kewpie-doll shape. She had a strong jaw
too. Her braces didn't really matter. Stork Collier was attracted first by her eyes. They were large and soft and
shaped like a doe's. She had a little acne on her chin and
forehead, but it didn't bother the Stork. Then he was attracted by her speech—she was English. Anyway, she was
born in England and had lived there for most of her life
before her family came to America. Her father was some
sort of scientist who did all kinds of experiments with coal.

The way she talked and the way her eyes looked made her seem always a little frightened, even though she walked very straight. It was a desire to protect her that most stirred in the Stork.

She had sat in front of him in Biology class during the first semester. They became lab partners the second semester. Just when the Stork began to conceive of himself as a fit object of interest for a nice Christian girl, Mary Jane Bloxham pledged a sorority, her braces came off, she got her hair bobbed, and began dating an ex-Navy lieutenant almost all at once. But she did seem to like the Stork well enough for a while, long enough to go on one date and to give him the sense that his loneliness was a condition that would be altered in the course of time.

Their third collaboration in the laboratory and their only date are interesting and, in relation to Gene Collier's development, the passage of his soul through time, and the crucial decisions of his life, they're very important.

When the Stork arrived in the laboratory that third Wednesday, he was aware of a very strong formaldehyde stench. Mary Jane Bloxham was in a tither before a large bowlegged frog whose supine position in a tray told of its clinical demise better than words. Mary Jane was slouching (a sure sign of trouble) and absently knitting her hair into a ragged braid (it had not yet been bobbed). She grasped his arm for support and said, "Look, Everett, isn't it just ghastly." She always got his name wrong when she was upset. The Stork saw merely a dead frog; in his life he had seen dead rats and chickens and pigs and ponies. "And we're supposed t' cu-ti-topen." The Stork decided he loved the way English girls talked on the basis of Mary Jane Bloxham's Midland's accent.

"Don't panic, Mary Jane. The thing's dead, after all. We ain't doing anything wrong." The words were empty but the intention and tone were reassuring. To a certain extent, Mary Jane Bloxham had been seeking to elicit just such

words from Eugene Collier; the situation almost required
that such a scene be played. To a greater extent she was
weakened and repulsed by the ugliness and the death in her
pan. To the greatest extent the prospect of dissecting and
observing the creature's vital organs scared the hell out of
her.

This was the day the Stork had looked forward to, especially that part of him that enjoyed the crack of leather
against bone and muscle on a football field. Fatty Conklin
had told him that someone was bound to faint dead away,
probably one of the biggest guys in the room. "It'll be a real
wild scene," promised Fatty.

The lab instructor was a burly young woman the kids
called Milton because she looked like Milton Berle in drag
—buck-toothed, horse-faced, the works. She deliberately
wore a blood-smeared white smock for the edge it gave her
over most students. This, the first dissection of the year,
was the day she also waited for, but there was no glee in her
voice or demeanor; rather, a cold precision that clearly
indicated her professional reliability (and superiority) in
moments of stress. For all the sweet young things and even
some of the big city show-offs this was indeed a time of
stress. It was no accident that on this, of all days, the lab
was poorly ventilated. Milton would have her dissection.

"Don't you hate her?" asked Mary Jane Bloxham, still
looking pale and holding on to the cold marble of the
counter top.

"You want a drink of water or something?"

"No, thank you, Everett."

"It's Eugene."

"Sorry. Knew a boy at home named Everett. You remind
me of him."

"She's a type."

"Pardon."

"Miz Milton. She's a type. I've seen them a lot around
football. Assistant coaches, mostly. They ain't got much

power themselves, so when they get in a position to lord it over someone else, they try to make him miserable."

"Sade-ists, that's what they are," said Mary Jane Bloxham, and the very name had a power to it; it was as though the word pinned the cruel Milton squirming and wriggling to the center of the lab floor. Mary Jane became palpably stronger; her posture improved markedly as she seemed to realize that the ultimate weapon was hers.

"Say that word again."

"Sade-ist."

"What's it mean?"

"That's just someone who gets pleasure making other people feel sad."

"There's a word for that, huh?"

It was clear that Mary Jane Bloxham thought of the next hour and fifty minutes as a trial by formaldehyde, and it was obvious by the jut of her jaw that she willed herself not to be found wanting. The Stork sensed that she was very well bred and that her old man must really be something. "You an only child?" he heard himself ask; he had never asked that question before in his life.

"Yes."

"I guessed it."

"How?"

"Don't know. Just did."

"Ladies and gentlemen." It was Milton. All the girls whose heads were not reeling—there were three—consciously detested her. "In each dissecting tray has been placed a frog with the dorsal side down. Please look now to see that this has been done." She turned slowly in the center of the room with the graceless movements of a work horse. "Good. Now if you will place a pin through each of the extremities; be sure to be firm. We wouldn't want any movement after you begin to cut, would we?"

"Sade-ist," said Mary Jane Bloxham angrily. Fortunately frogs were such horrid creatures in her eyes that the element of pity that might have caused her open rebellion was not present. A low-grade disgust stayed with her as she saw Eugene insert the pins quickly and firmly.

"I want you each to participate. Science is sharing. You haven't learned anything if you haven't learned that."

The room was very warm. The Stork pulled his sweater up over his head. A boy on the other side of the room was doing the same thing.

"These are female frogs you will be working with. The internal organs of the different sexes are essentially the same. They have been purchased and shipped here at great expense to the university, so it is important that you do exactly as you are told and not mutilate"—a word she strung out like a prisoner on the rack—"mutilate the specimen in the tray before you."

The fine blond down on Mary Jane Bloxham's upper lip collected a great deal of moisture. Rivulets of sweat ran down the Stork's face and splashed from his chin directly onto the dead frog's stomach.

"You can read a great deal of material on what makes any specimen tick, but it is only through dissection that we fully come to understand the true meaning of life. The first cut is crucial; I suggest you practice it a few times before you actually try it. These specimens have been prepared for dissection; there will be no blood." Bela Lugosi could not have given that final word more syllables.

The thud was so soft, even Mary Jane Bloxham, who saw the whole process, from tottering through collapse, couldn't believe it wasn't an act of some sort. "Oh," was all the small girl who was his partner sighed. "He's fainted," Mary Jane screamed and went running over to the boy who had pulled off his sweater at the same moment as Eugene; he was himself on his dorsal side, ice cold, and pale as the gray-ceilinged room.

An assistant lab instructor appeared from nowhere and hooked a hand under one limp arm; Eugene grabbed the

other and they dragged the fallen boy through the doorway, his chin on his chest, toes pointing straight up, into the
hall. Gene was told to return to his frog as soon as the
victim had been seated with his head down around his
ankles.

"The cut," explained the controlled voice of science, "is
like a printed capital I. A short horizontal slash across
. . ."

Mary Jane Bloxham, already standing rather tall, seemed
to grow even more erect before the Stork's eyes. She
tugged down on each seam of a pleated gray skirt and
strode to the center of the lab, where Milton revolved
slowly counterclockwise. The confrontation required her
turning for another few seconds. ". . . the lower abdomen
and a long vertical cut . . . please stay at your places; if there
are any problems just raise your hands."

"Sade-ist." Mary Jane did not holler the word; she said
it strongly, clearly, definitely; turned and walked out of the
stinking room, taking pains not to slam the door at the last
moment.

Milton gave no sign of her deep pleasure. Eugene carried
on and saw his first frog spleen. Mary Jane Bloxham was
transferred to a section of Biology that studied Botany. She
refused to apologize to the lab instructor she had publicly
defamed.

Mary Jane was sitting under a tree reading a slim volume
of poetry the next time he saw her. It was a fairly mild, late
February afternoon; Mary Jane was rushing the spring. Eugene asked if he could sit down. He did not realize that she
was hoping for someone else: The trapper always has great
hopes, but selectivity in trapping is not easily achieved.

Naturally they talked about her act of defiance, of motives and punishment. She said something the Stork
remembered, not every word exactly, but the general line
of reasoning and some specific phrases. What she said was:
"You know, Everett, t'wasn't th' frog exactly that caused

me t' act. No' teven th' boy who fainted in there. Really, no' teven that she is such a sade-ist and tried t' make everyone as sick as she is. T'was that th' whole thing was a lie right from th' beginning. When they tell you that you're learning about life by cut-ting a dead thing that's a lie. And when they kill things in order t' study them, that's a sin.''

The Stork had never heard anyone talk that way before; never heard the words come out so smoothly, as though they had been written down and were being read. Except in the movies, of course, but that's what made those people movie actors and not real people. "Can we go for a walk one day next week?"

Mary Jane Bloxham agreed without meaning to. "I'd like t' go t' the Gardens if it's nice," she said because she had planned to go there and read anyway, so the day would still be mostly hers.

That's when Eugene brought her the Mary Jane candy bar he ate. It was a clear, sunny Saturday morning, the first one in the month of March, 1950. The brave hint of warmth was only a vague promise of renewal—what the mountain people around Hundley called Fool's Spring.

Mary Jane had mastered her very slight skin problem and the Stork had gotten over his disappointment at not feeling disappointed with having missed most of the football season. So each had reached that certain plateau of maturity necessary for serious, subjective, philosophical investigation. Only the proper setting was required. What the locals called the Gardens was it.

The name was a misnomer. There were no gardens at the Gardens; very few people even knew how the name had been derived. The Gardens was an incredibly clear pond stocked with great jumping carp, bordered by large sitting-rocks, ancient beeches, tall firs, and some meadow land.

The two did not hold hands. Stork Collier walked slowly, head down, avoiding with his heels every crack in the pavement along Conduit Street. His hands were in his back pockets, and for the first time since his injury, there was a natural spring in his step. Mary Jane Bloxham wore that gray pleated skirt, a heavy knit sweater, and a large maroon shawl. Her arms were crossed over her chest and the shawl enveloped her and *The Poetry of Amy Lowell* twice. She walked tall with her chin slightly forward.

At the Gardens she sat upon a boulder, making sure to get as much direct sunlight as possible. Her sigh of contentment was meant as much to assure herself of her well-being as to announce it to Eugene and the world.

The Stork sat half in shadow on the cold ground with his back upon the boulder topped by Mary Jane Bloxham. What she said surprised him: "They say th' odds of anyone on earth finishing out their natural lives are less than fifty-fifty. Imagine, Eugene! They say th' next war is going t' be so horrible, you'd only die more horribly. Isn' tit too, too frightful?"

Eugene's silence was mistaken for incredulity.

"You see, every year some country or other will get th' secret for the bomb. When enough of them have bombs, surely one will go off. My teacher says it's got nothing t' do with meaning t' do wrong. It's just that there will be so many bombs, one is just bound t' go off. It's simply mathematical."

The Stork was staring at the surface of the pond. The steady breeze put a grainy texture on it, almost like liquid wood. Each time a fish broke through and made an impertinent circular ripple, which began to widen immediately, the grain of the water blown by the breeze immediately obliterated it. The phenomenon absorbed Eugene. No circle lasted more than a few seconds. He was unaware of Mary Jane speaking until she had stopped. "Lookit the way the circles are brushed away by the breeze," he said. She didn't. "Sometimes I feel it's goin' to be that way with me."

"What do you mean, Everett?"

He went on. "I don't know, I just feel that a man just ain't free to develop in his own way. There's always big pressures, always people tellin' you what's right, how you're supposed to act, what you're supposed to do. . . ."

"Look, Everett!"

"Eugene."

"Look at th' bird in that nest. Oh, look at th' babies!"

A nest in an overhanging limb of the great, old beech tree above their heads. Three robin chicks—comical, scrawny, cheeping for food—all but fell out of the nest while the mother made repairs. "Oh, isn' tit beautiful?" It was as though Mary Jane really expected an answer.

He gave a truthful answer: "Part of me thinks it is. Nature and all. Those helpless little things and that brave mother. 'Course it's beautiful, and there's a part of me that just feels so good when I look up an' see it." Mary Jane had stopped listening. "But there's another part of me, an' it has a real hard time being around anything beautiful. I don't like that part—it scares me—but it's real, an' it isn't the strongest part of what I feel when I see something really fine, but it's there. I would never do anything to destroy something beautiful, but I know lots of guys on the team who would. It's just that there's a part of me that doesn't want to see any beauty, that would sooner look away or get up and leave. Really. Can you believe it? It's got something to do with the part of me that wants to do something very bad, without any reason or anything, just to do it because you shouldn't." It was the longest statement Eugene Collier, Jr., had made on this planet.

Mary Jane Bloxham thrilled at the bliss in the nest above her. "Thank God for God," she gushed.

The mother robin, flying home with a twig in her mouth, dropped it in the pond, where it began to send out ripples, which in turn were smoothed away by the prevailing breeze on the water.

Eugene sensed that he was about to do something foolish, perhaps even bad, for no reason he was able to communicate to anyone. It is a paradox that so many young men see the possibility for such a life in the service or at sea, where in fact they become minuscule working parts of demanding and total organizations. Some men even believe they are most free in prison. Perhaps it is true that there is no better place to lose yourself than in one of these appallingly unfree situations. The Stork might have been liberated on the football field or meeting his responsibilities at West Virginia University. As it happened, he was not. Gene believed that he was attuning himself to a new destiny. He had cut himself loose; he would drift, no longer confined by the circular ripples, but perhaps to be carried on the cutting edge of a wave. Fine. Foreign countries, strange languages, new faces. An alien life.

Although Gene was thrilled at the deepest levels by the prospect of doing something rash, and felt genuinely mysterious, there is a more simple and reasonable explanation for his behavior. Eugene Collier, Jr., had simply run out of patience. If he had been asked to fell the tallest fir in Hundley, he probably couldn't have done it, for he no longer thought of himself as a stroke-and-stroke-and-stroke-and-stroke human being.

Gene joined the Army the next day in Morgantown. The years of the Stork ended abruptly. He wanted to leave almost immediately. He packed his bag, wrote a letter to his father merely stating the facts of the matter, and lay down on his bed in the quonset in a state of mind somewhere between fear and intense excitement. He packed no books.

When the bus that was to pick up volunteers as it wended its way south to Camp Gordon, Georgia, arrived in front of the recruiting office in Morgantown, it was already 8 A.M.; its arrival was an hour and a half late. Gene's getaway from the campus was perfectly clean: Fatty had been on an all-nighter; nobody had seen him walk into town with his suitcase; Ben Crowder would certainly be the most surprised man in the state when he got the news. "Maybe," Gene thought, "I should have left a suicide note, 'cause I'm a dead man as far as some of those people are concerned."

The date of the Stork's death and Gene's departure was March 5, 1950, four years to the day after Winston Churchill's visit to Fulton, Missouri. The term "cold war" had been minted, coined, and widely distributed. The conflict took the form mainly of propaganda and political jockeying; shortly tanks and planes and bombs and bullets and guns and men would take the place of the words and bluffs and emotions.

The bus ride was awful; it was also exactly what Gene Collier desired. Mostly the bus with its few recruits scattered widely and sprawling listlessly over the seats followed the back roads, stopped at Abingdon, Virginia, Asheville, North Carolina, and Anderson, South Carolina, where it picked up frightened boys. Usually the boys were alone, or perhaps accompanied by a woman, either someone very young or fairly old. Technically speaking, none of these "recruits" was as yet in the U.S. Army, for the formal induction ceremonies were to take place upon their arrival at Camp Gordon. Mining towns and mill towns went by the large tinted window, as well as miles and miles of grazing and farm land, all of which were superimposed on Gene Collier's reflected image. Gene did not use the nineteen hours of the trip as a period for analysis or self-appraisal; he simply dedicated them to that part of himself that had asserted itself, the part that desired irrationality and an open-ended life.

Nineteen country boys got off the bus at Camp Gordon at 2 A.M. They were lined up in the darkness and marched for the first time in their lives. To a chilled barracks in which the bunks had springs and nothing more. "You mens will git your mattresses tomorrow; you'll have to make do fer t'night," they were told by a tiny Negro sergeant who was kind enough not to berate them for disturbing his own sleep. Gene took his raincoat from his suitcase and rolled it into a pillow. The arrival—its time, the setting, the inconvenience—seemed remarkably appropriate, and he was quietly pleased by the discomfort.

4

Mens

An Army career for Gene Collier was far from a leap into the abyss. If a boy wished to avoid the mines, the Army was always a most attractive and popular alternative. Tater and Billy Ames and lots of other guys joined up right out of school. On a weekend in Pleasants you always saw a soldier or two in uniform somewhere or other, usually strutting up and down in front of Mom's Malts and Popeye's Billiard Parlor, where most of the kids hung out most of the time. And as far back as he could remember, Gene always heard tell of some cousin or other who had run off to join the Army and broken his poor mother's heart. For lots of kids in the West Virginia hills, joining the Army was a standard operating procedure.

Morning was announced by a metallic voice on the barracks intercom: "All new recruits will assemble on the company street outside the barracks in twenty minutes. All personal belongings will remain in the barracks, which will be locked for the day. Twenty minutes."

It was still dark when the boys lined up. Actually, they

didn't line up at all but formed a knot of bodies with twisting, craning heads. The only light came from a bare bulb above a small building labeled "Orderly Room"; it lighted the expressions of confusion and fear in an extraordinary way. One face would always be highlighted, or perhaps only a feature or two, with other faces more dimly perceived in the background. The entire effect was of a charcoal sketch with all the careful chiaroscuro in the foreground. Although the faces circulated and were markedly different structurally, a characteristic expression in the eye—as though of trying to look backward over the shoulder without turning the neck sufficiently—made them seem remarkably the same.

It was warm. Gene guessed it was not yet 6 A.M. and already the breeze had an unnatural warmth that worried him a bit. This might be the sort of place where the midafternoon heat robbed a person of even his private thoughts; the sort of place where all you could think about was how best to conserve your energies, how to ration water, how to use the shade.

The small sergeant of the previous night came out of the Orderly Room holding a clipboard. He walked before the gaggle of recruits. Most of the boys were grateful to see him again, and he seemed to appreciate the fact: "All right, mens, we got a long day fer ourselves. A long day. An' "— he looked toward the east—"a damned hot one. So . . . we need some sort of organization. Right?"

One of the boys said, "Yes, sir."

"I am a Sergeant. A Sergeant. That's what these stripes mean. Sergeant. You don't say 'sir' to a Sergeant. Ever. It's an insult. You say 'sir' to an officer. Right?"

The sergeant's voice was gentle, his manner reasonable. Few of the boys could appreciate how fortunate they were. When they had had sufficient experience with other Army sergeants, they would have conveniently forgotten this man.

"Now, I'm going to pick out three mens. Don't mean they're better'n the rest of you. It's just a way of getting some organization started." He selected the three tallest boys in the group and brought them forward. Then he got their names, checked them off on his list, and proceeded to announce: "These mens are your squad leaders. Whatever happens today, don't lose your squad leader. This one is the first squad leader." He placed his hand on Gene Collier's back. "The following mens are in the first squad." He called off five names, simple American names, "Childs, Cream, Hudson, Johnson, Jones. Now you mens come forward and line up next to your squad leader. That's right. Now stick your left arm right out 'til it's touchin' the tip of that other man's shoulder. Git it straight, git it straight." He did the same for the second and the third squads until he had a rectangle of men with a little tail; he did it sweetly and quickly. "I'm curious," he said, almost to himself but sufficiently loud to be heard by all, "which squad'll be the best one today."

The next ten minutes he devoted to left turn, right turn, about face, forward march, platoon halt, at ease, and attention—rudiments of movements and deportment that he conveyed in a command voice so authoritative it induced immediate obedience and a high degree of performance. It was too dark for anyone to have yet observed his name printed over his heart; it was "ARNOLD."

Breakfast was served by squads, and Gene Collier, as the leader of the first squad, was the first man served, Sergeant Arnold preferring to wait at the end of the line and keep an eye on his chicks. The cooks were exceptionally polite, but with a manner of concern heavy with mockery. "Good morning, gentlemen, it's a pleasure to have you with us," said a gorilla in a white T-shirt and chef's cap.

"How would you like your eggs?" he asked Gene.

"Sunnyside."

"Fine. And would you like some homefries?"

"Yes."

He scooped some on Gene's tray. "Enough?"

Gene saw the huge pot of homefries. He did want another scoop. "That's fine," he said and immediately regretted the lie. His first meal in the United States Army was very good: The toast was porous enough to absorb the egg yoke and firm enough not to turn soft; the coffee was strong and not bitter; the juice cold; the homefries had just the right bite to them. Of course a man could not judge his future on the basis of one breakfast, but Gene believed this fine food augured many good things. "Seconds?" the cook shouted. A few of the boys went back to the counter. Gene got a second cup of coffee.

The sun was up. It was already warm when the squads lined up and marched across a parade field, past a long low hospital, over railroad tracks and badly paved roads, to a large wooden building that said "Central Supply."

The day was spent in a variety of activities in different rooms in that building: official induction; a battery of tests; the issuing of uniforms; the formal orientation and welcome by a representative of the camp commander. These activities took six hours. Most of the time was spent sitting in shady spots, waiting for the activities to begin. For lunch the platoon marched back across the parade field to the site of breakfast. Now, however, a different shift of cooks was on duty, a group much less friendly and considerate. Lunch was chipped beef on toast under cream sauce, a glass of lemonade, and a canned pear. Everyone cleaned his tray and waited for the "Seconds" call. A call that never came.

Gene Collier had never heard the word "orientate" before this day, but from breakfast until dinner he heard it a dozen times. He guessed it meant "to tell the truth," as in, "The Major is going to orientate you mens to being in the Army this afternoon. Be sure you listen up good."

The recruits—the formality of induction had made that word fully applicable—received their insignias, their nametags, their haircuts, their Army numbers (Gene Collier was RA 51 310 611), and a list of General Orders (to be memorized in twenty-four hours; "Not," as the pig-faced supply sergeant had shouted, "in twenty-three or twenty-five, but in twenty-four hours exactly!"). Then the men were marched into a small, air-conditioned amphitheater.

"Men. It is an honor to stand before you this afternoon." The major's voice was commanding; he was tall, square, and impressive in a tailored gabardine dress uniform. Actually, no one noticed these military attributes on first glance because half his face was scarred with deep maroon- and white-flecked remnants of a horrible burn. "Men, I wish to welcome you to Camp Gordon on behalf of General Steinert, who, unfortunately, is not able to be here himself. I know, however, what he would have said if he were here. He would have told you how privileged you were to be new members of an old team. A winning team. He would have asked you to look around the walls of this room and see the pictures of the great battles fought by the gallant men of the United States Army. Then he would have paused and said, 'Men, the United States Army, in over two hundred years, has never lost a war.' Think about that, men. We have never been defeated. And now for the sixty-four-dollar question—why do you think that is? Why have we never been defeated? Why are we the greatest fighting machine the world has ever known?" He did not pause; he stopped. Apparently he expected an answer.

After a nervous minute, one of the boys in Gene's squad raised his hand. "Stand up," whispered Sergeant Arnold. He did. "I think it's because the American soldier's the best-trained soldier in the world."

"Exactly."

The boy's eyes shone like the eyes of one who has achieved a life-long dream.

"And that is how we will train you. Every time you miss something one of your instructors tells you, you are risking your very life. Or the life of your buddy. And just because there is no war going on right now is no reason not to take your basic training—and your survival—for granted. The only reason there isn't an actual war is because the enemy knows that men like you will be ready to fight any kind of war on any terrain in any climate, and that you will never be defeated." The scarred major spoke on, going over the military history of the United States in detail. It happened to coincide quite closely with the political history of the United States.

"Besides," he concluded, "we have a secret weapon. We have something no other army on earth has. You know what this is, men?" He paused.

"No, sir."

"The buddy system. But it's up to you to make it work. Whenever your buddy's in trouble—anything from a broken shoelace to a bullet in his arm—it's up to you to help him out. Sure, men in this man's army have different ranks, but underneath, each of us is only as good as our support, as our buddy. The thing that really makes us the greatest fighting force in the world is even more than our training—it is *trust.*"

After a march to dinner (it was something called shepherd's pie and came as a mighty surprise to Gene Collier's palate) and a roll-call in front of the barracks, Sergeant Arnold said, "You mens will be getting your uniforms in shape tonight. I got you some mattresses, but not much of anything else. Tomorrow morning orders will come down on most of you. Reveille at six sharp. Before you fall out, I just want to ~ay what a fine platoon you mens were today. Fall out."

"Collier, Gene. Report to Item Company, 74th Regiment, 2nd Army Division. And good luck to you, son," said Arnold when he handed Gene his orders for eight weeks of basic training on the red clay of Georgia.

By degrees Eugene Collier, Jr., became a soldier. Every event—from the bestial growl that accompanied a bayonet slash to the skin-closeness of a dance at the U.S.O. Club—had the effect of making a young man believe totally in the present moment, in the illusiveness of time.

This great lesson began with his second day in Item Company. The first day he spent drawing his footlocker and supplies, marking them, and sewing on his name tags and insignias. That night his platoon sergeant told him to tie a towel on the end of his bunk. The soldier in the bunk above his was a frightened, bespectacled question-mark of a boy. Periodically throughout the night Gene's bed rocked with a sensual rhythm Gene could not ignore. It must have been well after midnight when he gave the upper springs a good kick and the rolling finally subsided.

He was awakened very early by a flashlight in his eyes. "Collier," the light said, "get your ass over to the mess hall on the double." It was gone. At the mess hall he was greeted by a toothless cook who asked him where the hell he'd been and told him he was the pot and pan man. Gene didn't know until his day cleaning pots and pans ended at about 8 P.M. that he had pulled his first K.P. He did, however, discover that the number of huge pots to be cleaned was virtually without end, that time was only exhausted by work, and that a man was a fool to rush since there would certainly be other chores when these were finished. So he rolled up his sleeves, disappeared into a great pot, and lost himself in the scrub-and-scrub-and-scrub-and-scrub mentality country boys develop when they are transformed into modern warriors.

The second lesson was related to the first: What is important is not only subjective, it is completely arbitrary. On the third day the company was awakened by shrill whistles and made to line up in formation three times between the hours of 10 P.M. and 2 A.M. The first sergeant called the roster slowly and said something about trying to find a missing rifle, but the platoon sergeants smiled broadly and winked at each other. On the fourth day the company was made to set up their tents in front of the barracks and live in them for two days. No water or soap was permitted for shaving, even though both were only a few steps away.

Gene Collier was, like most of the country boys, too disoriented to clearly evaluate his condition. The grumblers and complainers ("Latrine Lawyers," the platoon sergeant called them with a sneer) all came from big cities. The worst ones were from up north. Maybe they were right about how bad all the recruits were being treated, but it was obvious to Gene that it didn't do any good to complain.

Private Eugene Collier, Jr., RA 51 310 611, won three commendations from Lieutenant Grey, the Item Company Commander. He got the highest score in the P.T. test. His squad won the forced march race, as he finished with three helmets and two rifles, the handicaps of buddies less staunch and dedicated than he. Finally, he was named Item Company's "Soldier of the Week" for the week beginning April 27, 1950. For this achievement he was granted a weekend pass, which he spent in the Service Club drinking 3.2 beer, reading sports magazines, and trying to recall faces from his former life. Only his father's came, and that was because he could see his own face in the juke box and that reminded him of his father. But none of the faces, not Crowder's or Fatty's or Mary Jane Bloxham's, none of the people he had seen just a couple of months ago appeared. And then slowly another face—his grandma, and after that his ma. When his own face came again in the tinted glass, Gene assumed the cycle had completed itself. He was wrong. His face melted and was replaced by the horribly scarred face of the major at Orientation. That grotesquerie began to fade, to be replaced by Gene's again, but here another surprise—although the face was Gene's, the scars remained, seemingly grafted to the young initiate. "Hello, trooper." The face in the glass now was Sergeant Arnold's. It did not replace Gene's; it paired with it. In fact, it was a true reflection. Gene turned and looked dumbly at Sergeant Arnold in the flesh.

The sergeant had a container of coffee and a danish and was on his way somewhere. "Better watch that stuff. It might be 3.2, but it'll get the job done under the proper circumstances."

Gene continued to look stupefied. "Thanks, Sarge," he said.

"They done made a soldier out of you sure as hell," Arnold said as he left with a kind but mocking salute.

"Sure did," Collier said.

They called it "graduation"; it signified the end of the eight-week basic training course. There was a dress formation, a speech by Lieutenant Grey about how they were now the best fighting material in the world, and the distribution of certificates and medals. Each man received a piece of paper saying that he had completed Basic Training; everyone, including the complainers, was awarded a Good Conduct Medal, an act of kindness, Gene thought, that was as clever as it was forgiving. Most of the country boys, Gene included, had won marksman medals as well.

All the recruits were nervous, and beneath the festive atmosphere prevailing before the barracks of Item Company was a pervasive anxiety that threatened to surface if an essential matter was not soon dealt with. The company commander, his first sergeant, and the platoon sergeants, although seemingly concerned with baccalaureate speeches and congratulations, were, in fact, well aware of the general concern. Rumor had been rampant for days that orders had been cut and were already resting in the Company safe.

When it was decided that the men had been teased long enough, the first sergeant called out the roster and handed out new orders. It was understood that most of the soldiers would be put into eight more weeks of something called Advanced Basic Training in the Georgia sun. A few, those who had shown some aptitude required by the U.S. Army, would not. They would go on to school.

Private Collier had no true preference; after all, he had rejected school in favor of Basic Training; but so many guys were down on more training that he found himself hoping for something different too. As each soldier broke ranks and took his orders, his face clearly registered his fate. The reactions did vary considerably. Generally the guys who drew eight more weeks of march and drill and bivouac looked dejected, but a few laughed and shook their heads as though a joke really worth pulling on someone had happened to fall on them. Some merely shrugged and wiped their noses.

The winners were all ecstatic, but even here they were moved to ecstasy differently. Most whooped or whistled or shouted, but some looked, stuck the orders behind their backs or in their pockets, and then took them out for another look before smiling a very broad smile.

A high percentage of the PM's (for "Pissers and Moaners," as the shirkers and grumblers had been renamed toward the end) had avoided the curse of more training. Gene thought this benevolence from on high was excessive. He was assigned to Radio Operators School right there at Camp Gordon. The one week's leave time he was granted troubled him because he didn't have anywhere he wanted to go, and almost no money. He was, he felt, not yet far enough out of people's thoughts back home to make his reappearance either dramatic or important enough to be worth the effort.

Baker Company, 3rd Battalion, U.S. Signal Corps was a "paper" outfit for a week. A "class" of 120 men was expected the following Sunday (June 15) to begin a twelve-week course in the sending and receiving of international Morse code. Until the "students" arrived from scattered points throughout the South and East to begin "matriculating," the company consisted of three cooks, a first sergeant, a company clerk, the name of a new commanding officer none of them had ever seen, and a file containing the duplicate orders of 120 potential high-speed radio operators.

When Private Collier showed up with a bulging duffle bag one week early at Baker Company, he was not welcomed.

There is no better situation in the U.S. Army than being a member of a "paper" company—no responsibilities, lots of bunk time, card games, pool shooting, reading, and chow of an uncommon quality and quantity. Reluctantly, Sergeant Spitz took in the stray. His words tell all: "We've all broken our humps with the last group that went through here, and now we're on *our* time. If you do anything to fuck it up for us, kid, your ass is grass." Gene thought the sergeant was finished and began to turn away. "And," continued Spitz, "if you ever tell anyone anything, I will make it your word against mine, and I've been in for eighteen years." Still he wasn't finished. "Breakfast is at ten. Find yourself a bunk and keep a very low silhouette."

When Gene arrived in the mess hall for breakfast, the three cooks, the first sergeant, and the company clerk were eating at the same table. He waited by the tray stand. "That's the kid," he heard the sergeant say. "Well, c'mon in. Just he'p yerself," the oldest cook said. Sausages, scrambled eggs, toast, juice—the best breakfast he'd had in months. At the table they made room for him and asked a number of harmless questions.

He spent the afternoon walking, and then returned to his bunk to lie down for a while. Through a window he noticed a remarkable lavender sunset streaked across the Georgia sky and, then, believed he heard a whisper of music. Full consciousness told him that the whispers were in fact the sweetest and most melodic growls he had ever heard. He followed the sounds, which did not become significantly louder, to the next barracks, where Gene Collier discovered a tall black man, one of the cooks who never spoke, sitting on a footlocker and blowing introspectively into a shiny trumpet. The player surrounded and overwhelmed the instrument; it pointed directly down into his lap.

Gene stood unseen in the doorway as the musician breathed and growled and fingered an improvised blues statement of remarkable feeling and complexity. The lavender sky gave way to blue and that to a starry southern American night.

When the music ended, the barracks were dark. Gene clicked on a light and moved to the musician, probably to thank him, although he had no clear motivation when he acted. He pretty well knew he was going to say something stupid. The musician's nametag read "BOWENS"; Gene Collier said, "Mr. Bowens, that was the best trumpet music I ever heard in my life—real deep."

"Deep," repeated Mr. Bowens, his sad eyes smiling for a fraction of a second.

"It's like you play what you feel. Never heard anyone could do that."

"Hope you liked it, Mr. Collier." Sergeant Bowens began wiping off his trumpet and putting it away. "Want to hear some more music?" he said. Gene nodded. "You got any civvies?"

"Just the shirt and pants I come in with."

"They'll do just fine. Meet you at the Orderly Room in twenty minutes."

An adventure. Something he could yield himself up to. "Hot dang," Gene said out loud in the shower room.

When he saw Sergeant Bowens in a plaid sport jacket, gray slacks, and cordovans, Gene Collier was struck not so much by the clothes as the fact that the man who wore them was as tall as he was. Gene waited outside while his benefactor arranged for passes, still another blessing of belonging to a company that was not yet a company. As Bowens handed Gene his pass, he said, "My name's Byrum, what's yours?"

"Gene."

"Glad to know you, Gene." Their hands matched one another perfectly, in texture as well as size.

Gene didn't ask where they were going, but Byrum Bowens was carrying his trumpet case, so the destination was music. After a bus ride into Augusta, and a taxi ride cross-town and cross-tracks, the site appeared—a rickety building near a dilapidated church. The building had a porch, on which some old Negro men were rocking and passing a glass back and forth. All the shades were down in the building, but one could sense activity within.

Gene anticipated a similar room to the one he visited with Fatty up in Morgantown, and his anticipation made all the difference in his present excitement. Byrum and Gene had spoken little, just enough to establish that they were, respectively, from Cleveland and West Virginia, had been in the Army for almost six years in one case and two months in the other, had attended college for about a semester each, one with a basketball scholarship and the other with a football scholarship.

Gene walked into one large room full of tables and people with skins of every shade from beige to blue, bodies ranging from tiny to immense, drinking everything from Coke to moonshine. Yes, there were smoke and revolving pink lights; men leering at girls and girls pulling down at dresses with one hand and primping hair with the other. There were jokes, cruel and dirty. There were sneers and shrieks. But everyone there had a single higher motive, something that transformed them and gave them grace: they all came to hear the music of Byrum Bowens, who played with an owl-faced drummer, a great mound of piano-player, and a serpentine bassist. When Bowens' horn produced the first three notes of a song Gene had never heard before, the room became silent; everyone retreated behind his own eyes, lost in feelings and private thoughts by the time the rest of the group joined in. Gene's eyes caught bright reflections from the trumpet, which became his grandma's scissors, his father's eyes, and Hamlet's dagger. The overwhelming feeling, however, was of sadness. There was grace, but there was mostly sadness. The music went on forever.

Byrum Bowens was an important man in the club. During the breaks people came to the table where he sat with Gene. Even the more informal approaches were deferential: "Hey, man, you're really makin' the hawk do some talkin' tonight."

"Thanks, man."

Byrum Bowens had a very studious face; his eyes looked inward as far as they did outward. His long face was deeply lined, and his hair had begun to recede. He introduced Gene as "My man Gene," and drinks were sent over all night, sweet-tasting stuff that the waitress with hooded eyes called "Seven-and-Seven." Then the music became celestial—circular and whirling back upon itself.

If Gene was drunk in the taxi, it was a condition that brought out the very best within him, particularly his essential good nature. A tongue that was slow and somewhat thickened was a small price to pay. "By-rum," he said more than once, "you're th' bes' damn trumpeter in th' 'orld."

"If I ain't," said Bowens, his eyes bugging out for emphasis, his voice rising in pitch, "then eggs ain't poultry . . . grits ain't grocery . . . an' Mona Lisa was a *man!*"

They had just missed the bus; another would come at 3 A.M. It didn't matter. A detail. They sat on the curb, eventually sinking back on the sidewalk for comfort, gazing at the sky, particularly rich with stars. Gene fell asleep.

When he heard, "Hey, boy," Gene snapped up immediately. But the face in the patrol car made it clear that only Bowens was its object. When the cop got out of the car and came to the curb, Gene automatically stood up. "If you're waitin' fer the bus, there's a bench fer that purpose right over there." Gene walked toward the bench.

Byrum Bowens did not.

The events that followed have remained vague in Gene's mind. The essential facts are these: Bowens would not move; the cop said "boy" repeatedly and pointedly; there was an arrest—all done quietly. At one point Gene moved back to the curb and began to talk to the cop in a conciliatory tone. He did remember the cop's face, swollen and extremely genial. He remembered Byrum's words that he did not understand: "Listen, Gene, there ain't no mistake here. This cat knows what he's about and so do I. We're both doing what we got to do. So go on and sit on that bench over there and catch the next bus back."

When Private Collier saw Sergeant Bowens in the mess hall later that week, they looked sheepishly at one another and spoke only of the end of the "paper" days. Perhaps the two men would have become friends in time, perhaps there would have been other trips to the club where Bowens played, perhaps even words to describe feelings that were beginning to rise to the surface in Gene, not to be blown away—perhaps. But a week after Baker Company's full complement arrived and began to distinguish three "dits" from four on the earphones, Private Eugene Collier, Jr., RA 51 310 611, and lots of the others, received orders for Korea. The war that wasn't a war to keep the peace that wasn't a peace had suddenly taken the form of men dropping bombs and shooting bullets at other men.

5

Status

Watch a good pool shooter run fifty balls, and you will learn
something about continuity. In such a run there will usually
be five or six fairly difficult shots; two or three others might
be very difficult indeed. Watching a good run by a good
player, a person generally remembers all the very difficult
shots and some of the fairly difficult ones; this sort of memory, we are told by apologists for the human race, is perfectly reasonable and clearly a matter of what passes under
the catch-all of "Human Nature." Such logic suggests that
a man who can first master all the parts of the game (the
making of difficult shots) will then master the whole thing
(be able to run fifty balls).

'Taint so.

There is such a thing as the rhythm of continuity and it
is something more than one plus one plus one plus one. It
is a thing that sweeps certain players along so they can
make shots in a run they might never have made before
and, when absent, may cause a superior technician to falter
over a shot of only moderate difficulty. The whole of a thing

has a quality, a texture, a rhythm all its own, perhaps related to the sum of its parts, but essentially it is a force unto itself.

There was a continuity to Gene Collier's Army career totally unrelated to specific events. But relating that career, unfortunately, becomes too often an exercise in merely recounting certain specific, difficult shots.

For example, there was the incident in the mess hall the day Private Collier was shipping for Korea. His orders had assigned him to a transient company on the post for two days, after which time the men would be shipped by train to Fort Lewis, Washington; then take a flight to Okinawa and another to Japan; the entire process culminating in a troopship cruise to Pusan, Korea. He arrived on July 8, 1950, the day after Harry S Truman named General Douglas MacArthur the Supreme Commander of all United Nations Forces.

An Oriental sage has said that even a journey of many thousand miles begins with a single step. For Gene, his particular step established the rhythm of the journey. Since he was to be very transient in a transient company, Gene lived rather casually out of his duffle bag for the two days. His fatigues were somewhat wrinkled; his boots were laced halfway, his fly was not entirely buttoned most of the time. He went to the last meal he was to eat at Camp Gordon in this state; the train was scheduled to leave that night from Columbia, South Carolina, at 2000 hours. With a tray full of food and still somewhat bewildered about the events that were dominating his life, Gene Collier walked across the tiled floor of the regimental mess. A single voice pierced the din of voices and the sound of metal touching metal; it was an outraged voice, a voice practiced in command. It was not at all clear what the voice was saying. It exploded a second time, and the entire hall fell instantly silent. Still the words were unclear. Collier continued walking toward an empty seat, only slowly becoming aware of the silence and the fact that all eyes were on him. The voice crashed behind him a third time: "You. Soldier. Stop where you are." The words were unclear because the breathing of this man who produced them was terribly strained. Gene turned and saw the scarred face of the orientation major not ten inches from his own. At close range he saw that a great deal more of it was scarred than appeared to be from a distance; a skin-colored powder covered the forehead, nose, and one cheek. There was an incongruous female cosmetic odor to the face. The deeply scarred portions had an ugly scabrous edge that could be seen clearly at close range. There was lunacy in the eyes.

The silence prevailed. When the major spoke again, his voice was resonant enough to shake the pans in the kitchen. "Soldier, where do you think you are?" Gene looked around, as if to find a clue. "You're a disgrace to the uniform, and I will not have you degrade it. Button those buttons." His fingers flicked a loose button on Gene's shirt and one on his fly. "Tie those laces properly." The major kicked Gene's instep stingingly with a polished toe. "Collier. I won't forget you. What's your status?"

The question made no sense to Gene; what the hell did he mean by "status"? When it was screamed again into his face, he searched for an answer to the question he could not understand. An answer came; Gene believed it was a mistake to utter it. He withheld the words.

"What's your status, Collier?"

"I'm in the Army."

There was some laughter, abruptly shut off by a withering look. Did the grotesque face actually turn white? "You'll be hearing more from me, Collier." The major straightened, cut a clean about-face, and strode out of the hall. Slowly the mess hall sounds returned to normal. Gene Collier remained the object of numerous eyes for a few minutes after he sliced into the meat loaf with his fork. "I know him," said a freckled corporal sitting next to Gene; "he's a son-of-a-bitch that really won't forget."

The major did not forget the episode. Gene Collier did not forget the episode. But their paths diverged markedly —that night Gene was headed west; the following Wednesday the major was reassigned to Army Headquarters in Munich. Merely an episode. Over in a few minutes, but the episode left him utterly bewildered, and that bewilderment formed the tone and texture of his life for the next few years.

Here is another representative example. Upon receiving an eight-hour pass from Fort Lewis and a night on the town in Tacoma, Private Collier elected to eat the best dinner in town—at the restaurant in the Wiltwick Hotel—and to see the best movie—*The Asphalt Jungle.*

A simple matter, you might think. As he entered the lobby of the hotel, he was followed in by a number of male and female dwarfs, perhaps a dozen. Gene had never seen a dwarf before in his life. Now he was surrounded by them, by their peculiar voices and incredible bodies. They must have been some sort of entertainment or novelty act, for most of them lugged instrument cases along with their suitcases. Collier stood like Gulliver in their midst, seeing their eyes, the wrinkled faces, and uncommon torsos quite closely. He froze. They, in their confusion to find the desk, circled him twice and then moved off toward the elevators, leaving him unwilling to go on to dinner. A deep sadness came over him: not a "There-but-for-the-grace-of-God" sadness, but something much deeper and more irreverent, something related to revulsion and akin to emptiness. It gave way to confusion, and that to bewilderment. Gene had a Coke at the bus station—it caused him discomfort on the bus; he returned to an empty barracks six hours early. He did not understand his reaction; it was as though another man within him, one much more sensitive to things than he had ever been, had been overwhelmed.

Collier's bewilderment had a physical dimension. He was never alert anymore. He wished to sleep most of the time. His face took on a dopey cast, with his eyes rounded and the brows raised. Also, he began to develop his father's mannerism of scratching the back of his head when it didn't itch.

It didn't bother him particularly that the war he was going to was not clearly explained to him or defined. That was irrelevant. He had had eight weeks of basic training; he had had a number of superb adventures; he had eaten Army food and worn Army clothes. It was assumed by both signatories of the contract that he would fight when called upon.

The flight was exciting and rough. Gene's stomach was one of the few to remain stabilized. It was grueling; there were numerous refueling stops and a detour around some threatening weather. The plane was followed by lightning and buffeting winds all the way into Japan.

Aboard ship from Japan to Korea the men were briefed: The North Koreans had attacked the South Koreans. The United Nations decided to help the South Koreans. The United Nations didn't have an army, so the United States was going to act as the United Nations' army. The guys we were helping were known as ROKs—troops of the Republic of Korea. The guys we were going to fix were known as Gooks because they were sneaky and not worthy of a respectable title.

On the ship the new men (Gene included) were equipped —rifles, helmets, full field packs—and given specific assignments. He was welcomed into Able Company, 17th Infantry Division, 8th Army, by the company commander, a waddling, bespectacled young southerner, a first lieutanant. Gene became a rifleman in the third platoon. The leader of the second squad was Sergeant Isaiah Tall Saddle, a full-blooded Oglala Sioux and one of F.D.R's most decorated warriors in World War II. He had recently been busted for rowdiness while drunk and was on his way back to top rank. This turn of luck placed Eugene Collier, Jr., in excellent hands and provided him with the finest on-the-job training for war it was possible to receive.

Pusan, Korea, looked pretty much like Charleston, West Virginia, when it came to the buildings, but not when it came to the people. The number of people Gene saw as the truck rolled slowly north through the city was staggering. They moved quickly in bunches in all directions across and up and down the wide streets. Many were on bicycles. It looked to him like a mob scene in a silent movie. The day was overcast, and the lighting added to the quaint cinematic effect.

The only signs of war were the warriors themselves, the endless green trucks loaded with confused, anxious American soldiers. Planes—ours—were coming in low over the city.

Then a closer look, not at crowds or their movements, but at a face or a hand gesture. A toothless man whose pushcart had broken. A young woman (a girl) with a baby strapped to her back. A huge poster of a white-haired, kindly Oriental face over the entrance to an official-looking building. A young boy in the distance kicking a ball, soccer-style, through the park. A man with a wagon smacking a bone-thin gray horse with a rolled newspaper. But mostly the impression of tremendous numbers of people.

A continuous buzz echoed through Collier's head and ran down into his hands and feet.

None of the small local people paid much attention to the soldiers. Most were preoccupied with getting somewhere other than where they were. They moved freely and gracefully in loose-fitting clothes, which were generally white and often highlighted with some bright design. Most days were sunny; there were numerous awnings on buildings and many people carried sun umbrellas. Most of the Koreans wore conical hats of straw that made them appear to have balance and control, no matter how active and confused their bodies were.

Gene Collier was struck by the strange familiarity of this alien scene. "Don't seem like no war to me," said the soldier crammed next to him on the truck.

As the soldiers rolled northward in the covered truck toward combat, combat moved southward toward them. About thirty miles outside the city soldiers became more evident, as did a strange sound barely audible in Pusan itself. It was exactly like the "pop" of a good hit on a tackling dummy. A high-pitched squeal, barely heard but more perceptible as the truck rolled north, preceded each "pop." "Mortars," said Sergeant Isaiah Tall Saddle, his face reflecting deep concern. Private Collier, seated directly across, found the expression reassuring.

Sergeant Tall Saddle said in a low voice, "They say MacArthur's in charge. It's bound to be tough." When he talked others craned to listen. He didn't elaborate.

"Tough on who?" a voice from the darkness in the truck asked.

"Ever'body," Tall Saddle said, and he spit out the back of the truck.

Occasionally along the road the convoy passed a line of ROK soldiers moving in the opposite direction. From the rear they looked like Americans to Gene.

An argument broke out in the darkness. Two guys were going at it pretty good. One was willing to bet twenty bucks he was right; the other thought fifty bucks more manly. The issue split most of the truckload right down the middle: Half thought Korea was an island, half didn't. "Hey, Sarge, what it is, an island or not?"

"Sure it's an island," Tall Saddle said. He smiled and might even have flashed a wink over to Gene. "Pay attention," he said suddenly and pointed to a flat stretch of rich blue-green that ran in rectangular segments far beyond the highway on both sides. "Purty, ain't it?"

"Yeah. What is it, Sarge?"

"It's your first rice paddy. And if you have to fight in 'em, you'll have an extremely memorable military experience." He curled a lip and lowered his chin into a cup formed by his large brown hand.

Soon after, the truck began a series of fairly sharp in-

clines, and Tall Saddle's expression eased. Gene was thinking of nothing, hearing a faint buzz and snatches of music
he didn't realize he knew. The ground became rocky. Collier noticed a number of ridge lines to the west; the terrain
was very much like certain parts of West Virginia he had
seen on bus trips with the football team. With one important exception: There were few trees, and those he saw
were small, with more growth from side to side than upward. "Tough terrain," said Tall Saddle, "lots of diggin'."

The truck stopped in a great clearing. Hundreds of U.S.
Army trucks. Half a dozen tanks. Thousands of soldiers and
tents. Shouting. Whistling. Much activity. The "pops"
came very regularly now. The men of the second squad,
third platoon, Able Company, 17th Infantry Division, 8th
Army, trusted their leader implicitly. So, by the way, did the
company commander. The result was that Tall Saddle's
squad got the word fastest and truest. Very often before the
company commander had made up his own mind or had a
decision passed along from Headquarters.

"This looks like our home for a few days," he said when
his men left the truck. "There's a field kitchen, so the
chow'll be purty good. All in all, purty duty until the Kores
decide to test us." Sergeant Isaiah Tall Saddle was the only
American soldier who referred to the enemy as "Kores."
Gene Collier never referred to them at all.

Four days of cleaning equipment, sleeping, and sun-
bathing. Unless, of course, you were unlucky enough to
pull a guard duty or a K.P. Tall Saddle's men tended to pull
very few such details. Gene had almost begun enjoying this
phase of Army life when an enemy mortar attack was reported at another staging area a mile or so up the main
road. It was heard clearly well before it was reported. Even
though the "pops" were quite loud, their regularity made
them seem anything but formidable. Certainly, destruction
should have a random chaotic sound. Half a platoon wiped
out, Tall Saddle estimated.

Combat meant walking in squad formations up and down

ridge lines until a shot was heard. Then returning fire in the general direction. And after a while movement cautiously in the same direction until another shot was heard. And digging; man, was there a hell of a lot of digging. Usually as soon as a fairly safe, fairly comfortable hole was dug, the platoon would move on. Gene never saw anyone actually hit, although at the staging area there were plenty of wounded; nothing that tough to look at though. For the first few weeks or so most of the wounded men were ROKs, but then more and more were Americans.

Gene Collier didn't exactly remember his specific initiation to combat. It was no big deal to him. He had been the wide-man-right in a squad formation going down a cart-road when he saw some tall reeds to his right break in half at just about the same moment he heard a machine gun firing. He didn't panic; he didn't freeze; he didn't philosophize. He yelled: "Take cover," and dove in a ditch. He felt nothing. He fired his first shot of the Korean Conflict toward a hill a machine gun might have been on. Sergeant Tall Saddle disappeared in the reeds. Twenty-five minutes later a grenade went off. Ten minutes after that the sergeant emerged from the reeds.

The argument about whether or not Korea was an island was again activated. It became the most common subject of off-duty conversation. Next was what they were all going to do when they got home. The only man who spoke less than Tall Saddle was Gene Collier. Everyone saw that he was a loner, but somehow they also sensed his bewilderment, for his isolation was never because of arrogance or disdain. One of the fellows in the squad—as a matter of fact, it was the guy who first insisted that Korea was an island—nicknamed everyone. Gene was, for a short while, known as the Mechanical Soldier. "Yeah," said the Islander, "just wind him up in the morning, and watch him do everything by the book." The name didn't really stick because the Islander was pretty much the only one to use it regularly, and the Islander was the first man in Able Company to be killed.

The squad was out trying to make contact with the enemy when a machine gun opened fire from on top of the ridge, over five hundred yards ahead. Really a dumb thing to do, giving their position away like that. Tall Saddle waved the men back out of range. The private who was now ready to bet a hundred bucks cash that Korea was an island never pulled back. Tall Saddle went out and found his body the next morning.

That day marked another turning point. Each time the squad went out, thereafter, they made contact sooner and with forces of increasing strength and firepower. "Man, these Kores can fight." By week's end the camp was hit by mortar and machine-gun fire. Intelligence reported Gook tanks in the area. Able Company moved out smartly.

No one said the word "retreat," not even Sergeant Tall Saddle. Most of the men believed the company's movements were simply a means of by-passing an obstacle. Gene realized that when his squad went out in the mornings the sun was now on his left. They were probing their way southward.

The United Nations Forces retreated within a semicircle around Pusan. It was a tough goddamned semicircle. The Gooks controlled the entire peninsula but for that armed semicircle. The month of August was mean. Men and supplies poured into Pusan. The enemy hit it with everything they had. Something had to give.

6

Bei feng

The three men in the room were incredibly different, physically and temperamentally. Yet their lives had been knit together by a good many elemental things, most basically by the fact that they were among the very few who had survived the torturous trial of the Long March. They were very considerate to each other and very tolerant of their differences. They referred to one another as *tung jr,* or comrade. It was both a manner of address and a statement of fact.

Meetings between these three always had a purpose beyond mere sociability. This latest was indeed somber, for the thin dark man with the graceful hands had to inform the tall, slightly paunchy man with the mole on his chin that his son had been among the first members of the Chinese People's Volunteer Army to have been killed in Korea. Thus at the outset did Chou En-lai relay the information to Mao Tse-tung. The third man, the wrinkled little Chu Teh, registered no particular expression.

The essential purpose of the meeting had been strategic;

the men had met each week since late June to discuss intelligence on the war. Comrade Chou's written request that
the three meet one day earlier was very irregular. There
was an ineffable suggestion in the ambiguous wording
which Chairman Mao regarded as foreboding. He was,
therefore, not unprepared to hear about something
unusual and perhaps painful: the fate of his son, An-ching.
Similar information had come to Mao periodically throughout his life. His first wife, Yang K'ai-hui, had been killed by
the Kuomintang, and then a sister, a brother, and several
uncles and aunts.

Chou presented the information in the form of a report
from An-ching's military superior. Chou did not slide the
document across the lacquered table, or even hand it directly across. Rather, he stood, walked behind the expressionless Chu Teh and placed it on the table near Mao's left
hand. The larger man read the report. The most difficult
problem was that the cause of death was indeterminate.
"Chien," said the Chairman. *"Chien."*

Chu Teh took a cigarette from a leather pouch and began
to screw it deliberately into a holder. Chou En-lai returned
to his seat.

Chien means "family." "It is a double sword-blade,
chien," Mao said and looked about for something to settle
his eyes upon. The others realized they must wait while this
man dealt with the first stages of his grief. He settled his
eyes on a small photograph of the Peking Summer Palace.

When the three men had met in September of 1950, a
situation of great urgency and danger had arisen. General
MacArthur had authorized a surprise, amphibious landing
on the Korean western coast. It was a daring tactic and
almost immediately had achieved three desirable conditions: 1) It relieved the pressure on Pusan; 2) It met with
little effective resistance and quickly became the base for a

widening fighting front; 3) Much of the North Korean force would be caught in a pincers movement; they could not be expected to withstand the pressure for very long. The tactic had impressed the three men, each of whom had had enough personal experience in such matters to maintain at least a partial objectivity and, therefore, a measure of respect.

There was an obvious countermove—the injection of a new element into the equation—at a very great cost, however: massive numbers of the People's Liberation Army. Independence had been newly won and now still more fighting was required. An economy in woeful condition, and a new investment of men and matériel to be risked. A new country to be fed and housed, and strong bodies to be diverted elsewhere.

In late September U.S. forces pushed northward from Inchon toward the 38th Parallel. Foreign Minister Chou En-lai was authorized by the Standing Committee to inform the Indian ambassador that if and when any troops other than South Koreans entered the North, China would be forced to intervene. The word was dutifully passed along the diplomatic corridors toward Washington.

In an emergency meeting on Wake Island, General Douglas MacArthur assured a fretful Harry S Truman that the Chinese were in no condition to intervene in any significant way, given their limited resources and the manner in which the United States had just raised the stakes.

On October 7, U.S. troops crossed the 38th Parallel.

At the meeting following this incursion, the wizened Chu Teh spoke at length. This was rare for him. When he spoke, he brought to bear all the lessons learned from a bizarre and painful lifetime. This was the man who had isolated himself on a river steamer for weeks so he could struggle directly with his opium addiction, and finally overwhelm it by will. This was the young Kuomintang police commander who had led an ill-fated uprising against the government in

Nanchang. The rich landlord's son who gave all his family's wealth to the Communists and saw much of that family slaughtered. The man who had joined Mao early in Hunan and helped organize a successful peasants' revolt and the autonomous Kiangsi Soviets. The commander of the Fourth Red Army with Mao as political commissar, the "Chu" half of the "Chu-Mao" twins, as they were known to their troops. This was the man who saw all lost in the South when he was overruled by the Party as to which tactics would succeed against Chiang's superior numbers; the result was a disastrous defeat and the most costly retreat in military history. This was the man who led one of the columns on the year-long, six-thousand-mile expedition for survival northward to Yenan. Along the route some men had been forced to drink their own urine and even to eat the sparse flesh of dead comrades. This small man, as well as the others at the table, was among the handful who survived.

"We three know that nothing important in the world of men is ever easily achieved," Chu Teh said. His voice was very low. "That is a lesson that must be retaught too often, I am afraid." The other men both looked directly at his eyes. "We have no choice but to send troops in great numbers. Tactically, we must relieve the pressure on the men who will be caught in the vise. We must also challenge the drive northward very strongly. Politically, we have lost all if we permit the imperialists to maintain a presence on the people's soil, especially in view of all the sacrifices that have already been made. In essence, comrades, we actually have no choice. It is only the reluctance to cross the river yet another time, so to say, the hope that another severe sacrifice would not be necessary, this is what makes us wish to avoid recognition of the true situation." Chu Teh had not raised his eyes from the table's edge during his advice. He suddenly looked up and opened his lips to speak further. But he thought better of it and remained silent.

Chou En-lai read various reports of political and military significance. His manner was curt and he was partially distracted. He concluded with these words: "It would be possible to have an effective air defense in a matter of six weeks. Troops rushed in from Manchuria could engage the enemy in perhaps a week's time. It is entirely likely that the front could be stabilized by the middle of next year and the price for their aggression made so great that a cease-fire could be established shortly after that. I agree with Comrade Chu, however, that we must move; the questions that remain are only, when, where, and with what force."

The Chairman nodded. "We must have specific forms of action to recommend to the standing Committee. With proper alternatives. I, personally, have only one other concern. The soldiers who engage the enemy should be volunteers."

"What members of the People's Army would not be?" asked Chu Teh in a whisper.

"There are many who have eaten army food for too many years, who have seen too many different faces sleeping next to them and worn out too many shoes marching on the road. Not every soldier should be required to make this expedition. Remember, there may be others required before China is through." It was considered a minor stipulation to the other men and to the members of the committee.

Chinese People's Volunteers entered Korea from Manchuria three days later.

Mao's gaze left the photograph. He quoted some lines of an ancient, anonymous poet:

> Do not let me hear you talking together
> About titles and promotions;
> For a single general's reputation
> Is made out of ten thousand corpses.

Another long pause. Then he smiled strangely. "But, of course," he continued, "we have no choice in these matters since we are all ruthless men."

Chu Teh finally lighted his cigarette. And the three men began to speak in more normal tones and rhythms. The word *"ming,"* or fate, was used repeatedly in the conversation by Chou and Chu Teh; it was meant as a salve or healing ointment for the Chairman's pain of loss. "I would suggest, my friends," Mao said after all their business had been completed, "that if we all believed so implicitly in *ming,* we would not have dared to risk what we have for China. We would not have challenged the gods so brazenly. We would not have refused to recognize our inevitable defeat so consistently. No, comrades, there was a *bei feng* [northern wind] in China not because fate willed it, but because we stood up in Yenan and blew."

7

Jersey Red

Gene Collier missed the very toughest fighting up around the 38th Parallel in the early months of 1951. He had, however, seen enough mutilated bodies around Pusan, enough petty cruelty and personal degeneration to make him deal with life and the world as he had neglected to before. It was, perhaps, the lifeless look in a street urchin's eye as he tried to sell his sister's services that began to end Collier's numb bewilderment. It may have been the sister's grateful expression when the deal was consummated and she led Sergeant Tall Saddle gracefully into a nearby alley.

Gene Collier followed a girl similar to Tall Saddle's into a storage shed behind a Pusan bar later that same night. In the chill darkness he smelled the oil of her hair as she tried unsuccessfully to undo his belt. He heard his own heavy, nasal breathing. Then he realized that he had raised his hands as though he were a prisoner.

The belt finally unhitched, she began to unbutton his pants, and Gene felt first his penis' throbbing and then its pressure to free itself. "Mo-nee now," she said sweetly.

"Later," he said, not believing that the word was his.

"Mo-nee." He felt her hands fall away. He could now just make out her body, withdrawn, in the darkness.

"I'll pay you, just keep goin'."

"Mo-nee."

He withdrew some bills and coins from his pocket and handed them directly to her as though it were an exact-change transaction in the market. There was a chink of coins and then one of her hands caressed his stomach, his thighs. The other tripped expertly over the buttons on his pants and pushed enough clothing aside to let his penis force its way out. When she touched it, her hand was cold yet the sensation for Gene was intensely warm.

The girl was expert; tender and thoughtful, even though the situation lent itself to a much more mechanical approach. She took time with her stroking caresses. She told him it was "beeg one." And she all but bent him into position over her after she raised the skirt of her *cheong sam* and slid to the floor. Gene Collier felt suddenly very experienced. "I don't want to hurt you," he said. She coughed or giggled. And then he tried to hurt the girl, but she took his thrusts so expertly, glided and slid sideways from them so that none of the plunges came directly into her. The man upon her growled regularly, as though each sound activated a new thrust. Suddenly he felt an incredible release —solder suddenly made liquid—and his spine, the back of his knees tingled. His full weight fell upon the girl, but she was already in the process of escaping under his arm.

When Gene Collier realized that he was lying prone on the floor of a dark, cold shack in Pusan, Korea, with his pants and shorts down around his knees, his first feeling was laughter: He saw himself the butt of a joke so funny even he had to appreciate it. Then he felt terrific relief: He had finally accomplished the initiation that separated him from the men in his world. Then he felt foolish again, so he got up, wiped himself off with a handkerchief and dressed, running his fingers through his short hair as he reentered the bar.

The final feeling came later, an hour or so after he joined some of the men back in the bar. It came when the girl, on her way outside with a fat, greasy corporal, passed Gene and scanned his face without a flicker of recognition or memory. The moment activated a deep and lasting sense of shame. Gene Collier had seen and done a great many things that offended and eroded the better part of his nature. Perhaps this episode with the Korean bar girl put him at rock-bottom, led to the destruction of that better nature.

More likely, though, the shock of recognition brought about by a fall to the depths is not the result of a single blow, although that's how it often appears because a particular limit seems to have been reached. That limit is the end of a process. What remains encouraging (to the onlooker only) about a fall to rock-bottom is the relationship between the rock, the fall, and the impact. Where there is movement and impact, there is the possibility, at least, for reversal.

Gene was altered by the sum of individual sufferings, shames, and humiliations he had seen and experienced. And the alteration had some obviously beneficial effects. The faint buzzing in his arms and legs and head that had been a condition of living for almost a year ended abruptly. His body relaxed; he was loose-jointed, exactly as he had been in a football game after he had been hit a good shot and realized that he would be able to take whatever they threw at him and still do real fine dishing it out too. He developed a different sense of time: He felt, now, that time was not provisional, not transient, but in fact a resource he must learn to value and spend. This vivified young man seemed ready to begin to accept the role of personal artist: molder of self and shaper of time.

But.

There was a residue of other, earlier choices that held

him as the glue of sleep on eyelids can keep the morning eye closed against its will and can blur vision even after it has been opened. Or, to use another, more familiar metaphor, Gene was ready to make some ripples of his own, but the prevailing breeze would not permit them to become visible. Private Collier was reassigned to permanent guard duty on Koje-do.

The Inchon strategy and the trap which resulted had caught so many Gooks unaware and helpless that many thousands were taken prisoner in the first few months. Their numbers increased rapidly and with the passage of time were augmented by numerous Chinese. A small *"do"* (or island) barely five miles off the southern tip of Korea was selected as the perfect repository (à la San Quentin) for these captives. Koje was little more than a barren rock-pile on which was built a stockade that ultimately held, during the heaviest season of spring '52, 130,000 Korean and 20,-000 Chinese prisoners of war.

Gene Collier was there only until January '52, so he did not witness the riots of May, or the humiliating capture by the prisoners of the base commander, Brigadier General Francis Dodd, or the bloody slaughter that followed by way of reprisal after Dodd was released. Gene was not on Koje during those remarkable events; he was in another, very different prison camp. But his time and duty on Koje were far from uneventful. Least significant, perhaps, was his promotion (rather tardy owing to his several transfers) to P.F.C.

P.F.C. Collier was one of the few regular guards on Koje who was not an M.P. This is merely a fact; in and of itself it has no real significance. His treatment of prisoners, however, did differ markedly from most of the other guards.

"Permanent" guard on Koje sounded at first like dreadful duty, akin to "permanent" K.P. or "permanent" message-runner. It wasn't. It amounted to eight hours on duty out of every thirty-six. Night duty was spent in one of the towers spaced about every fifty yards along the outer fence, periodically running a searchlight over the nearest compounds. Two men were assigned to each tower, so loneliness and boredom were more matters of choice than necessity. A small heater was sufficient to warm the small glass and wooden chamber.

During daytime duty each guard was personally responsible for a small compound building and its inhabitants. He was expected to examine the prisoners and their quarters daily, to rectify any breech of camp rules, discipline, or authority in any manner he chose and to report them to his superior. Punishment was generally arbitrary, immediate, and violent in nature; a short, blunt rod was the common instrument for meting it out. Less common but widely used was what the guards humorously called "The Five of Clubs"—a tightly clenched fist.

P.F.C. Collier was known among his prisoners as "the careless one." They did not mean that he was either slovenly or inconsistent; they meant, quite literally, that he was without regard for adherence to the rules of life within the barbed wire on Koje-do. Many of the restrictions beyond those of incarceration itself seemed unduly severe and arbitrary to Collier.

He tacitly permitted reading material and messages in the compound, any personal items the prisoners had managed to hold onto or manufacture, the communication and exchange of thoughts. He did not choose this approach; it was almost as though the approach chose him. How could he behave otherwise? The approach was effective. The prisoners were cooperative and understanding, self-interest being a strong (and conscious) motivation among them. The specific benefits to Gene were both great and small: He expended minimal effort in his task; it was not particularly unpleasant; he did not sink deeper into his own shame; he was taught some conversational Korean phrases; he received an expert haircut each month from a prisoner called Moon who had been a barber before the war.

P.F.C. Collier might have remained on Koje-do for the duration had he behaved in his formerly characteristic manner and kept his mouth shut.

Sometime after midnight on December 25, 1951, Gene was on duty with a young M.P. everyone called Jersey Red because he had red hair and came from New Jersey, but really because he made it clear that was how he wanted to be known. Jersey Red was a kid, even younger than Gene, who talked tough in a way that scared Gene a little.

The night was clear and cold, with a strong, gusting wind coming off the Yellow Sea and causing the windows in the tower to vibrate at various high pitches. A new load of prisoners had arrived earlier in the day. They were piled in temporary huts—dirt floors, bamboo walls, thatched roofs —until room could be made for them elsewhere. There was no hurry. The huts were directly below the tower, wired off into a separate compound. Until events unfolded, Gene Collier did not give the men in those huts or the conditions they had to endure this bitter night the least thought.

No, he was thinking about home. Not his house or even his family. He was thinking about being truly home. The entire concept was summarized by a memory: The Stork had felled a tall hemlock on a hill about a mile or so to the east of Hundley. He had worked fast, even for him, so he could have some precious minutes on his back looking at the sunset before his father came by in the wagon to pick him up.

Gene remembered how cool the ground was beneath his sweat shirt and moist pants. The sky in the east had begun to darken, for the sun had fallen below the hills to the west. High in the sky he noticed a lone hawk, soaring in great circles. The bird remained in sunlight; its body seemed bright in the reflected light. Twilight. No longer day, not yet night. The air heavy, the silence palpable. Home was a

matter of feeling connected to things. It was a condition of
harmony so deep that even the parts could not be separated. There was no such thing as parts!

When his consciousness brought him back to Koje-do, it
carried with it a topical conclusion: "When a man's at
home, no one could make him do the things they do over
here." He didn't know if he said the words aloud or if he
merely thought them.

His reverie, he discovered, had been broken by Jersey
Red getting up and going over to the window. "There they
are," he said.

A number of soldiers approached the foot of the tower.
Jersey Red stepped outside and challenged them. His voice
blew away from Collier's hearing. "Halt, who goes there?"
The response came faintly: "Forget that shit. It's us.
We're coming up."

The tower shook as a number of men came up the ladder.
Gene didn't move. Soon the room was filled by three men,
plus Jersey Red and Gene. An M.P. sergeant Gene had seen
around but didn't know did most of the talking. All three
men placed open hands above the heater and then applied
the warmth to their faces. "Witch's tit," one of them said
three or four times.

"We got thirty bucks says you won't do it," the sergeant
said to Jersey Red.

"Are you shittin'? Of course I'll do it. What the fuck is
there to it?"

"Well, we got thirty bucks says you won't."

"You're on."

"What if you don't get one?"

"How the hell could I miss?"

Jersey Red took his rifle off a rack on the wall and moved
outside onto the platform, followed by the three other soldiers. Gene saw him aim down toward the thatch of the
temporary compound. There were three shots. The wind
absorbed them as though it were the ocean. Gene remem-

bered the faces distinctly—the cheeks and eyes highlighted, the other features in shadow. They remained outside for a minute. Nothing stirred in the yard.

When they came back inside, Jersey Red said, "Give me the bread."

"What if you missed?"

"I didn't."

"What if?"

"Then I'll try again on Thursday."

"Give him the money," the sergeant said.

"Thanks," said Jersey Red. "Maybe now when Jersey Red says he'll do somethin', you guys'll believe him."

Disbelief of what he had seen had frozen Gene Collier.

In the morning screams were heard from the hut. Two men, dead from loss of blood, had been discovered by their fellow prisoners. The morning guards got them quiet soon enough and carted off the bodies. A lieutenant ordered a search of the prisoners for hidden weapons; none was found.

The Stork might have remained too incredulous, too confused by the diversity of the world to have acted. Private Collier, RA 51 310 611, the isolated, confused, bewildered and displaced, would certainly not have interfered. But something stirred in this rock-bottom Collier.

He requested to see Colonel Bragg, the adjutant base commander. Denied. A second request. Denied. A third request. Approved. P.F.C. Collier advanced to the desk, stopped, and executed a decent salute. "P.F.C. Eugene Collier reporting, sir."

The colonel did not look up from his papers on his desk. "At ease, Collier. State your business."

"Sir. Those men killed in the temporary detention hut. They were shot by a tower guard real late three nights ago."

"We're conducting an investigation, Collier."

"But, sir, I saw it all happen."

"I'm very busy this morning, Collier."

"But, sir—"

"Excused, Collier."

P.F.C. Collier was relieved of his next tower shift and confined to barracks until further notice. Further notice took the form of orders to rejoin his old outfit, Able Company, 17th Infantry Division, 8th Army. He carried an invisible burden with him as he left: a vague but troubling sense of guilt.

There was a truce in Korea that wasn't a truce; intermittent and vicious fighting erupted continually in a random pattern. Able Company was then north of the 38th, moving on a Gook area called the Iron Triangle.

Gene went by ferry, truck, jeep. Over some highways he had traveled before. Past familiar ridges and rice-paddies. When he finally made contact again with Able Company, Collier discovered that all the personnel had changed. It was a situation too well suited for a relapse into the stiff, buzzing, bewildered Mechanical Soldier who had first come to Korea. He resolved to fight those tendencies within himself. Events made that struggle insignificant.

His first day on patrol Gene got separated from his squad by withering machine-gun and rifle fire. He was pinned in position while the nearest squad members were able to pull back. The distant "pops" came at a faster pace than he remembered before. Gene decided to ride out the storm; no great piece of strategy since he was pinned in a small hollow in a clearing twenty yards from any other cover. Every time he poked over the roll of the ground, bullets sprayed the air above him. He got as comfortable as he could and waited. He had two thoughts: one, the war he had left seemed to have a lot less firepower; two, he didn't want to die.

He was very cold and extremely uncomfortable; he did not move for three hours. At the moment when his discomfort counterbalanced his desire to continue living he raised the muzzle of his rifle beyond ground level. Nothing. He raised a hand. No fire. His helmet. Silence. He decided to go the twenty yards to a small clump of trees. Suddenly. Directly.

As though to confuse any enemy who might have been reading his mind, Collier's knees began churning even before he had decided on the proper moment. The proper moment must be improper. He looked just a bit like the Stork as he took his first strides bent over and then was running erect, stiffly, and with great flat-footed strides toward the trees. He heard a tremendous noise, a roaring sound almost. Perhaps his blood rushing through him. A yard or so from the trees he dove and slid over the snow toward safety under the first line of small trees.

His face was in snow. He was alive. He heard some branches swish and the snow squeak. As he picked his head up, his eyes saw three pairs of boots. P.F.C. Eugene Collier, Jr., was taken prisoner by soldiers of the Korean People's Army on January 7, 1952.

PART II

REMOLDED THOUGHTS

8

Mr. White

Collier was marched through the winter gloom up the hill and over the ridge where a machine gunner had commanded the valley and had managed to hold him in place until, like a stray, he was rounded up. A small, agile boy led the way; his uniform looked very new. Collier could not see the two soldiers behind him very clearly until he was halfway down the far side of the ridge, when they made him stop and sit on the trunk of a fallen tree.

Their jackets were made like the quilts Grandma Gossett produced from scraps, lots of square puffs of cotton covered over with cloth and all sewn together. The smallest one even wore a quilted cap and quilted pants. All the men were similarly flat-faced, and Collier thought of them only as three interchangeable parts of a trap that had worked. They acted as though they hadn't really wanted to catch him very much. They stole quick glances at their dubious prize.

Nothing very specific stood out in the memory of Eugene Collier about the first hour or so of his capture. He remembered, however, sitting on that tree trunk waiting for something to happen and staring at the eyebrow of the young one who had led the way. The boy stood in the snow three or four feet to the side of his prisoner, looking intently up the slope. Hairs as black and shiny as you'd get on a really expensive fishing lure. And perfectly straight up and down, as though each hair had been painted stroke by stroke to produce a perfectly graceful sweep. The boy was young, seventeen perhaps, but that brow would give him the look of innocence for many more years, perhaps forever.

The soldiers spoke in bursts, shorter and seemingly more intense as the sky darkened. Collier looked blankly ahead of him; he heard and thought of nothing. Finally, up ahead, other soldiers came down the hill and the captive was prodded on a few paces until he realized that the two groups were expected to meet where the tree line began. When the groups met, there was only the language of face and eye between them. Collier sensed clearly that his capture, rather than being a source of pride, was an encumbrance.

He was struck by the fact that the uniforms of the soldiers were noticeably different in texture and color: Not all wore quilted jackets and caps; not all their caps had earflaps; two of the men had brown wool gloves, the others all wore green. Each man's clothing was colored like a paint sample on a chart that ranged from gray-green to forest. The soldier walking on Collier's left carried the captured rifle so it swung loosely by its sling at the end of a tired arm, although his eyes remained on it almost constantly. Was it admiration? The other flanker continually examined Collier's boots with what appeared to be anticipation, if not envy; his own were of rough hide, loosely stitched and packed with dirty cloths.

With darkness came the first stars and, behind Collier, a perfectly white half-moon. The clarity above him threw the dapple of frozen mud and ice patches into relief before him. It made the dark blur of the trees ahead seem particularly threatening. One of the men up front began to speak, finally, to someone else in a relaxed, conversational tone.

Collier realized that he was very hungry. For a moment he felt a part of another life, one of a group of West Virginia hunters returning from a cold day on the slopes, tired, hungry, but with a catch that would make their families proud. But who would he be returning to? The inevitability of the answer—No one!—destroyed the mood utterly. And Collier was again the captive of strange, flat-faced men, moving down the far slope of a mountainside in a strange country. His hunger, which he had shared with the hunter of his fantasy, returned to him with a pang. He swallowed saliva. His neck felt suddenly cold, but he did not move his hand toward the collar of his field jacket.

His neck. Cold? No. Not really. It was the neck of someone else, the footsteps in the snow of someone else, the perspective and perceptions of someone else—someone close to him, perhaps, someone with whom he had an empathetic bond, but distinctly not himself. Of course, *he* would always be nearby, close enough to give advice, close enough to care intensely, but *he* would not be wracked with hunger or fear or longing or able to feel a hundred other unpleasant sensations of the prisoner. *He* might occasionally move inside Collier, but never really attach himself to anything that was Collier; rather, he would remain free-floating yet stable, like a small gyroscope that needs only space and a tiny point to rest upon. Usually, he would be outside Collier, somewhere back over his shoulder, elevated where he could see more of the whole picture and hear the distinct snow-crushing footsteps of seven soldiers and their tall captive. He would advise the captive to comply. He would give him all the help and advice he possibly could. He was quite sure he wouldn't be caught, tortured, and killed in a Gook prison camp. He, goddamn it, would not die in Korea.

When the group arrived at the tree line, a distant voice hurled a question in two alien syllables. A voice behind Collier shouted the same syllables in reverse, and after the slightest pause the group moved into the trees. It had either begun to snow or the freshening wind was blowing some flakes off the peak. The ground fell away sharply beyond the trees, and only Collier failed to notice that the steps were taking them all below ground, until he was there. It was a huge, square, underground room covered with wire mesh, newspaper, and tattered cloth. There were large electric light bulbs that did little more than throw off orange candle flame. A very young soldier was lighting lanterns. Only very slowly did the darkness edge away and Collier begin to see hundreds of soldiers, most of them stretched out on mats laid on top of some large green tarpaulins. In the far corner a man was cooking over fires made in holes in the ground. There was a whisper of sound, human speech, so controlled as to seem more the sound of the earth itself than the talk of underground men. The experience was so utterly unexpected and strange that it reinforced Collier's feeling of separation from himself. The Collier who was sure to survive identified much more easily with the clear winter night aboveground. He was a curious onlooker in the artificial world below.

A squat, angry-looking man approached Collier, who had been neglected momentarily by his escort, and pointed to his cartridge belt, which Gene unhitched and handed over instinctively and immediately. Seeking the fullest measure of compliance, Collier also emptied his pockets: a handkerchief, some Korean coins, a Saint Christopher's medal he had found in a Pusan bar, and his wallet. Collier found himself searching the face of the man opposite, who he assumed was an officer. Collier decided this from studying his riding boots and his military bearing, and from the fact that he allowed the collar of a dark sweater to show evenly at the neck of his military shirt. His features were remarkably fine; the eyes seemed Western and extremely bright and bold. Collier told Collier that this was a man you must respect. His captor pointed in turn to his helmet, his field jacket, and his boots, each of which Collier removed and placed on a small table. Losing the boots was a source of worry to Collier; he tried and believed he succeeded in showing no expression at all, whatever had been asked of him.

Three days in the same corner of the hole in the earth. Huddled on the edge of the tarpaulin, chilled and sleeping fitfully with his hands inside his pants, his knees at his chin. No guard; none required. Collier went generally unnoticed —a glance sometimes from some of the men coming and going but never a clear gesture or word of recognition.

The roof over the hole was opaque during daylight and in some spots even transparent. Collier could trace the passage of clouds. He wondered how far they could go— around the world? Could they ever be blown over Hundley? Over any place in West Virginia? When he had to piss badly enough, he stood up. Even that only attracted the notice of a few men. Apparently not the right ones, for no one approached him. Eugene Collier, Jr., began to piss in his pants. He moved toward the table near the center of the dirt floor. A few soldiers jumped up and moved quickly toward him. He stopped and raised his arms above his head in the familiar surrender position. One noticed his wet pants, so Collier was led through a tunnel to another chamber, one in which the stench was so overwhelming he did not dare to breathe through his nostrils. This opportunity to relieve himself completely might not come again, so he proceeded quickly. The lack of paper or even dry leaves created a chafing discomfort that was to stay with him for many days. He was so raw for so long that the misery seemed to afflict the other Collier as well. Anyway, it drove him away for a while.

What he thought was just a tin of hot water, brought to

him by the boy who had been one of his captors, was in fact soup. What he thought was the same soup the following day, was tea. The dark-grained, chewy cake he received at midday was millet; Collier thought it was a strange-tasting nut bar. Ignorance, chills, and wild, half-awake dreams and fantasies obliterated uneven segments of time.

Awakened during the evening of the third day, first by the sounds of a churning motor and then by a kick in the ass, Collier was prodded forward by the squat man he believed to be an officer he could trust to a thin, very composed man. The two men spoke about Collier as if he were not there, pointing at him with their thumbs without bothering to look at him. Some of the men resting along the wall sat up and leaned on their elbows. The verbal exchange apparently had become a serious argument. The thin, composed man's face became defiant; the other shrugged and walked away briskly. Collier's boots and field jacket were brought to Gene by the boy who had brought his food. Collier almost said "thank you," but elected to remain silent in word and compliant in gesture. He put them on and followed a new leader. The wallet was taken by the composed man.

The vehicle was, of all things, an old Chevy pick-up, its present light-gray color being not the only, just the most recent, attempt at a new exterior. It was badly painted and seemed unintentionally camouflaged. There was a grumpy olive-skinned driver, dressed in a quilted green uniform, at the wheel of the idling truck. Collier sat between him and the composed man for many hours.

The words "squat" and "composed" require some clarification. Collier's reaction to the people he had encountered since his capture (or rather, who had encountered him) was elemental; although his eyes recognized individualized, complex personalities, his mind registered simplifications: "young," "dark," "thin," "squat," "composed."

The composed man spoke the words as though he had

learned them phonetically only, perhaps from phonograph
records. He spoke slowly, often emphasizing the wrong
syllable: "You are now a prisoner of the Chinese People's
Liberation Army. Yes? I am taking you to a camp in which
you will be interned until the aggression of your government is ended." The words in English came as a shock to
Collier, not their meaning but the words themselves; they
almost slipped past before he realized that the sounds also
held meaning for him. This man is Chinese, Collier decided
with satisfaction. But the sounds produced a greater effect:
Collier realized suddenly how long it had been since his
ears had heard words in English, how long four days as a
prisoner of war really were and how many more days might
stretch before him. He realized, fleetingly, that words can
measure time as well as clocks, better maybe.

"I will tell you what our activities will be for the next few
days. So you will not be in ignorance and behave . . ."—a
pause here while the man flipped through his supply of
verbal modifiers—" . . . carelessly." Collier had enough
time to apprehend the intelligence of the sharp-featured
oval face on which there was no identifiable expression
while he spoke in English. "We must try to collect other
prisoners today. Tomorrow we will go to a camp at which
you will be processed. Then you will be interned. You are
fortunate. Our Korean colleagues do not place the value
upon prisoners that we do. You understand."

It was not put as a question, so Collier gazed blankly.

"You understand."

Collier nodded so deeply as to approach a ceremonial
bow.

Collier sat between the driver and the composed man.
The pick-up was shifted roughly and much too quickly over
frozen dirt roads. No heater. A cold breeze blew in constantly through vents no one had bothered to close; Collier
steered his eyes from the vent handle.

That other Collier, the safe one, the confident, suddenly

returned with a plan, something rather daring. He communicated the gist of it to the one who was a prisoner. He'd
have to be awfully quick: two swift, disabling blows, first
against the composed one and then the driver; both doors
kicked suddenly open and each of the men shouldered out
onto the road. Then a joy ride (the sort of filmland adventure he'd been looking for all his life) behind enemy lines
to freedom. Imagine! No, not a serious voice, Collier; more
like a wild urge, something irrepressible, but nothing serious. You'd have no chance, so forget it.

Once in the truck Collier closely observed the relationship between the two men. Both, he assumed, were Chinese. Members of the same army. The English speaker was
certainly the driver's superior in power as well as rank.
There appeared to be neither friendship not antagonism
passing from one to the other across Collier as he sat between them. Whatever bond did exist was purely one of
function: The driver could not interrogate a prisoner in
English; the interrogator probably could not drive the battered Chevy. If he had allowed himself to continue thinking
further on the subject; that is, if he weren't just concentrat-
ing on keeping his mind off that open vent, Collier might
have concluded that he was captive of a very different army
from the one that had abandoned him.

They made three stops at underground encampments
very much like the one from which he had been fetched as
the truck careened northward in the gloom of the Korean
winter. At each one the composed man returned to the
truck without prisoners; he brought only packets of paper
tied with coarse striped twine. The road improved
markedly after the first stop to a narrow macadam surface
that was edged with bomb craters, but nowhere had it been
hit directly. The final stop was for fuel and food—balls of
rice and stringy meat eaten with the fingers from a metal
dish, the sweet gravy drunk to the final drop. The driver
licked his dish and then his fingers slowly with a thick
tongue.

Nightfall made driving, even at moderate speeds, extremely difficult, so the composed man said something to the driver, who slowed and drove the truck into a clump of small trees, scrub pines and firs exactly like those that begin to dominate the landscape when you get north of Pleasants, West Virginia. The man's tone in speaking to the driver seemed to Collier to be joking or maybe even teasing, but he must have been incorrect, for the driver seemed to scowl as he got out of the truck, took a bedroll from the rear, and moved with it into the trees.

Collier thought he heard a lightly mocking voice say to him, "Now's your chance," but he wasn't listening very carefully; he accepted the fact of his capture, his imprisonment. To a certain extent he saw his situation as justifiable punishment, but he would have been hard-pressed indeed to convince a rational man that it was really so; a rational man might not have accepted the burden of guilt that Collier carried from Koje-do.

Another day of hard driving. Great discomfort for Collier. Nowhere to rest an arm or stretch a leg. He compensated somewhat by alternately tightening and relaxing various muscles in his body. The exercise did more to pass the time than induce bodily comfort. The day was a continuation of all the days since his capture: chill, bleak, appropriate.

The tall man had been speaking for some time before Collier became aware of the fact. His lack of awareness resulted from several things: his preoccupation with his discomfort, the high level of noise from the motor and the road, the unlikeliness of words after so many speechless hours. The words he missed were these: "Perhaps I should not tell you the things I am about to. . . ."

These words were not particularly revealing. Perhaps this was a technique his captor used in order to get compliance without coercion; perhaps he decided spontaneously to be of some help to Collier in preparing for his adjustment. Collier, having missed the preface, tended to accept what followed as a factual statement.

" . . . Most prisoners, when they arrive, are unprepared for the choices that are offered. They feel that imprisonment means the loss of all choice. We. We feel to the contrary that internment is a failure if it does not lead to the making of right choices." The composed man spoke like a teacher explaining something to a class of particularly slow students rather than to Collier. "It is important, therefore, to understand this from the beginning. And to make the proper choice the first time." In the Collier lexicon, "choice" was a word as unused and vague as "soul" or "love."

"There are no roadsigns in this place," that other, distant, voice said. "How the hell do they travel around? You'd never be able to find your way out of here even if you did manage to escape."

The truck sped through the gloom of evening just about the time Collier noticed that they were passing through small villages with greater frequency. Then the villages became almost continuous. Some large buildings loomed on the road before them. The macadam was replaced by cobblestones in concrete. This was Pyongyang, a city Collier would reside in for one and a half years; he never learned its name.

The Chevy swung off the main road and was soon on dirt. The driver was obviously relieved: He turned toward the composed man and smiled a long, deep smile. His companion made two nasal sounds and the driver nodded and attended to the bends in the road.

Huge wooden gates and a sudden "s-s-s-s" from the composed man forced the driver to stop the truck a little too abruptly. The driver shouted something out of the window and the gates parted unevenly and slowly. The truck entered a huge frame building, dimly lighted, that looked like some sort of storage warehouse to Collier. As a matter of fact, at one time it had been used in that way; now it was a prison.

As Collier descended from the truck, the circulation returned painfully to his rubbery legs. He felt grateful at first when the driver took his arm, until he realized that it was a rough rather than a helpful grasp. The little driver, sullen and preoccupied most of the time behind the wheel, was transformed all at once into a proud captor before his fellow soldiers. The composed man followed with the packets of papers. The driver bent and jerked Collier around dark corners and along corridors until his colleague spoke to him. Collier was left in front of a door formed by wide slats of rough wood. Light came through cracks in the boards, and Collier could make out a man seated behind a desk.

The composed man knocked and opened the door after a moment. He pushed the prisoner inside with a brusque shove. He placed the papers on the desk, said some whispered words and departed, leaving the two men alone in the room.

In one corner a round coal-burning stove threw off the first warmth Gene Collier's body had absorbed since he left Koje-do. "You may step closer to it, if you wish." The white-haired man behind the desk spoke English like an Englishman. Collier assumed he was either a professor or an aristocrat. A small pointed white beard, high forehead and cheekbones, a compact body completely at ease in a loose-fitting black sweater and dark pants. Tapered fingers of great length and delicacy were clasped across his chest. The confidence and ease of the man struck even the cold, confused prisoner and made him defensive, as though he were in the presence of someone special whom he had to please.

"My name is Bai. In English it translates as 'White,' which is indeed an anomaly, is it not?" Collier nodded. "You have been conducted here by Captain Gao. He and I are the only people here who speak English; when you have something to communicate or when we wish to make certain that you understand something fully, we are the ones with whom you will be dealing. Have you ever known any Chinese persons before?"

Collier nodded.

"Would you care to elaborate?"

Collier shook his head.

Then Mr. Bai said, "May I have your dog tags, please?"

The prisoner's hand moved instinctively toward his neck. "Wait a minute. Is this legal?" a voice asked Collier. "Is this legal?" the soldier asked before he pulled them over his head.

"Of course. How else will the Red Cross get word to your family in America?"

"Oh."

"Collier, Eugene. RA 51 310 611. Blood type O. Protestant. Is that information correct?" The prisoner nodded. "Are you familiar, Comrade Collier, with the Chinese water torture?" At the final word, Collier's spirits and then his chest and shoulders caved in. "A joke only, forgive my bad judgment. You have every right to know quite seriously the nature of the situation in which you find yourself."

Mr. Bai wrote some words in Chinese characters on a sheet of graph paper before him. Then he placed a pair of spectacles on his large forehead, looked up, and asked, "Where are you from in America, Comrade Collier?"

"West Virginia." Collier's partner had deserted him; left him without a strategy or a single word of advice.

"Then you must have had your training at Fort Jackson?"

"No, sir. Camp Gordon." Eugene Collier felt many things when he spoke those words, but the strongest was gratitude for this man who cared about his past, when even he was inclined to forget most of it.

"Then you must be adept in some field of radio work."

"I was just beginning to learn to send Morse when I was shipped over."

"Of course, of course. And what does your father do to support his family in America?"

"He works in the mines."

"Mines?"

"Coal. Soft coal. Bituminous." Eugene felt as though he would like to sit down and really have a talk with this fine old fellow.

"Coal. Of course. Collier—coal. It makes perfect sense." Gene was confused by the disjointed reaction. "And what is the level of your education, Comrade Collier?"

"Two and a half years of college," Gene said. He had told lies before, usually in meaningless things. Saying he read a book when he hadn't or seen a football game he'd only heard about. Here the motivation was the same, although the situation was far from meaningless. Gene Collier felt a need to meet this man's expectations, even if he had to create the expectations, too.

"Is it not unusual in your country for the son of a collier to attend a university?"

"I played ball, a football player."

"Of course, of course. Perhaps, Comrade Collier, I should not tell you the things I am about to, but you have been frank with me. I wish to reciprocate." The kindness of his captor suddenly made Collier feel terribly vulnerable.

Mr. Bai pulled down his glasses and seemed to be reading these words from some point beyond Collier's left shoulder. "The Chinese Liberation Army does not regard you as a prisoner of war. We regard you as a criminal. A criminal. And the crimes you have committed, which range from exploitation of the world's poor to the destruction of valuable property and resources and human life, must not go unpunished. Your government is the chief instigator of criminal behavior in the world. We recognize that you, yourself, Comrade Collier, as an individual, instigated nothing. We believe, furthermore, that you were essentially ignorant of the crimes in which you were participating. A pawn merely. But you are not entirely guiltless. In this, as in many things, ignorance is not the equivalent of innocence. As a criminal against humanity, you must be reeducated and transformed before we can release you with some assurance that you will not revert to your former criminal behavior. But before any part of this necessary process can begin, Comrade Collier, you must recognize and confess the full extent of your guilt. This is essentially a matter of choice. You may, as do some of your fellow criminals, choose to deny that guilt. We have no choice but to treat such men as hardened criminals, unwilling to transform themselves. Should you require some help in learning of the full extent of your complicity in criminal behavior, this can be supplied. The question is one of recognition of guilt." Mr. Bai was finished. Collier followed little more than his general tone. He did not, unfortunately, understand the process that Mr. Bai had outlined, nor any of the options open to him. He did, also unfortunately, come away with the sense that Mr. Bai knew things about him that Gene didn't even know about himself. Particularly the stuff about guilt.

"You will need some time to think over my words, and your choices. Time is what we all have too much of and yet never enough, eh, Comrade Collier? We will provide you with seventeen hundred calories per day, the same ration as a field soldier in the People's Liberation Army. Are there any questions for the present?"

The question leaped out and asked itself: "Is there any chance of sending a letter home?"

"Perhaps, Comrade Collier. Perhaps. I look forward to seeing you again in the anticipation that you will make the correct choices, but the process is a painful one either way. Transformation is never easy."

9

On the Seventh Day

In the West it was called "brain washing," and it had connotations associated with horror movies: "truth" drugs, shaved heads, incisions, dungeons, torture, hypnotic-suggestion, mad doctors with fangs, subhuman assistants. Such an image of the process was somewhat helpful in enabling the citizens back home to comprehend the startling fact that among thirty-six hundred American prisoners of war, there was not a single escape and, even more curious, no known attempts. And an incredible degree of compliance and downright collaboration. This could be accounted for logically in America only by the fact that, à la Fu Manchu, these stunted beasts were doing something to our boys' brains that turned them into zombies.

In the People's Republic the process was not generally known. The *People's Daily* had mentioned "thought remolding" among certain Party cadres in the north who had abused their authority, even to the extent of indulging in "profiteering, abuse of workers, rape and other decadent sexual offenses." There was no mention made of the application of the process in Korea or precisely how it worked.

"Thought remolding" was little more than applied Mao-ism by way of Taoism out of Yin and Yang. It was, perhaps, Mao's greatest contribution to Marxist theory: there were, he discovered, two distinct kinds of contradiction; he called them antagonistic and nonantagonistic. The latter could be resolved, indeed must be resolved peacefully; the former, unfortunately, required some form of violent confrontation. So the conflict in Korea was between governments whose interests were essentially antagonistic; resolution required bullets, bombs, and blood. (Of course such a resolution would only be temporary anyway.) The conflict between, say, Mr. Bai and Comrade Collier was nonantagonistic and could be transformed into harmony if one, the other, or both of them realized that on a personal level there was no need or basis for conflict. Since Collier was the prisoner, it would be pretty much up to him to become the transformee.

The first stage in the resolution of nonantagonistic conflict was the passage of time and thought. Time to contemplate alternatives. Time to fear and create fear. Time to evaluate the means of coercion Collier would have used if he were in Bai's place. Time to separate rationalization from understanding (a process that had begun in Collier when he was first captured). Time to think about guilt, about sins of omission, commission, and complicity. Time to stew in his own juices. Time.

Collier was taken down a dark corridor by two soldiers who alternately gave him instructions in Chinese. The faint light from the hallway illuminated the room's few features. It was a ten foot square with rough wooden floor and walls and a high sloped ceiling covered with some fibrous insulation. There was a small opening, a window, under the eaves of the roof that was covered only with a thin wire screen. A large, heavy-lidded crock in the corner. A wooden bed-board attached to the wall by chains at each end held a straw sleeping mat and a quilted blanket that could have been made by Grandma Gossett. Nothing else.

One of the soldiers told him to take off his clothes. Collier did not understand. The man repeated the command. Collier tried to smile. The soldier pulled down the zipper of Collier's field jacket, and the prisoner got the idea. Collier undressed slowly, stopping after removing each article, hoping that just that piece would be sufficient. He proceeded slowly to nakedness. One soldier examined the naked American shamelessly with his eyes; Collier sat down on the edge of the bed-board with his hands on his knees and his knees pressed together. The other soldier brought Collier a gray-blue shirt and pair of pants that were of very rough material and the weight of a cheap summer suit. They were short in the arms and legs. The shirt had no buttons but strips of cloth to be tied up the front. A pair of straw slippers was thrown on the floor; they conformed to Collier's feet exactly. Collier wasn't sure if he heard the soldiers laugh to each other after they slammed the door behind them and had moved down the hallway.

The room was generally cold. But it varied significantly in temperature. In the darkness in which he had been left, Collier moved slowly; the floor turned colder as he approached the outer wall and the wall opposite his bed. He struggled into the bed and under the quilt—it was too short so he had to make a diamond out of it and tuck the corners under his feet and sides. Gene Collier lay on his back, his arms forming a pillow. Some light came through the small opening under the roof and he began to make out the limits of his room. "Man, it sure ain't much . . . but I'm living." His feet were very cold. His ass was raw. He was as weary as he had ever been. That night he slept on his back for the first time in his life. He woke often, but while he was asleep he snored pitilessly.

Mr. Bai and Captain Gao talked long into the night in

English. An important decision had been made on the basis of Bai's short interview with Collier: Collier would remain in the Pyongyang center rather than be shipped north to the Yalu. Bai's prisoners were personally selected. Usually they were black men or poor whites who were more than modestly educated. In other words, Bai sought to screen out men for whom the antagonistic contradiction would always remain on a personal level. With one or two exceptions that he deemed necessary for experimental purposes the thirty-six prisoners in Pyongyang comprised a control group of the nonantagonistic. The extent to which "thought remolding" succeeded in Korea is now known, both in the West, where behavior of American prisoners has been conveniently forgotten, and the East, where techniques and applications of the process are being refined. Like any process, it has its limits. Ordinarily one would not expect a prisoner to resolve his contradictions with his former "enemy" so completely that he would refuse repatriation to his own country when the war ended and prisoners were exchanged. And the fact that only twenty-one American prisoners of war chose to go to China or remain in North Korea rather than return home suggests precisely where the normal limits exist. They must touch somewhere near the province of a man's consciousness that he calls Home.

"We'll give Comrade Collier six days, eh, Gao?" Mr. Bai poured tea from a kettle on top of the stove for himself and the captain. Both men were relaxed and warm.

"That is your province, Mr. Bai. But why so short a preparation for him?"

"There is a quality about him which I believe I have read correctly. And if my perception is correct, there is not the need for excessive isolation." Mr. Bai poured the tea slowly into the small cup; he dwelled for an absent moment on the swirl of leaves in the cup. "As I have mentioned, I find guilt to be the best initial motive for making the men wish to begin to resolve their contradictions. Often, it takes a good while to discover the source of guilt. As with the Negroes, for example, it took quite a long while indeed to discover that there was no basis for their guilt other than the vague, but very strong sense that they actually had come to accept the myth of their racial inferiority. In this Collier I believe we have close to a guiltless personality. No, no, I do not mean quite that. I think we have a life so extraordinarily unexamined that questions of guilt, innocence, yes, even love, fear, and hate have been only superficially dealt with. Such a personality—and I have only an intuition that he is such—can be made to transform itself significantly in a short time if a proper sense of guilt is induced. Yes, I think six days are sufficient as a beginning." He carried two cups of tea to the desk.

"Xie-xie," said Captain Gao.

"English please, Captain."

"Of course. Thank you." Gao took his cup with two hands locked by the thumbs; he brought this cup within a cup to his face and inhaled deeply. "May I," he said, looking up again, "tell you something confidential that I have wished to mention for some time now?"

"Certainly."

"It is this. When I was assigned here, I was very disappointed. I do not mean to offend or disrespect you. I had heard of your work at Yenan, of your collaborations with Chairman Mao. It was natural that I should have been pleased to have been thrown by fate [*ming* once again] into proximity with some of your knowledge—"

"May I interrupt you for a moment, Captain?"

"Certainly."

"Fate did not throw us together like a pair of dice. I selected your record from a great many at the Language Institute. Proceed."

If Bai had expected Gao to be surprised by this revelation, he must have been disappointed when the younger man said, "That pleases me indeed, but it is not my chief concern. You may or may not be aware that my family was killed by bombs during the revolution." Mr. Bai nodded. "American-made bombs dropped from an American-made plane—their gifts to Chiang."

"Certainly that sort of collaboration is no surprise to you, Captain."

"Of course not, but I saw this war as an opportunity to make them pay in some measure for my family. At first I was bitter because I was not sent to the front, but now I am troubled even more." Both men observed a natural pause to sip the tea. "This process of change that you are directing can be very dangerous. I find that as I am exposed to more and more American prisoners whose thoughts I am to help to modify, I am myself transformed. They have become only men to me, victims, not objects on which to avenge my family. My thoughts, too, are being remolded in the process."

"Then what is the problem?"

"Is it not obvious? Have I not lost my firmness, my socialist resolve?"

"Mao has said, 'If you wish to know the taste of a peach, you must bite the peach.' If you wish to transform men, you must transform yourself. Always we Communists transform. Time is with us. When the situation is antagonistic and requires firmness, conflict, and even personal sacrifice, you will know the difference, my dear Gao."

"How can you know that, Mr. Bai?"

"Because you are not a fool, Captain. You have begun a process of struggle within yourself as well as with the pawns of the world's oppressors. Our revolution will not be over and soon stagnate. Nor will it lapse. It will be, thanks to men like you, Captain Gao, a constant struggle, with periods of strife and self-doubt, but it will be a process of beneficial transformation such as the world has never known. You and your doubts are precisely the things that will create China's future. So drink your tea with an old man who is feeling many of the same stresses himself." They smiled at each other with tired eyes.

The six days for Comrade Collier to which Mr. Bai had referred were six days of total isolation. He was awakened by a sharp rap on the door. His eyes opened in sudden wakefulness. The room was bright with morning light filtering through the small opening and diffused unevenly into high and low corners. There was a strange, deeply submerged happiness in Collier in having wakened into this particular world.

Another rap on the door. Collier, wrapped in his quilt, unthinking, jumped off his bed-board and shuffled to the door with the intention of opening it. He was neither surprised nor particularly disappointed to discover no method of accomplishing the simple act. Another rap, somewhat sharper, accompanied by harsh-sounding Chinese syllables. There was, appended to the door, a covered shelf, which itself was enclosed by a sliding door. Collier slid the small door open: food—tea, a bowl of warm, soggy oats, and a large, enameled spoon. Breakfast was tasteless, but sufficiently familiar as ritual to elevate Collier's submerged happiness a few degrees. A rap (how many minutes later?) indicated he was to return the bowls and utensil.

Collier, still wrapped in his quilt, walked the limits of his room a great many times, lengthening and shortening his steps until he was, alternately, a child playing "Giant Steps" and an old man shuffling out to get the mail. He lay down periodically. He examined the crack in the corner. He drew in the foreshortened rectangle of sky intensely and for long periods of time.

Another rap. A cup of water and a large bowl of dark rice with spinach leaves. This enameled spoon had a different design on the handle. Collier prided himself in noticing the change. The spinach and rice tasted of the earth; he began to salivate with new appetite as he emptied the bowl. Not long after the second rap and the return of the cup, the bowl, and the spoon, the pressure to relieve himself physically began to increase. It was a feeling of embarrassment only that caused him to avoid the crock. He thought of other possible uses for the urn: "Maybe I'm supposed to put my clothes in it when they're dirty. Maybe it's for water. Maybe it's for maybe. . . ." When necessity caused him finally to piss in the urn, the room was almost in darkness; nevertheless, Collier looked over his shoulder once or twice before commencing. When he heard the echoing splash it made at first, he aimed closer to the edge of the opening and managed to create a quiet, clockwise spiral. Later that night after he had found a fairly comfortable resting position on his hard sleeping mat, he struggled not to have to use the crock to move his bowels. The struggle somehow induced its usage. Gene Collier moved toward it in the very cold darkness, untied his pants, and lifted the lid. He tried, and succeeded sufficiently well in keeping his skin from contacting the cold, ceramic rim. The reminder that he was unable to wipe himself brought him again to the depressed level of the first day of his capture, and he moved with graceless steps back to his mat. The lid was heavy and fit the crock so perfectly there was barely a trace of an odor in the room; by midmorning of the second day, there was no odor at all.

The second day was also sunny, or at least bright. Collier deduced that his window faced north because the sun was never directly visible and small puffy clouds (Grandma Gossett used to call them "mashed potatoes") moved across steadily from left to right. He spent most of the time sitting on his bed, his feet resting lightly on the floorboards. But his chest felt different; there was a fullness, a congestion, that made him edgy and continually anxious. He was certain he had been misplaced. He stared at the door for over an hour. Then he moved to it and sat cross-legged under his quilt with his ear to the crack. He heard some footsteps, some distant voices, a laugh, an automobile changing gears too quickly. With the recognition of each new sound his anxiety did not diminish—it increased. He thought of pounding on the door and shouting, but he knew that such an act was a sign of desperation, not merely anxiety, and could be used against him in some way by his captors. When the evening rap came, it woke Collier, who had fallen asleep with his head against the door. Water, brown rice with black beans, another enameled spoon.

Collier spent the greatest part of the third day on the floor against the door; it was warmer than the rest of the room. He was terribly cold most of the time but tried not to think about it. He decided he would ask to see Mr. Bai when the evening meal came. He bit off his thumbnail very carefully and used it as a pick to clean his teeth. An examination of his straw shoes gave him no clues of their origin or method of construction. Then he sat with his back against the door and, holding a finger up as a marker, he began closing one eye and then the other, trying to compare the points of view afforded by each eye. The blurred effect produced by his tears added a dimension to the game that he decided not to pursue. The pressure in his chest had built to the point where only rage or tears could have eased it. Had the Stork still existed in Collier's life, rage would have been the more likely release. Collier's tears filled his eyes and ran down his hollowed cheeks; they ran slowly over the chin, down the long neck in two separate rivers. Where the downy hair high on his chest began, the tear liquid moved randomly and was slowly saturated. His tears had come without volition and he could not will them to cease. He heard the guard coming slowly along the hallway and he began to grow angry; the combination of anger and tears produced an uncharacteristic petulance in Gene Collier. As he started to shout, he forgot Mr. Bai's name. "Tell

. . . tell . . . tell . . . him I need some toilet paper for Christ's sake. I can't live like a goddamned pig." Even while he shouted, he heard the cup and bowl placed on the ledge. The rap on the door punctuated the word "pig."

Gene Collier cried a great deal more on the fourth day. He thought of the three or four times in his life when he had gotten lost. He remembered going out in that blizzard to help find Jethro Cowley's kid, who was sleeping nice and warm in the garage the whole time. But Gene remembered the feeling of the exact moment when he saw that he was in deep trouble. Finding that mineshaft to crawl into when he was too cold to go on searching had saved him, but that was just luck—it had nothing to do with saving himself or with not saving the boy. By the end of the fourth day the pressure in his chest, the anxiety he felt, the tears, the petulance, these had all become conditions of his existence.

When he awoke on the fifth day, Collier asked himself, quite seriously in reasonable tones and in these words, "What was my crime?" He devoted sixteen consecutive hours to finding the answer to the question. No answer came at first. He recalled hooking the defensive end in the Stenneton game and getting away with it all through the game, but, he told himself, "we lost anyway." Of course he knew that such a crime deserved no such punishment as this. It did have, however, the effect of priming the guilt pump, for literally hundreds of deeds and thoughts and words that he had never considered came to him. They ranged from the things he had said about girls to fellows on the team to times when he wanted to go out back and have it out with his father. A toy soldier he stole from Mr. King's Notions Store. Looking in the kitchen and seeing his mother naked when she was bathing. Cheating on exams in school. Masturbating in the woods a few times. Wanting that woman at the top of the stairs that time in Morgantown. Wanting Mrs. Philpotts, too. Having that bar girl in Pusan. Could it have been lying to Bai about college? Hundreds of things of all sorts—great, medium, small—all thrown together to produce a single, overall flow of guilt. Then the guilt pump had run dry. And so had Gene Collier's spirit at the end of the fifth day.

Awakening on the sixth day, Gene Collier said, "But what about all the good things I did?" Almost all the good things he thought of were bad things that he didn't do, and, as he admitted to himself toward evening, things he couldn't do because he was too scared or shy. Around midday, Collier said something smart, "But Bai couldn't know about any of those things I did. It's got to be something I did in Korea." Then he thought again about that girl in Pusan, but he didn't see how Bai could possibly know about that. At last he thought about trying to turn Jersey Red in for killing those prisoners, and he was proud of himself until after dinner. Tea, brown rice and bean shoots, a small enameled spoon, the spoon of his first meal. As the room darkened, Collier saw again, very clearly, the highlighted faces out on the tower, the look in their eyes of . . . nothing at all. And he did not truly know if he had been paralyzed with disbelief or if he, too, had felt nothing about the men below under the thatches. Or—now he felt close to something that seemed immoral and maybe criminal—if he himself believed the men below the thatches were truly men. He did not sleep very well on the sixth night. The date was January 17, 1952. For most of those who knew that date, it held no particular importance. Eugene Collier, American P.O.W. in Korea, did not know the date; it was his twenty-first birthday.

The door to his room opened the next morning. Mr. Bai, Captain Gao, and a soldier holding a tray with tea and cereal stood before the supine prisoner. "Comrade Collier," said Mr. Bai, "I hope you do not feel neglected. This is, indeed, the only way to adjust to prison life, believe me. Have you been reasonably well?"

"I need some toilet paper."

"I am afraid we cannot oblige you or ourselves in that respect, Comrade. But I will have some grass brought to you. Perhaps we can have a serious talk after your breakfast."

"Do I have a choice?"

"Comrade Collier, there is always a choice if you but learn to discover alternatives." The guard left the tray on the floor near the door before it was closed and locked.

10

Kao Li-ye

"I must ask you, Comrade Collier, do you wish to stand, or would you prefer to sit down?" Mr. Bai raised his brown hand to forestall Collier's response. "The reason I now ask is that often in the past when I have offered some of the young Americans a seat, they very firmly rejected the offer and stood, almost at attention, for the entire interview. A very unproductive exchange it was, I can assure you. So now I always begin with the alternatives clearly stated at the outset. A seat or not?" Mr. Bai had the rhythms and general disposition of a small lean cat.

Collier nodded and said only, "Seat."

Mr. Bai pointed with the tip of his short, white goatee to a straight-backed chair near the stove. It was so pleasantly warm in this room, a man would be a fool indeed if he deliberately did anything that might shorten an interview. "Place the chair opposite my desk, Comrade Collier, so we may see one another's eyes at fairly close range. Two men cannot have the conversation I anticipate without fully exploring the facial expressions as well as exchanging the words. Also, I cannot apologize for your initiation to the camp; it was, as I mentioned before, necessary. It is a strong likelihood, however, that you will not be exposed to such a long solitude again. That should please you."

Collier was irritable, owing to his isolation and the discomfort caused by the severe chafing around his ass. His irritability may have been helpful to him; it gave him a critical "oh yeah" attitude, and he questioned things in Bai's words he might normally have taken as fact. Like the "however" Bai just added to his sentence about not being locked away again for so long. He didn't actually say Gene wouldn't be locked up like that again, even though that was the way he probably wanted it to sound. Mr. Bai was full of "howevers" and "perhapses" and "somewhats"; today Gene Collier was ready to catch every one of them.

"You should see your face, Comrade Collier. You look as though I were trying to trick you out of the deed to your land. I am not. It would be more productive for both of us if you could, perhaps, relax just a bit."

Collier shuffled his feet and ran his hand through his hair, but his expression remained essentially unchanged. He didn't hear his own voice until a full second after he had begun to speak. ". . . wonder why you always call me 'Comrade.' I'm not a Communist."

"Don't you think it matters, Comrade Collier, how people refer to each other? Doesn't 'Sir' mean something? Or, as they call Negroes in America, 'Boy'? Shouldn't we get in the habit of calling each other by titles that do not separate us? 'Comrade' is merely one such possibility I happen to favor. But if it bothers you, I will desist."

Gene Collier had never considered the matter before.

"If you wish, however, you may call me 'Comrade' since I am a Communist." Mr. Bai's face broke into a big smile. Gene noticed that his teeth were small and almost black.

Gene shook his head.

"Do you think that would make you a Communist, too?"

Gene shook his head.

Bai's expression changed. His lips closed and a strange look came into his eyes, as though he had once seen something no one had ever seen before, but it was a quiet look. He said, "Chances of your becoming a Communist, Private Collier, are impossibly slim. A very small percentage of the people in my own country are actually Communists; it would be unusual indeed to find an American soldier, an enlisted man, no less, who could be made over into a Communist. . . . Are you aware that each time I say the word 'Communist' your face registers an involuntary reaction, as though the word carried with it a foul odor?"

"Well, I just don't happen to believe in it."

"What do you truly know about communism, Private Collier?" Gene shrugged. Then Bai said something strange; the last part, especially, stayed with Gene. "If you make an attempt to learn about it and then find it has no application to your life or if you are not perfect enough to find the fault within yourself, then it would seem reasonable for you to reject it, Private Collier." No one had ever used a phrase like, "not perfect enough to find the fault within yourself," right to Gene's face before. Of course he wasn't perfect, no man was; but you didn't have to be perfect to believe in whatever you wanted to believe in.

"No, we could not make you over into a Communist, even if we wished to." Mr. Bai withdrew a small pamphlet from his drawer and handed it to Gene. It was a tattered, smudged copy of *The Communist Manifesto.* "We have processed your papers and sent them to the Red Cross. The rule we have as to correspondence is as follows: You may write one letter of reply for each letter you receive from me." Then the meeting was over. Gene stood and began to return his chair to its original position. "No, you may leave it." Gene moved to the door and Bai said very casually, "You will be working with Captain Gao, so you will probably see very little of me in the future. His English is not

perfected yet, not sufficiently colloquial; if you can help him
to improve, we will both be grateful."

After he had been back in his room for a few minutes,
Gene tried to reconstruct the interview. It had all gone by
so swiftly in retrospect the only things that seemed to matter were what words you called people by and that thing
about not liking something because the fault was in yourself. Mr. Bai, who had continued to be pleasant enough,
was now a severe annoyance to Collier, not by what he did
but by what he could make Collier feel—the things in himself Gene did not comprehend or want to deal with. The
less he saw of Bai, the better it would be.

In the next few weeks of his captivity, Gene Collier's
condition underwent a great many changes, most of them
beneficial, some prompted by forces working from the outside inward, some pushing the other way, and some just
moiling about at random. After three tight-lipped awkward
meetings with Captain Gao, during which Gao explained
how fortunate Collier was to be in such enlightened captivity, both men began to relax and discover that the voice
of their humanness was carrying more and more of the
conversation. The periods of Collier's isolation, at first irregular and often as long as four days and never less than
two, diminished and became more regular. This happened
after he recognized in Gao an elemental decency and sympathy. The camp, Gene was told confidentially, was an experiment in "the humane remolding of misguided criminals." The phrase meant nothing to him.

The captain, Collier discovered, had been a young
teacher in northern China when the precarious partnership
between the Communists and the Kuomintang was joined
and an anti-Japanese war finally became a reality. "I was not
then a political man," he told Gene, "but as you can see "
—he touched the collar of his uniform—"that condition
has changed." He told of how he discovered that only the
Communists seemed willing to struggle against the Japa-

nese as true patriots and how, by degrees, he had been won over to their point of view. "As a teacher, I had always taught the importance of self-knowledge, until I came to realize that I had been teaching in a vacuum. There is no true self-knowledge that excludes the man who has made your clothes or grown your food." It was here that Collier noticed Gao's composure disappear; his expressions became just slightly smug, his voice a trifle harsh."Probably you have heard of *yin* and *yang*," he said.

"No."

Gao explained. Gene was almost ready to understand the concept of the tension between opposites and also the harmony between those same opposites. Gao drew the circle and the curved line that divided it into contending, fluid opposites. He shaded one half. Gene had seen the symbol before, but couldn't recall where. It was over a bar in Pusan. "It would seem," said Gao in an embarrassed way, "as though you and I are *yin* and *yang*."

Gene Collier said something remarkable: "Maybe, but I think I'm both *yin* and *yang*, and probably you are, too."

Gao experienced a teacher's encouragement from the surprisingly good response of a student. His voice softened and he said, "Unfortunately in the West they do not know that *yin* and *yang*—negative and positive—are only one set of antagonisms among eight principle lines of tension. The others are *xu-shih*, empty-solid; *leng-je*, hot-cold; and *piao-li*, outer-inner. They, also, must be placed in harmony for health and growth."

"What was that last pair again?"

"*Piao-li*. That is the antagonism between the inner, the essential character of a thing, and the external demands placed upon it by the world. I can tell you from personal experience that it is a very difficult harmony to achieve." And Gao busied himself with some papers on his desk. The meeting was over.

Confinement was initially the greatest force acting upon

Collier. Eugene Collier had never before been un-free to the extent of being circumscribed by four ten-foot walls, by clothing and sleeping and toilet accommodations not the least bit of his choosing or liking, by physical discomforts he could do nothing to lessen, by food that was alien, by a small window to the world he could not really look out of but which provided others with the means to look in upon him. Inevitably, and rather quickly, the unyielding limits of his situation forced him to turn inward. What Collier discovered there was wreckage.

Not the wreckage of, say, an edifice that had been badly built or had been destroyed by a natural disaster; rather, the wreckage of an edifice that had never been built at all —the parts of what was to have been the superstructure lay about rusting, the lumber for the foundation forms warped and weathered into tortured shapes, the cement having leaked out of the bags and solidified into abstractions in the rain. Tools, broken and useless; machines on their sides. No, not the wreckage of what had been and had failed; but the wreckage of that which had never even come together in the first place.

The enforced peering inward brought out variations on the same theme: a football team in which all the assignments were confused and mistimed; a band in which the players played different music at various tempos; of books in which the pages were unnumbered and whose words lacked logical continuity. When Gene Collier was forced to look inward in Korea, he always saw incompletion, situations of various kinds in which the parts never came together properly. But he also saw his perception of Home: the refracted twilight, the heaviness of evening, the soaring of the eagle, the pine forest, and the uniting of himself with all the parts in the picture.

Confinement was an important force for change in Collier, but so was its antithesis—long periods of searching discusssion with Gao, a good man and very subtle teacher.

He seldom led Gene in a particular direction but preferred to follow where Collier went, picking up things the younger man dropped along the way, often branching off on an excursion of his own. Gao, like all true teachers, developed respect for the integrity of Collier's search. The respect in time became a deeper liking. Gene's personal, intellectual quest, after six weeks, took on a central theme: the coming together of broken parts. The theme had various forms: questions about Gao's life; questions about the forces that shaped men; analysis of his own actions and his motives; criticism of people and institutions that had touched him; criticism of himself. Gao underwent the same interior examination, but since this had been an ongoing process of many years' duration with him, he had no revelations.

At a subsequent meeting with Gao, Collier had a specific, political question. One that had an honest and dishonest dimension. He really hoped for an answer from Gao that he could accept; he also hoped the question would upset the captain, cause him anxiety. He asked: "If harmony is the resolution of conflict between the outer and inner, how can the workers be in harmony if they lose their chains? I mean, aren't those chains necessary to balance the inner force?" Unfortunately, the contentious motive was stronger when Collier asked his question, and his voice made it sound more of a challenge than he had really wished.

Captain Gao's English pronunciation and usage had improved considerably from his exchanges with Collier, although he still felt a bit uncomfortable with idioms that departed greatly from logical content or construction. But as a theoretical Marxist, he was impeccable. He noticed the tone of a political adversary in Collier when he asked this question and he thoroughly welcomed it. "It depends precisely which 'chains' you are talking about. Your father, he is a worker, a coal miner, is he not?" Gene's eyes widened and he nodded. "Well, even if the workers in America were to unite under communism, they would still remain workers, still be required to go down and bring out the coal. In that sense, the demands of the world are the 'chains' that bind all of us. But if the workers would throw off the 'chains' of those men who draw unearned benefits from their labor, they would harvest the full fruit of their own labor, not merely part of it, and they would be free to develop a healthy balance between the true *piao* and *li.*" Again the embarrassment. Gao was sensitive about his "preaching"; among other men, where there was opposition and a very different Marxist interpretation on some matter or other, Gao could be as clever, as firm, as convincing as he had to be to win his point, but contending with a captive over the "ABCs" of socialist thought robbed him of a good deal of bravado.

Gene was given and read more political material, a series of pamphlets entitled "The Little Lenin Library." He asked his teacher a great many questions, ranging from the meaning of "dialectical materialism" to the impossibility of a workers' paradise where the state decided to eliminate itself. This did not result in his becoming a Communist, for Mr. Bai was absolutely correct in estimating the chances of such a conversion as impossibly slim, and actually Bai had serious doubts that such a transformation could ever be useful politically. However, for the first time in his life Gene was exposed to a teacher who could thoroughly, logically, and systematically answer all his questions. Such a method of thought, if not the man who employed it, might be valuable if Gene ever began to build an edifice out of the wreckage in his world. He thought fleetingly of Mrs. Philpotts and what she had said about learning.

Just about the time Gene Collier accepted the hard fact of his permanent isolation, Gao told him that he had been elected camp librarian. Yes, that was the word Gao used— "elected." Collier, of course, was so surprised by the word "librarian" that he did not even think to question the electoral process.

The room into which Gao led Collier was a small, cheer-ful room with flowered curtains, Chinese prints on the walls, portraits of Marx, Lenin, and Mao Tse-tung on silk; wicker chairs, a large table piled with recent American magazines. A wall of unpainted shelves and boxes of vari-ous sizes on the floor, all overflowing with books and pam-phlets.

"That is our library," Gao said, pointing to the boxes with his chin. "Tolstoy, Hugo, Dickens, Steinbeck." Gao thought on, but came up with no other names. "You will organize it."

For three hours each day, Gene Collier oversaw library activities; that is, after an initial period of arranging and cataloguing the books by title, author, and subject, the camp librarian sat in the relative comfort of his domain and read. It was two weeks before anyone came in for a book. The first American Collier saw since his capture was pecu-liarly unrepresentative; he was a bald-headed young man with a facial tic that caused him to wink an eye and purse his lips at the same time. He did not speak, but went along a shelf of books and seemed to select one purely on the basis of color and weight: He chose a middle-sized, tan copy of *Tortilla Flat*. Like all the other prisoners who visited the library, this first one was accompanied by the same severe sullen-faced guard.

With the coming of spring and the reactivation of the truce talks at Panmunjom, Captain Gao Ma-ting began to think of his return to his village of Yang-Xien when the war ended. He contemplated all the work that had to be done there and how much resistance and confusion there would be; also the many hours he would spend with farmers trying to show them the advantages of sharing one another's land and tools and skills. It could all fail, of course, but that, at least, was a task truly commensurate with his talents and training. It was the work for which he had sacrificed so much. It was life-work. The spring of 1952 embodied for him the most unpleasant contradiction: the need to stay and complete a hateful task; the desire to move and begin life's labors. Gao Ma-ting showed very little of the conflict within himself to Gene Collier. To anyone.

The next time the two met, Collier surprised Gao by confessing his complicity in the Koje incident. By asking very careful questions, Gao quickly established that there was no overt involvement on Collier's part. He did, however, discover Collier's essential insensitivity toward the men under the thatch as well as his belated desire to attain some sort of justice for them. "It could be a great many things," Gao said, unable to mask his disappointment, "the least of which could have been the imperialist myth that life is meaningless in the Orient. But I feel it probably has as much to do with the false sense of superiority you were made to feel toward Chinks and Gooks." Collier understood only much later that Gao had been hurt by being told of the episode, and he was, in a rather direct fashion, attempting to repay Collier in kind. More importantly, Gao's reaction showed Collier a part of him always hidden behind the rationality of dialectic thought. Collier felt drawn closer to both the man and the mask.

At Gao's request, Collier signed a peace petition. It was general enough to meet any of Gene's objections. Ironically, one portion condemned the treatment of Chinese and Korean prisoners by the Americans. "These things," Gao said, "are of negligible propaganda value, but Mr. Bai feels they must be done, more out of form than for any practical reason. Of course, when you go home, you will probably tell the authorities you signed only after you were tortured." The words were intended as further reproof and also as a recognition of what time and the world can do to a man's memory and his tongue.

"What would my name be in Chinese?" The question,

coming so totally out of the blue, caught Gao slightly off guard.

"It would depend on where in China you were. There are still many different dialects."

"Where you're from, what would I be called where you're from?"

"In Shensi they don't see many Americans. But why do you wish to know?"

"No particular reason. I just would, that's all. Curiosity, I guess."

"Well, we usually take the first sound of a Western name, and that becomes the Chinese family name. In your case the people would probably call you *Kao*, since it is one of the common family names in Shensi. Then they would attempt to find a combination of sound and meaning for the given name, so that it still sounds like your true name but also has a Chinese meaning—perhaps *Li* and *Ye*. So you might be *Kao Li-ye* . . . Col-li-er."

"But what would it mean?"

"*Kao* is merely the sound of your name now . . . Mr. Kao. *Li* we have discussed; it means 'from the inside' and *ye* is 'in addition.' So you would be *Kao Li-ye,* or Mr. Kao, a man who has something inside also."

Gene Collier had been a prisoner in Pyongyang for almost eight weeks. The mornings had become pleasantly warm, and the crock in his room was almost full of his waste.

11

Choose Life

"If I may make an unpardonable pun, Private Collier, the crock in your room is now full. And right on time, too. You see, it is not so much a crock as a clock." Then Bai laughed his high-pitched, black-toothed laugh. Collier liked Bai less as he had come to know Gao better. "Don't you see my joke, Private Collier; isn't crock the way most Chinese in your country would pronounce clock?" Collier didn't see but felt his growing dislike for Bai justified.

"Well, that is a shame; nevertheless, your crock runneth over. What do you propose we do with it?"

"Empty it."

"Of course, but where?"

"Anywhere. I don't care."

"It is a shame you are not a peasant; you would know so much more than you do as a man with two and one half years of college."

"We don't have peasants in America." Collier was feeling cranky because he believed he had been robbed of his conversation with Gao.

"That, too, is a shame. Do you know what night soil is?"

Collier knew but didn't remember that he knew. For a while, when he had been in Korea for a few weeks, there had been a "honeybucket" joke every day. Usually there was an unsuspecting guy falling in one, not getting out until help came in some unexpected manner. Gene never thought the jokes were particularly funny.

"Night soil, Private Collier, is a euphemism for human excrement which, when allowed to stand under proper conditions, can be used as fertilizer for crops."

"Yes, I know."

"Have you ever done farm work, Private Collier?"

"No, not really."

"Would you like to try?" Mr. Bai's eyes narrowed and widened suddenly and a look of expectancy froze on his face. This is not a frivolous question, is what the look communicated.

"Yes."

"It is spring and we do a great deal of our own planting here. Captain Gao has recommended you as a particularly likely candidate. The work is strenuous . . . but of course you must know that even though you are not a peasant." Mr. Bai rose, turned his back on Collier, and went to a file cabinet from which he extracted an envelope. It appeared to be a letter of some sort. He took the letter, which consisted of a great many pages, from the envelope and handed it to Collier. "We must keep the envelope, but its contents are entirely yours. It is a regulation not of my making." The eyes had narrowed again and the brown face seemed vaguely apologetic. "Captain Gao will give you writing materials if you wish to respond, Private Collier. Today your services as librarian will not be required."

Gene took the pages and was about to leave when Bai's very old hand touched his wrist and caused an embarrassed pause. "I will give you time in your room with your letter."

When Gene was returned to the room, the small patch of

sky had turned from morning blue to eternal gray; a rain was falling lightly and an occasional drop came in under the eave of the sloping roof. The crock, Collier discovered, had been emptied but not cleaned. He imagined a similar crock —a huge one—into which all the crocks in the camp were emptied. And then (why not?) an immense crock into which they dumped all the huge crocks in Korea. And then? Collier started to laugh, almost nothing more than nasal snorts at first; the snorts were transferred after a few seconds to low throat sounds. Gene imagined gigantic crocks from every country in the world emptied into one stupendous *Crock,* and his laughter came forward into his mouth. And then his head fell back as the laughter developed its own momentum and began to control him. He felt himself giving way to a laughing fit—how long since he's had a laugh like this one? Ohmigod, look . . . that stupendous *Crock*'s got a crack in it. The whole world's a cracked *crock.* His laughter heightened in pitch. It had almost become a scream.

Guards went scuffling down the hallway. Unheard by Collier, who, goddamn it, would have his laugh. Every time it seemed to diminish, something, probably the laugh's impulse to sustain itself now that it had finally broken free, carried it to new heights. Collier was crying and sucking for breath. Now on the downside of the laugh, he relaxed and enjoyed the easy glide back to the mundane. Occasionally he felt ripples that recapitulated the heights of his joke and the confidence that he had really had himself one hell of a laugh. "Oh my," he kept saying, "Jesus Christ," and taking in great gulps of air. There were a few false starts at another ascent, but he kept sliding back to "Oh my."

He could not recall laughing that way before in his life. He knew he had, but when and where and at what, he couldn't remember. And when would it happen again?

The pages of the letter, onionskin paper, had fallen to the floor, and as Gene stooped to retrieve them he sneezed, suddenly and without restraint. It seemed like a fragment of a new laugh to the guards listening on the other side of the door.

The large, childish scribble on the page told Gene immediately that the letter was from his father. The letter was torn in a number of places, the result of his father's pressure and the paper's delicacy. The upper right-hand corner of the first page—there were ten pages—was blacked out. Gene heard Bai's voice: "You will discover, however, that certain things have been, let us face it, censored. I, myself, would not order such things, but these are the regulations that restrict me"—or some such crap as that.

Dear son:

It certainly was good to get news that you are alive and we hope well. We are all fine. Your mother just reminded me that you couldn't have heard about your grandmother. She died almost three months ago. In her sleep, so that part of it wasn't too bad. Life treated her hard but all in all more fair than lots of other back hills people. You probably only remember her complaining and with an edge on most of the time. She wasn't like that when I married your mother and when you were a young boy. She would sing songs she learned when she was a girl. Her voice was not half bad either. She was a great help to us in those days. She used to be a real practical joker. One time she really did boil my socks in the coffee pot and poured the

page two

stuff in a cup I was just about to drink it too, when your mother caught my arm and told me. You see I used to complain that her coffee tasted like boiled socks. She did lots of things like that in those days. I can't truthfully say we'll miss her though. Her life was very hard down near the end. She hollered in her sleep about men coming to get her with the worst cussing and screaming I ever heard come from a woman's mouth. I know she's better off where she is. A cemetery back country in Weyland right near her husband who died over twenty years ago.

The girls are fine. You wouldn't recognize how they have changed. They don't even seem to look much like each other any more. They both said to tell you how they hope you are well and will come home before long. The news seems [ten words blacked out] home so we can have the kind of talk I guess we should have had a

page three

long time ago. You know how hard it has been for me to understand what you did? Especially after it looked like things at the university might really work out for you. By the way, you probably don't know that Ben Crowder ran for Congress in November. He didn't win though. I guess that means the voters are smarter than I ever gave them credit for. But I really would like to know what made you quit it all like you did. And why you never even talked it over with me—or anything for that matter. You are my only son, Gene.

Of course I joined up myself, but it was back in 1918 and it really seemed like a war where a man could do something about the world that he and his family, including his children, were going to live in. But this [eight words blacked out], even if

page four

it wasn't actually going on when you joined up. Have you [eight words blacked out]? Have you [ten words blacked out]? Are they as [fifteen words blacked out]?

We listen to the news on the teevee. I guess I should say we watch it. Yes, we got a teevee. Things are better for us all around I must say. Not because of grandma, but because things have gotten better at the mine. Actually there are very few men going down into the mine these days. The company has begun doing what they call strip-mining, where they have these great digging machines that sort of peel the surface off the hill leaving the shale and underneath that as much soft coal as you could ever imagine. They still do some shaft mining but anyone can see that there's no future in it. Strip-mining is where the future is in West Virginia. We got a new contract. I get to work in the open air in clear daylight. Can you imagine!

page five

I used to worry that you would have to go down into the mine some day. Probably you worried about that too, maybe that's the reason you joined up without ever talking about it to anybody. Who would have guessed that there would be a day when there would be coal mining and no mine! Not that the company has become so free with their money. I'm sure they're making more than they ever did. They must be. Otherwise why would the men be doing so well with this new contract and everything? I guess it is no secret but you know I've always believed the union was in cahoots with the bosses. So if we are doing good the company must be doing even better. That isn't right of course but what is a working man with a family supposed to do about it? But as I say things are pretty good. The teevee especially. Probably you

page six

don't get to watch any teevee where you are. It's really something. There is a guy—Milton Berle is his name—and he comes out every week dressed up as crazily as you can imagine. Most of the time dressed like a woman. You know I am not an easy one to laugh but he sure does get me going. And not just me but your mother and the girls too. The best thing on the teevee though are the programs that they put on on Sunday afternoons. Programs with important men in the country, men like [blacked out] and [blacked out]. Not just politicians but professors and writers too. And they ask them some very tough questions. Your mother teases me because I always fall asleep in front of the teevee set when those programs are on but that doesn't mean that they are not my favorite. It looks like next year I will get a vacation. Can you imagine how far we have come when a coal miner in West Virginia gets a vacation? With pay I mean?

page seven

I spoke to a lady from the Red Cross. She said they are doing everything [seven words blacked out]. I wanted to send you [four words blacked out] but she said she didn't think they would let a [blacked out] go through. [Twenty words blacked out]. Are they treating you ohkay? I mean are you getting enough to eat? On the teevee there are programs about the talks they are having over there about ending the war. I don't see any reason for it to continue. I don't see [twelve words blacked out]. Do you think I could send you a book? Son, the truth is I feel very guilty about how

I never raised you. How I just about let you raise yourself. You've got to know though that I never had the time to spend with you to talk with you to encourage you even in playing football if that is what you wanted to do. It wasn't completely my fault though. The mine leaves a man weary as hell most of the time and even if it isn't physical it's as if something just flows

page eight

out of his inner spirit. That's why the men coming along with this new kind of mining will have it better. They will be able to get close to their own kids. Down there it is as though you are losing time always and when you get out you just want to think about yourself. Well, it isn't thinking so much as brooding. And I'm sorry but I couldn't help myself. Still, all in all I think you turned out to be a fine boy.

When the war is over and you come home is still time enough to talk out a lot of the things that need talking out. My guess is that you are well. Have you lost much weight? What is the food like? Are there many [five words blacked out]? Don't lose your spirit. I once was in charge of some German prisoners

page nine

in Paris and I remember what good spirits they were in. People who don't know about these things think being a prisoner is very awful, but it all pretty much depends upon your attitude.

They are thinking of renaming the football field over at the high school in your honor. There was a clipping saying that in the *Speculator*. I was going to send it but the Red Cross lady said that clippings were frowned upon. I don't know why they would be, but I didn't send it. Actually it didn't say they were going to rename it just that it was proposed and they were considering it. When I think that I never saw you play a single game of football I get sad and angry with myself.

It was a shock you know getting word that you were [seven words blacked out] when the last we heard was that you quit school. We didn't know where you were and your mother was worried sick. I guess it proves that when a father and his son miss connections there are things wrong on both ends of the line. Your mother didn't want me to mention this part about your not writing to

page ten

us for so long but I felt I had to say you were wrong about doing that. Very wrong.

Son, remember the good things in life. All the people back here who care about you. This was [twelve words blacked out]. I never really told you what a good boy you were, how you never caused your mother and me any real trouble—except for not writing. This is a good time to begin. You are and have been a fine son, don't worry about that. I cannot wait until we can be together again sitting in front of a fire talking or maybe just sitting and watching the [six words blacked out] on the teevee.

Your sincere Father

Gene Collier, who for many weeks had had no possessions, looked for a pocket in which to slip the letter. It struck him—no need for pockets. Communism must do away with all pockets; he'd tell Bai that next time. He thought of hiding it in the crock and began a laugh that had no hope of becoming airborne. So he placed it under the sleeping mat for safekeeping. He would have to read it many times before he could reconstruct the world from which it came.

Then, still not conscious of a particular reason or motive, Collier began to do leg stretches, the sort he had learned for loosening up before football games. One leg thrust out forward, the other trailing behind, and then he circled his forward thigh with both arms and let his body fall against the tension of the legs. Little bouncing movements as his body fell against himself and was pushed back up. Short grunts with each dip. Then some jumping jacks. Sit-ups. Push-ups. All of this activity done awkwardly by a body beginning to regenerate itself, a body that longed to throw a block or dive on a fumble. One of the guards finally determined what these new sounds indicated; he said a phrase to his partner which would translate roughly: "Like that crazy one." And he screwed his face into a quizzically unpleasant expression.

During his sit-ups Gene had realized by the absence of any rolls of flesh on his stomach, after his shirt had risen up on his back, that he had lost weight. Although he had slipped out of good shape—as attributable to the nature of duty on Koje-do as his confinement here—he was surprisingly strong and energetic. On his feet again, he clenched his fists, brought both arms up into blocking position, and darted around the room throwing high pass-protection blocks into the faces of invisible rushers, his grunts as vicious as the slash of his elbows.

He ran across the room, took a leaping step up against the outer wall and vaulted up toward the small opening. His large right hand knocked out the screening and its fingers hooked a firm grip underneath the narrow outer ledge. Collier was anchored outside the room. The other hand then came over and he pulled his body up the wall; his head filled the opening.

Off to the left was a city; a smoke-haze settled over it. It had been heavily bombed, but not since Gene had arrived; the smoke, he assumed, was from attempts to dig out and rebuild. Straight ahead was a low mountain range; it seemed blue and white in the distance. Old mountains, he concluded, not a sharp angle anywhere. In front of the mountains and as far as he could see to the right were fields, flat and gray with large patches of snow and slowly melting mud.

The sky was uniformly bleak, no variation to speak of; the gray was a little brighter as a backdrop where the mountains dipped. Two thin jet trails far off to the north. It was a scene, a day unlike any he remembered at home. He had the feeling, a fear, that every day was just about the same in this place.

His hands and arms began to tire. He decided to hold on longer for exercise. No movement out there. Nothing. Not a car. Not an animal. Even the smoke above the city sat on it like a lid. His arms began to quiver. Slowly he let his feet slide down the wall until he was all dead weight. His knuckles began to turn white. He was just about to drop to the floor when the door to his room flew open. It was Gao and the two guards. "Collier," Gao snapped, almost as a command. Gene eased his grip and came down the wall slowly, almost as though it were a rope. He turned and faced Gao. "Just looking," he said.

"The guards thought you were trying to kill yourself."

There was a moment in which Gene Collier scanned the faces before him, dwelling longest on Gao's. He started to laugh again; not the epic *Crock* laugh, but a gentle, thoughtful laugh that you offer to people who mean something to you. He then said, "Not me, Gao. I'm planning to live forever." The words escaped from him without Collier being certain whether they were true or sarcastic, or both at once.

"You are expected at the library," said Gao.

"Not today. Bai said—"

Gao nodded to a guard, who pushed Collier forward with a short-armed thrust in the small of his back. Gene turned quickly and said, "Easy, man. Just you take it easy." The threat on his face was unmistakable.

12

Liquid Birds

That afternoon, when Gene Collier arrived at the library, he met six other Americans. He was escorted into the familiar room; he noticed today, for the first time, that there were no windows. Four of the men were black; two were white. They were all dressed in identical gray uniforms and seated in an irregular semicircle. Although he had assumed that every prisoner had come into the library at some time or other, these men were new to him. A guard, the one who escorted prisoners to the library, stood menacingly in the corner.

They were all tall, thin men with taut faces and bright, darting eyes. Each was in a relaxed sitting position, some with legs extended and toes pointed upward, some with the heel of one foot resting casually on the kneecap of the other leg. The ease, however, was incomplete and incongruous with a tension that remained in the hands and face. Gao introduced each slowly as Gene took one of the remaining seats. Almost every name Gao uttered was a first name: "John Thomas . . . Evan Charles. . . ." As he proceeded, the

spaces between first and last names lengthened: "Malcolm
. . . Greer . . . Angelo . . . Carmine. . . ." It was not at all
clear if it was a reading of last-name-first in the American
military fashion, and Gene could make no connections between the name and the nod of identification that accompanied it. Gene assumed that he was the new addition to
the group, but the assumption was refuted by Gao's introductory statement.

"It is extremely unlikely that any of you will have met
each other before. You will comprise a basic work and
discussion group."

Gene, as did all the others, found himself furtively
searching the faces of the men in the room for some sign;
whenever glances locked, both men quickly broke them off
and tried to concentrate on Gao, who faced the semicircle
and was intent only on the completeness of his message
and the accuracy of his English. "Three evenings each
week, we will meet in this room and discuss issues of the
gravest political importance." He paused, trying to remember something: " . . .There will also be occasional reading
which will raise important theoretical problems." Gao was
unaware of the fact that the attention he was receiving was
a sham. The members of the would-be discussion group
had passed from curiosity of each other to suspicion, an
attitude that was to soften over the following sixteen
months of captivity but never to disappear. How could any
of them be certain that one of the others was not a spy, a
counterspy, an informer, an opportunist, or, worst, a pa-
triot. "Your days will be spent in a variety of labors, most
immediate of which will be the preparation of the field for
planting our spring crops."

Each man was asked to say a few words about himself,
and each followed Gene's pattern of name, outfit, and
hometown. Except for the last man, a light-skinned black
man, who rubbed his chin and said, "You all should know
that I've been climbing the walls here for I don't know how

many days. And. . . ." This word was his transition; it was
drawled and held a long while, seemingly to allow the
speaker time to think what he was going to say next.
". . . I wouldn't have been here in the first place if some of
my so-called buddies hadn't copped out on me. And. I
don't know why I should trust any of you cats. And. Well,
my name's 'Specs,' last name Tibideaux, but it don't spell
nothing like it sounds. And. They call me 'Specs' because
of my glasses, which I *lost* when I was *taken.*" At this last
word, perhaps because of its double meaning, the speaker
smiled. "But. I got no choice, you know. I've got to trust
you. Just like my buddies. If I don't, it'll be worse than the
solitary. And. Now that I've said all that, you got to be
thinking I'm the guy to watch out for. Well. Anyway. I'm
from D.C. King Company, 36th Regimental Combat Team.
Eighth Army. P.F.C."

Gao looked at "Specs" strangely. It was as though he had
heard the man speak many times before but now had become confused by the rhythm and idiom of this man when
he addressed his countrymen. He appeared puzzled when
he said, "If I take Private Tibideaux's words aright, he is
anticipating some problem of cohesiveness to the group for
fear that there will be a lack of sincerity on the part of one
or more members? We hope that does not occur. Although
we feel we have treated you most liberally, especially in
view of the treatment our own soldiers are receiving at the
hands of your government"—did his eyes seek out Collier
or were they just happening to pass over him at that moment as they moved from face to face?—"you must realize
you are prisoners and there is a certain amount of coercion
possible in any situation. We will punish anyone who un-
dermines the working of the group." Gao was the brand-
new teacher letting the children know how tough he could
be, wisely veiling his threats: "a certain amount of coercion" was infinitely more effective than a specific punishment, even something as harsh as a week in solitary with

Das Kapital. "Probably, however. . . ." Collier noticed all the
qualifying words creeping into Gao's usage; he must have
been talking more with Bai. Gene reminded himself to say
something about it in private. "Probably, however, you are
affrighted that you will be betrayed by one of your own
after you are released and go back to your own government. Well, that is as good a problem in socialism as any
with which to begin this little group. How you deal with
betrayers in your own society is a very practical matter. I
would suggest, gentlemen, that you were betrayed by people in your government and that is why you are here now.
You have an adage, do you not, about closing the door to
the kitchen after the rooster has escaped with the pie?"

Collier and Tibideaux, sitting opposite each other,
looked across sideways as if to say, "Dig him!" and "Crazy,
man!"

"Sir." The speaker was a blond boy whose name Collier
had lost; it was either Malcolm or Greer. "The labor we're
supposed to do, will it be assigned or will we choose it
ourselves? The reason I ask is that some of us may have
some specific skills which could be utilized."

"You allude, Private Malcolm, to the division of labor, of
course. That, unfortunately, implies a diversity and sophis-
tication of function we do not possess. We have neither
farm machinery nor irrigation; we have no animals and only
the most rudimentary tools. We require peasant labor
only."

There was the deepest sort of silence.

"Oo-ee. If there is anything lower than chopping cotton
—" Tibideaux threw his hands up in mock despair and
looked heavenward.

Tibideaux's face intrigued Gene Collier; he had never
seen one even vaguely similar. The kinky hair was clearly
the longest in the room, suggesting that "Specs" had been
a prisoner for the longest time. Gene felt around on his
neck and discovered that his own hackle hairs had thick-

ened and formed full curls where none had ever grown before. He had been shaved by a young guard expertly every third day in his room, after his initial week-long confinement, but he had never considered the length of his own hair before studying Tibideaux's head.

Tibideaux's hair was parted cleanly down the middle. Did he own a mirror? A comb? Were not all the prisoners kept in the same primitive condition as Collier? These were more questions Gene would have for Gao in private; nevertheless, the hair was peculiar. No single feature characterized that face; all worked together to produce a . . . a Tibideaux. The eyes, under a broad, wide forehead, were perfect slits; the pupils slid sideways, revealing more white than brown. You knew he was looking at you only when you were certain he was looking at nothing else. There was a gap between his front teeth exactly the size of another such tooth. He had the highest, fullest cheekbones imaginable. Gene Collier thought this was one of the most curious, most devilish, most interesting faces he had ever seen.

Tibideaux was speaking. ". . . there is another thing we have to face here. And. That is the fact that although we are all Americans, some of us are more American than others. If you get my point." He exchanged glances with the other dark prisoners.

Angelo Carmine, or Carmine Angelo, responded wearily: "Look. We're all in the same boat here. We're all prisoners of war. It's a new ball game. Let's not rehash all that crap. Why I've had colored guys in my platoon who. . . ." He continued on, but nobody listened. Tibideaux had gotten up, walked to the table which had American magazines scattered over it, and picked up a copy of *Life.* When he turned around, he held the cover directly over his face, and there was a lithe, brown-handed man with Douglas MacArthur's face glaring defiantly down at the group. It was the perfect joke, perfectly executed. Collier saw Gao's face beaming, his eyes so lighted with laughter he wanted to touch him. Never had he seen Gao smile before; and now he saw one of the deepest, most joyful smiles ever.

More important than Tibideaux's silent put-down of Angelo, or Carmine, was the sense of freedom engendered by his movement across the room. It was contagious. That simple independence of motion established a tone for the group far beyond anything Gao could have promoted with well-intentioned words. A very dark, large-headed black man—his name was John Thomas—began to reason with Angelo (or Carmine) along lines of, "You can't know if you ain't been black." Within minutes everyone had spoken; the subject slid from racism to materialism to imperialism to militarism, but none of those terms was used and Gao never spoke but listened very carefully. The discussion went on for hours, although no one was aware of the time passing. "Gentlemen," said Gao finally, "you will be given paper and a pencil when you leave. For our next meeting, you are to present us with a detailed autobiography."

The meetings of the discussion group were held irregularly, but there were always three meetings within every seven-day period. They were not only irregular, but extremely uneven, in length as well as interest and openness. Never did they attain the depth of exchange of the first one. This was due, at the outset, to the weariness of the men as they slowly adjusted to peasant life. It was due, also, to Bai, who appeared on occasion to deliver a lecture filled with pedantic terms which required a prior knowledge of the particular subject that only he happened to possess. Gene planned to tell Gao the problem in hopes that something would be done about Bai in the future.

Gene and Tibideaux labored together; rather, they shared a single back-breaking task. Their first day established the sort of toil they were to perform almost daily for six months.

It seemed darker than usual when the sharp rap came to Gene's door, but the food was there as always, oats, tea, an enameled spoon. When Gene had finished and replaced his bowl and cup and spoon, there was not the customary second rap; instead, a key suddenly sprang his lock, the door swung back, and a guard stood before him with an oilskin poncho, a pair of green stockings, his old army boots. They were held inches from his face, so Gene quickly put them on. The guard pointed and grunted his charge down the dark hallway where Collier encountered another man under guard dressed exactly as he was. Tibideaux's voice said, even before Collier recognized the face, "Hey there, country boy, bet you'll be more hep to this peasant shit than I will."

Collier said nothing.

Gao met them at the door. He seemed weary and a bit angry. He explained the task quickly. They had been selected to work together. They would grow the spinach, the beans, and the onions for the entire camp. There were some problems: the soil was poor; there was no watering system; night soil would be the only fertilizer; seeds were not very good or plentiful; there was no machinery or animals available. "The areas for growing are marked off with poles; the guard will show you. You may proceed in any manner you wish; your sole responsibility is to bring in a respectable crop." And then he snapped at the squinting Tibideaux, "Oh, I see what you are thinking: 'I'll do what I can and if it is not enough, well then. . . .' But I tell you directly, you have a responsibility and you had better meet it." Gao was almost shouting. The moment he realized it, he was particularly vulnerable and human.

"The local farmers have supplied us in the past. This year, however, we will have to supplement their contributions by growing much of our own crops."

Collier wanted to assure him the task would be done, but realized, even at that crazy time and place, he could not until he knew more. Tibideaux just shook his head.

"Each piece of ground is greater than a *mou*—that is

one-sixth of an acre." Gao was terribly preoccupied. "It should be sufficient for our needs if you are economical."

It was a raw, damp morning. Gene and his partner were handed strange-looking tools by the guard. Something that resembled a hoe tip (but this was almost twice as large and of a rhomboid shape) was wedged and pegged to the end of a hand-hewn, hardwood shaft—it looked like hickory to Gene. One edge was a fairly good cutting edge, and the corner that was less than ninety degress formed a pretty effective point. It could be used as a small shovel, too. Gene admired it immediately; he was impressed by the hammer marks still in the iron and the fact that he wielded another man's handiwork.

Tibideaux said, "What you call this thing?" The guard looked at him crossly. "Well, then, Collier, I'm going to call it 'my-tool.' And. I'm going to call yours 'your-tool.' But. When you say 'my-tool,' you make sure you don't mean your own. We can make an Abbott-Costello thing out of it." Then he stopped and took a golf swing with it: "Sure has a nice feel to it." The guard grunted him forward.

They walked along a path through a light rain and out across a rocky field to a point about half a mile from the prison. The guard pointed to three parcels of land which had been staked with tall bamboo poles. Gene shielded his eyes, without any reason to do so, except that he felt it was the proper pose to strike. Tibideaux had his legs crossed and hung on "my-tool" like a collapsed scarecrow. The guard, they discovered at precisely the same moment, had slung his rifle and was walking back to the camp. Each man suddenly felt a fearful confinement and looked at the other.

"Well, I guess he meant what he said. We can do it any way we want; all we got to do is grow the stuff. Sure isn't anywhere to go, is there?"

Tibideaux said, "You know how to grow that shit?"

"My grandma used to have a big garden when I was a kid. I'll figure it out. What we got to do today is start clearing the rocks and stones off the land."

Two tall men inched up and down the muddy length of the land picking up stones and scaling them away—Tibideuax sent almost a hundred onto the other plots before Collier noticed—digging out the larger rocks and making piles which they could clear away later. Slow work. Tibideaux chattered a good deal at first; after a while the stooping claimed his tongue and back. After about an hour Collier realized what poor condition he was in for working; using "your-tool" as a staff, however, he avoided the awkwardness that would have brought pain to his lower back, as Tibideaux had not. Also, he developed a method of scooping a stone with "your-tool," cradling it, and hurling it beyond the border of the plot. It was a technique that didn't work very well for his partner.

"Hey, Collier. You know what my real first name is, my *Chris-ti-yan* name?" Tibideaux asked that right out, for no apparent reason, as he tugged on a rock that looked like a long, petrified potato. "It's Reginald. Ain't that some shit! It's like my folks were hoping I'd be a butler, or something. Reginald. Hey, man, let's take a break."

"Let's keep going to the end of the row." That established a pattern: They cleared three lengths and took a short break. As the two men each rested in the mud on one knee, letting the driving rain blow directly in their faces, they did not speak. Each thought the same thought—food!

Half the field was cleared when Gene decided that he could no longer continue to work under the rain-slick poncho. He pulled it off with a grunt and placed it on one of the bamboo markers. "Man, you're going to take one hell of a cold like that," warned Tibideaux, but it was less than ten minutes before he shed his poncho and dressed another marker.

The guard was almost on them before they saw him. Collier didn't know if he had worked with such complete absorption out of fear or from the compelling nature of the work. His hands on the carved shaft, the metal working end a link between shaft and earth; everything connected

beautifully, from the idea in his head to the strong impedi-
ment sailing out of bounds. And when the connections did
not quite come off, something could always be done—more
strength, digging at a different place or angle, leverage
from Tibideaux's tool—to produce the result he wanted.

The guard shouted from about twenty yards away and so
disrupted Collier's involvement with the process that Gene
spun around, frightened, with "your-tool" raised above his
head. It was lunch. The guard placed two pails at their feet.
Tibideaux took the lid off one, Gene opened the other.
"What the hell is this stuff?" Tibideaux said; Gene looked
over and saw a surface of foam.

"I guess you drink it," Gene said.

"I guess *you* drink it," Tibideaux corrected.

Gene did. He lifted the pail and tipped it gently and kept
it tipped against his lips for a long time. When he let the
pail fall, the foam stretched over a wide area above his lips,
and those lips were smiling broadly. He exuded a burst of
air. "W-e-l-l," he drawled, "it's sort of warm. It's got an
aftertaste a little bit like burned wood. It smells a little bit
peculiar, like soap or something. It sure as hell is beer!"

"Beer!" Tibideaux's squeal made the guard take a step
backward. They drank the quart of Korean beer in alternat-
ing chugs, the man watching and waiting his turn deriving
almost as much satisfaction as the man drinking. The rice
cakes in the other pail were a pleasant bonus.

By evening, when they were marched back in, their bodies were weary—joints sore, backs painful, hands rubbed
almost raw—but each emanated a tired satisfaction from
his eyes and slow gestures, particularly when they separated in the prison-warehouse. Tibideaux's eyes closed and
he made a circular movement, as though he were polishing
a mirror in slow motion, with his cupped hand.

Collier dried his body with a coarse towel he was given
by the guard. He kept "your-tool" with him. Gene admired
it at close range that first night; he could hear the smith's

hammer pounding the metal head into shape. He ate his supper quickly so he would have time to think more about the process of making food grow in North Korea. But he was asleep after step one: Clear the land of all rocks. He didn't dream; he didn't change position a single time; he didn't alter his breathing pattern—his body slept.

It took them six days to clear the three plots of land, and each day was chill and rainy. Collier now knew from experience that he was right in believing that every day here was the same. Their hands were badly blistered, but on the palms and the meat of the thumb calluses had already formed. The bodies, although still very sore, were beginning to become inured to labor. Gene Collier's legs felt as they had when the assistant coaches drove him into running shape; they were pleasantly painful, a strange contradiction he thought only the athlete knew about; the toiler could evidently sense it as well. Gene and Reginald "Specs" Tibideaux talked almost exclusively during these days about states of body and mind. Tibideaux said that he felt "bittersweet" most of the time, and Gene knew what he meant.

"After a while, though, a man would lose his taste for this life, and then he wouldn't be able to tell the bitter from the sweet."

"I ain't sure there wouldn't always be new things to taste."

The discussion groups during these first weeks were dreadful. During the first few minutes, when the men exchanged details and impressions of their labors, it was all right. But they became easily wearied by abstraction, and abstraction was anything they couldn't eat, dig, or carry. Bai seemed unperturbed by a sleeping student or two and lectured unabashedly about the history of capitalism.

On the seventh day Collier and Tibideaux did not rest. But their labors changed considerably. Two things were different when they arrived at their fields. The morning was clear and sunny; the day was hot enough after an hour's work to prompt the men to remove their shirts. "Man, look at that poison running out of me," Tibideaux said about his free-sweating chest and arms. The work was different, too. Crocks of night soil had been placed in the middle of each field.

Collier's plan was to dig deep, narrow ditches where the rows of seed would be planted. He remembered Grandma Gossett's gardens; it seemed to him the rows were never closer than one foot apart. He told Tibideaux fourteen inches. Then the night soil could be poured into the ditches and covered over. By the time they did this for all three fields, the fertilizer would have begun to do whatever it did in the ground. Then the rows could be turned over and cultivated for planting. If the weather cooperated, they'd be eating beans and onions and spinach in nine, ten weeks. "We'll save the spinach for the sandy soil," he said to Tibideaux while thinking aloud. Both men were impressed with the statement.

Digging the ditches was more hard work. Tibideaux stood on one side, Collier on the other; they alternated swings, chopping deeply with their tools and pulling the earth up and toward them. Collier discovered that saying "huh" each time "your-tool" caught the earth made him feel better. Tibideaux tried first a "hee" but switched to and settled on "hah." Two swings, two side-steps, and sounds of "huh-hah, huh-hah" down the length of the plot; by degrees narrow furrows appeared.

During the break Collier noticed in the sky over the prison the tightest formation of birds he had ever seen; the circles in which they flew were also unusually small. Every time they swung away from Collier, they disappeared in a mist or pale cloud; when they reappeared again, it was always in a different close formation. The overall impression of the unusual sight was that of liquidity. Now a tear-drop, now a saucer, now a bent kite; a leaf, a fish, a top— then they disappeared into the mist or pale cloud and did not return. Gene Collier realized that he had seen something wonderful, and it did not frighten him.

When the beer guard came they explained to him with pantomime and pictures in the ground that they required a bucket attached to a pole so they could dip the night soil out of the crocks and into the furrows. "A honey-dipper," Tibideaux enunciated slowly a few times. "Hurry-dinner," the wary guard finally repeated.

The honey-dipper, hastily manufactured but effective, was there the next day, which was again clear and warm. "It's important to get this stuff down," explained Collier, so the open ditches were filled, and as soon as new ditches were dug, the "honey" was poured. Collier discovered quickly the quantity of night soil that would enable them to cover the entire area. So they poured a bucket every four feet, spread it with their tools, and covered it with earth. It stunk powerfully, and it looked even worse. Gene had a look on his face that got Tibideaux laughing his low-down laugh. Then Gene started. Then each saw himself through the other's eyes. Then each saw the pair of them together, objectively, as if from above. Their laughter mixed and blended, and they finally fell to their knees, weakened by the effect of their understanding and noncomprehension.

Later, during a more serious moment, Tibideaux said, "It's really something, you know, food turning into shit and shit turning back into food. It happens so slow, and most men never get to see it, but that doesn't keep it from being like a miracle."

And Collier said, "It's about the funniest damned miracle I ever saw."

"Maybe all I'll learn from the war and being captured is the difference between shit and fertilizer."

"Maybe," said Gene, "that's a pretty important thing to know."

Many days were spent preparing this poor-looking gray soil. Many more "huh-hah's" to turn it over again and make the mounds for planting. Planting, watering, waiting. Their daily task throughout the summer was the watering, and the waiting really ended the morning they saw a tiny bean shoot pushing through the earth. Collier and Tibideaux sat on the ground and stared at it reverentially for ten minutes. Laughing. Watering was extremely tough; the summer was dry, and water was taken from barrels with the smaller buckets and poured carefully on the root of each plant. Fortunately a truck was then available to carry the water barrels in with them.

The discussion group began to improve at roughly the time the tops of the onions began to push through the earth. There was no connection, of course, but the men began talking about their own work with greater relish, more pride and less self-consciousness. A week later they were addressed by Gao; it was a lecture—his first—in which he had invested a great deal of time and thought. The talk contained as many numbers as words. The effect of the statistics on the group was to start the men looking around the room for help and then shipping their minds far from their bodies. As he was about to begin, Gao reached under the table and brought out a small cardboard sign that read, "REASONS FOR WAR—NO. 1: RESOURCES." Gao was to introduce all of his lectures with similar signs. Although the men thought it a peculiar and rather unnecessary practice, they managed to hide their amusement in his presence.

Gao's thesis the first time was simply stated at the outset: "The world has limited resources; it also has an increasing population and a technology in certain countries and not in others that requires the use of the world's limited resources. Conclusion: The countries with the technology—the rich countries—will be increasingly in conflict for the world's resources; the poor countries will be in conflict with the rich countries for control of their own resources." The number of tons of cobalt in the U.S.S.R., barrels of oil in Malaya, potential kilowatts in Victoria Falls had a strange effect on Collier: they produced a cumulative, quantitative comprehension that grew, as Gao piled figure on figure for the better part of an hour, into a qualitative certainty. There would be wars for control of markets, minds, and raw materials for the rest of Gene's natural life—if he would be allowed to live out a natural life. It was, as Mary Jane Bloxham had once said, strictly mathematical. Gene Collier slept fitfully; he dreamed of a frigid, geometrical holocaust. He saw no liquid formations of birds.

On one occasion only did Collier work in the field alone. When he left the prison that morning, Gao was there to tell Gene that Tibideaux "was sick in the stomach." It was a watering day, a task one man could accomplish with difficulty, so the loss of labor was not crucial. The day was remarkable for one event. The sun was very high and Gene was sweating freely and hoping the beer ration would not be cut in half. A plane, a U.S. Sabrejet, small as a bird against the bright sky, circled over the mountains and flew directly toward Gene, dropping closer to the ground and seeming to slow appreciably as it approached. It made three such slow passes, apparently curious about the man below. Gene Collier did not wave; he did not feel the "Thank God it's one of ours" elation of the war movies. His reaction was very different. Terror. These plots of land had become his land and he was a peasant; the mechanical intrusion of the plane was a frightening threat. The plane and the man flying it were his enemies. They could destroy his crop, his life in a moment, and they did not have the right. Gene's helplessness made him angry, but he remained stooped, peering at the menace through narrowed eyes only after it had passed. Its noise, arrogant and vulgar, stayed with him long after the guard had brought the half-ration of beer.

Tibideaux and Collier brought in their first crop, the beans, in late June, in time to lay another. Then they harvested the onions and spinach. By August the two men had

become so deeply involved in the process as to be insepara-
ble from it. The fact that they were technically not free
occurred to them very infrequently, and when it did, it
came in the form of an omission or oversight on the part
of Bai and Gao that could be rectified at a later time without
significant personal loss. The first frost came to Pyongyang
on October 8, 1952; only a few dozen small heads of spinach were caught in the ground.

13

Relax, Charlie

While God sat—or did not sit—upon His Throne, concerned—or somehow managing not to care—about the
affairs of men, and while *yin* and *yang* contended and
blended interminably, Vice-Admiral Turner Joy sat at a
desk in a dark green tent set on a cleared acre of ground
called Panmunjom, framing the next day's reply to General
Nam Il. Vice-Admiral Turner Joy was the senior delegate
of the United Nations' Command at the Armistice conference. General Nam Il was the senior delegate and Chief of
Staff of the Korean People's Army. For nearly a year these
two men faced each other almost daily and, for the most
part, tossed prepared statements in each other's direction.
Fortunately, subdelegations had been meeting in other
tents and were making slow progress toward a truce agree-
ment. By the fall of 1952 the agenda had been formulated
and substantive agreements had been reached on most important items. Both sides accepted the restrictions on air-
field construction and limits on the rotation of military
personnel, as well as a generalized demarcation line and

ground inspection by neutral teams. Only prisoner-of-war repatriation remained a stumbling block. Return of all prisoners as opposed to voluntary repatriation was the specific difference; it would continue to remain the final impasse for many months.

Turner Joy was a man in his late fifties, a kindly, slouching, avuncular sort in appearance; and, when nothing of importance was at stake, he was rather jocular and easygoing. His eyes and the set of his jaw were most revealing. At rest or at play they tended downward like an old family dog who exuded a bemused tolerance; one sensed his wisdom and felt safe with him around. It didn't take much, though, to fire the eyes or bare the teeth; an intruder could do it, or any sort of challenge. If he ever were to catch an opponent in those teeth, you could bet he would hang on just as long as he had to.

Turner Joy carried none of the combative petulance with him when he left the brown "discussion" tent in the middle of the clearing each afternoon. He had the knack of being two different men on command. He enjoyed both his roles and, even more, the distance he could traverse instantly between the two. Turner Joy felt safer there at Panmunjom than at Kaesong, the first site of the talks, which was farther into Communist territory to the north.

He had come to like the life in the tent community; it offered him everything he enjoyed: food of his choice carried over from the mess tent across the road; press conferences; instantaneous communications anywhere in the world; a helicopter pad forty yards from where he sat; daily intellectual combat; solitude. . . . Vice-Admiral Turner Joy particularly enjoyed leaving his desk for a short walk into the field behind his tent, exchanging a few pleasant words with the guard and scanning the multiplicity of stars on a clear, cold night.

Nam Il was the same man at all times. His face always the same flat face, essentially expressionless except for two deep vertical creases falling from the corners of his thin lips to his chin. His ears were surprisingly large and stood out from his head, but this slightly comic feature was more than counterbalanced by dark eyebrows that appeared to form a single brow and small, piercing eyes; neither brows nor eyes moved significantly.

General Nam Il, like the other Korean officers but unlike the Chinese, wore an impressive military uniform: epaulets, a blocked cap, riding breeches, and leather riding boots. He spent at least an hour every evening polishing these boots himself, while he talked about the day's events with his staff. He was almost never alone; Turner Joy often required silence and isolation. Nam Il committed only the main points of his position to writing; Turner Joy composed whole pages every evening.

The site of the talks made General Nam Il uncomfortable. Of course his personal needs were well met; he was satisfied with his performance and the development of the talks; and he was only slightly annoyed at the ostentation and arrogance of the Americans. It was the site itself, the land, that was the source of his discomfort. The road that ran through the campground was the very road, much farther to the north, of course, on which his father had tilled soil for most of a lifetime. His father's land, less than an acre, a great deal for a peasant, was not of the same rectangular shape—it was a long, narrow "L"—but in color and texture the soil was the same. So Nam Il felt that he was literally on his home land. The presence of the Americans and members of the press, of the five main tents, the latrines, the huts, the trucks, the helicopter—the treatment of his soil as though it were neutral, as though it belonged to *no one*, that was the source of his discomfort.

Turner Joy wrote: "Yesterday you used the word 'arrogant' in connection with a proposal the United Nations' Command delegation now has before this conference. The United Nations' Command delegation has been in search

of an expression which conveys the haughty intransigence, the arbitrary inflexibility, and the unreasoning stubbornness of your attitude. Arrogance is indeed the word for it...."
He put down his fountain pen. Vice-Admiral Turner Joy never abbreviated "United Nations." He stood up, stretched, and slipped out of the tent. There was a chill, misty rain falling. The guard snapped to attention. "Relax, Charlie. It's just me. Trying to blow a little of the old stink off." He touched the guard's shoulder softly and moved far enough into the field so the sprinkle he made wouldn't be heard.

General Nam Il was buffing the heel of his left boot. He looked up and said to his fellow delegates, Lee Sang Cho and Chang Pyong San, "I understand their political motives, but what could motivate them personally?" It was not exactly put as a question because his voice did not rise. He looked directly at neither of his aides, but northward beyond the tent. One of his eyebrows was slightly raised.

14

Singing Wind

"We have not met like this for a long while, eh Mr. Kao?"

"Quite so, Mr. Gao."

With the arrival of winter and the end of work details, Gene Collier returned to the harsher conditions of his room during those morning and evening hours when he was not in the library. He huddled in his quilt near the window in order to have light for reading, but not so near as to be away from the heat coming from the hallway. Winter, according to Mr. Bai's process of remolding thoughts, was a time of withdrawal, a period devoted to reading and reconsideration. Labor, growth, and human exchange was the *yin*; isolation, introspection, and despair the *yang*. Clearly, Mr. Bai was interested in developing the whole man. The differences between Collier's living conditions when he had first arrived at Pyongyang and his present situation were that he was allowed in the reading room for an hour every evening, alone; he could take one book or magazine back to his room; he saw Gao less often and Bai not at all.

He read as long as the light from the opening permitted. As the light increased, he read faster; as it diminished, he strained and faltered, particularly if he had become interested in the subject. At night his body slept deeply; his mind flitted and dodged through and around book-induced thoughts. His reading position was critical, for although the window brought light it also admitted the cold. A spot between two small knotholes in the floor was a general point of balance. If the day brightened and warmed, Collier edged closer toward the heat. Balance, the harmony of contending forces; yes, even in something as trivial as this. Gene remembered one of Grandma Gossett's bedtime stories. They had all been discomforting and invoked bad dreams, but the one about the porcupines stayed in his mind longest and with the greatest clarity:

"Shut your eyes up, an' try to make pictures out of what I'm a-tellin' you. An' for heaven's sakes, don't do no peekin'. It's about these two porkpines I saw once when I was a girl, actually more what would pass for a young woman these days. It was when I was still livin' with my paw, back country up in Weyland. I got in the habit of puttin' some hog fat out for the critters in winter nights when it was freezin' bad. An' there was these two porkpines in partic'lar come around all the time. After a while, they just dug a hole right next to the cabin an' began to take up livin' right there. Well, one day my paw takes me over to the hole an' points out to me the way they're sleepin' in there. All sort of curled up an' cozy, but not really all that close to each other. He says, 'You know how in the Good Book it says two bodies is better than one because two can give each other warmth an' one cain't; well, that ain't specially true with porkpines.' You see, if they get real close, they hurt one another with them quills. But if they don't get close enough, they freeze. So they got to find out just the right point of closeness between hurtin' and freezin'. If they don't, their life just ain't worth livin'. An' that's exactly the same with people too. No matter what the Good Book says. Young Gene, you sleepin'?"

Gene had finished a novel called *Freedom Road*, about Reconstruction after the Civil War, in three days' time, a reading record for him. As in the other books he had read, sentences had been underlined and circled in pencil, with occasional comments of "wow" or "SOME STUFF!" stuck in the margins. With no completely logical reason for the conclusion, Gene assumed Tibideaux was the source of the running commentary.

Gao had requested the meeting, if "requested" was the appropriate word to apply to someone summoned by his captor. But when the captain addressed him as "Mr. Kao," some of the anger that had built up in Gene flew off immediately as though the unique address carried with it an apologetic overtone. This, indeed, was precisely how it was intended. "You see," Gao continued, "I have been away."

"You don't have to explain anything, you know."

"I wish to. Perhaps I should not tell you what I am about to, but once again I wish you to know what is involved in the choices you may have to make."

"That's just the sort of thing you'd say before giving me some bad news."

"Oh no, Collier, quite the contrary, quite the contrary. Before I tell you, however"—here Gene almost interrupted to tell Gao how he had begun to sound too much like Bai to satisfy him, but he just made a note of it and let it slide —"I have been informed that you have not composed a single letter. Not one. Your family being alive in West Virginia, it is of no sense to me that you should not wish to renew contact." Gao's face was expressive, it registered concern seasoned lightly with annoyance; his body leaned forward perilously across the table. In fact, if it were not for the table Gao would have appeared ready to spring at Collier. "They must have considerable worry at this point."

Gene Collier had intended to write a letter home often,

just one, but the intention became so familiar and reasonable a response the act itself seemed unnecessary.

"Truth is that I planned to write them a number of times. I did. Even had an opening sentence all prepared—'Dear Dad: I am not a *fine* son and have never been one, but that is subject to change.' I guess I'm just not ready to write him yet."

Gao's body relaxed a bit and his head and shoulders retreated before a situation he could not comprehend. Family, although it was no longer a thing for a man to worship blindly, nor an oppressive, authoritarian force to be feared, was, nevertheless, a link back to whatever it is we have come from, some understanding of why we have our father's hands, a mother's eyes, a particular grandparent's disposition. Gao, himself cut off from these links by American bombs, could not understand why a person would willingly choose such isolation. But Gao was not totally isolated; his village, the site of continuity, if not the continuity itself, provided him with a link sufficient for his needs.

"I have been home," he told Gene Collier. The simple statement was so rich in meaning the two men sat silent for almost a minute believing they were still engaged in conversation. "There is so much work to be done there"; Gao gave voice to his thoughts at a point approaching the conclusion. "My knowledge . . . I am needed so badly there, it is as though *I* have become the prisoner here." Then for a while the conversation was silent.

Until Collier said, "What are the choices I'm going to have to make?"

"Not choices so much as preparations. You see, there are very strong indications that your government is unwilling to pay the price of aggression for very much longer."

"Gao, what the hell does that mean?"

Gao smiled with the lower part of his face. "I have been told on good authority that an armistice will be signed in the spring."

Gene's gut reaction was disappointment. He thought the "preparations" Gao had referred to would have something to do with a work program in the prison. Gene Collier heard his own words a beat or two after they formed in his mind: "Just the same, I'm going to stay in shape for the growing season."

"Perhaps that would be wise. Please do not tell the other men what I have told you."

"Other men!" Gene's voice struck even him as being unusually resonant and deep. He had come to think of it as too high and nasal for someone his size. *"Jesus Christ, except for one or two zombies in the library, I haven't seen anyone since the spinach froze."*

The sounds of Collier's anger echoed through the warehouse. When they had finally been absorbed by the walls, Gao said, "At any rate, you must decide whether or not you wish to be repatriated when the armistice is announced."

"Repatriated?"

"Go back to your army."

"What's the other choice?"

"You may, if you wish, come to live in my country."

There were things that Gao had not told Gene Collier. He had not, for example, revealed that the interview was a probe of sorts, to see if Collier's refusal to return to America was a real possibility. Bai, anticipating the future propaganda value of those men who might refuse, had suggested raising the possibility in interviews with each man. In many cases the attraction of home, roots, and familiar patterns of life would be so great that any alternative would be unthinkable. On the other hand, there were men whose personal instability would ultimately prove an embarrassment should they accept the alternative. These, too, would have to be screened. There were, all in all, no more than five or six likely candidates.

The meeting with Collier was not, strictly speaking, a probe, and this fact related to something else Gao had not told Collier. Upon his return to the camp, Gao had been briefed by Bai on the movement that had taken place at Panmunjom and the reasonable expectations one might have of the talks' outcome. Bai then alluded to the disproportionate propaganda value a number of politicized "turncoats, as they are called in the West," would have in the struggles that lay ahead. Bai wanted Gao to continue with the group long after the armistice was signed. "Nothing quite of this nature has ever been attempted before. The possibilities to observe and learn things about these men should be quite special, indeed. Of course I could not have confidence in its success if I had not someone like you to share the responsibility, Captain Gao." With those words, Bai had begun to discuss the future.

Gao Ma-ting was annoyed on two counts: about Bai's presumption that he would stay with him and about the idea of staying itself. He had other plans—life-work, the rebuilding of a community in Shensi—for his energies when this war, this cycle of miscalculations, was ended. No, he would not accompany Bai and his group of "turncoats" to the People's Political Institute in Peking. His work was elsewhere with other men. In a modulated voice Gao Mating declared, "You are the political expert, Mr. Bai; it would be sheer arrogance for me to suggest that you may be placing too much value in the symbolic significance these few men may reflect."

Bai raised a finger that curved backward. "Their chief value would be as models of our thought-remolding procedure," he said by way of clarification.

To Gao Ma-ting it was a correction. "Nevertheless," continued the controlled Gao, "I must ask to be allowed to return to my village. I am called there. It would seem foolish not to allow a man to do the work he is called to do."

Bai suddenly looked very old. "Should I have to remind

a captain in the People's Army that it is not always for him to determine what is and what is not foolish."

Resentment ran deep on both sides. Never did it find expression in a raised voice or a rude gesture. Mr. Bai, in fact, poured the tea and served it as he might have for his superior in the Party. The resentment was implicit in the conflict of wills. Because both wills could not prevail on this matter, each man was angered by the willfulness of the other. Both understood that anger could do nothing to resolve the conflict, so they did something typically Chinese: they changed the subject.

"How are things at home?"

"We do not suffer so greatly from the war directly. Rather, it is a monumental distraction. We cannot get properly about the tasks that must be done."

They discussed specific prisoners at great length. They criticized political decisions that had been made in the past and the men who had made them. They recounted their personal experiences with some of those men, Bai, of course, having more of these anecdotes than Gao. They talked about cities they had each visited at different times and how each had changed for the better or worse. Finally, they discussed Gene Collier at some length; this was another thing Gao Ma-ting had neglected to tell Gene Collier.

"With this Collier, Captain, I feel we have gone as far as possible. There is no possibility of his becoming a political man."

"Not a theorist, that is true. Perhaps not even politically conscious. But he might someday be the sort of man who can function in constructive ways. There are times when such men are more useful than either theorists or organizers."

"Ah, hah. You are not speaking about Collier at all." Since time and circumlocution had dissipated much of the resentment, it was now possible for Bai and Gao to smile at the humor of Bai's observation. "You are speaking of

yourself, of your 'mission' in Yang-Xien. And you hide
yourself behind the example of this Collier. Really, Captain
Gao, shame on you." The humor of Bai, less sharp, that is
to say, more human, than customary, caused Gao Ma-ting
to smile; it signified the end of resentment between the
men.

"Of course you are the expert in these matters, as I have
already said, but I have always felt that there was value in
using some of the ones who choose to invade the Middle
Kingdom as workers." Bai smiled with black teeth at the
irony of "invade." "Not for their productivity; how few are
their numbers after all? Rather as working examples of men
who have been remolded. Examples not for the B.B.C. or
The New York Times, for they shall only misrepresent, but as
examples for our own people. That the devil can be tamed
and taught to sow a field and share his crops, that is what
a Gene Collier would show the peasants of Yang-Xien."
Only when he was finished did Gao realize the strident
undertone of his voice.

"Hear, hear, Chairman Gao." Gao Ma-ting blushed. Bai
continued. "Certainly it must have occurred to you that the
denizens of the Middle Kingdom will continue to see a
White Devil as a White Devil even if he is Nikolai Lenin
incarnate, which Eugene Collier is certainly not." Bai had
moved the conversation into repartee, and in so doing he
remembered his notorious reputation around the dinner
tables of the London School of Economics; he recalled
debates and his displacement and his triumphs with certain
English girls. Now he sensed the impending loss of Gao
more directly than ever.

"At any rate, with your approval, of course, I intend to
try to convince him to reject repatriation and return with
me to my home."

"Well." In turning serious, Bai's face aged. "You must
not 'convince,' because you cannot 'convince' a man about
such things. It is quite out of your hands. A man will refuse

repatriation only for one of two reasons. Either he does not know the true value of home; and Collier, I do not believe is such a one . . ." Bai paused, raised his spectacles, and squeezed the bridge of his nose.

"And the other reason?"

"Or, he knows the value too well, and is frightened by it."

"That is irrational."

"Precisely. And that is why on this matter a man cannot be 'convinced.' There are limits even to remolded thoughts. There is, however, something important that will help you with the Collier boy."

Gao asked "What is it?" with raised brows and an up-turned palm, fingers spread.

"I have in his file a number of letters from his family. All from the father, a rather literate coal miner. Collier, how-ever, has never answered the first letter he received; I have been keeping the others until he does. In my humble opin-ion, he belongs in the latter category: He is a man who values home deeply. This I conclude from the letters I have read and a passing knowledge of the prisoner himself. He may value it so much as to consider it unattainable; many such young Americans have these romanticized, utopian visions. And they are frightened to death by them."

Gene Collier increased the number of repetitions of each physical exercise after his meeting with Gao. He would not be shaken into confusion by rumors of an armistice, he would not get caught out of shape for the spring planting. Only the renewed vigor in his daily exercise marked the external change in Collier after Gao had begun to prepare him for the end of this segment of his life. That, and an interest in reading the novels and short stories of Jack London. The reading had a double purpose: First, it helped Gene believe that the snowflakes drifting through the opening in the room, like misdirected salt crystals, were nothing compared to the tundra blizzards which turned men into wolves and froze them both. Second, Gene extracted the idea of men being shaped by forces they could not possibly control, and certainly never understand, with a clarity and comprehension previously impossible to him. Of course his father's life had embodied that same lesson, and sometimes he even told his son how it was as clearly as Jack London did; but there was something about reading it in a book, in a story where a dying man is put out of his misery by his partner and buried with his lead dog, that made it far more real than his own father's life. The result of it all—the snowflakes, the small, cold room, the exercise, Jack London, and word of the war's end—was that Gene experienced a peculiar, almost belligerent perversity; it took the form of an irrational, "They-won't-get-rid-of-me-so-easy" attitude.

Eugene Collier's life had never been more ordered; and never before had his goal—the growing of beans and onions and spinach—been so tangible and worthy of his efforts.

The chief activity in life for a porcupine-man was, in fact, the continuous attempt to resolve contradictions: dark and light, warmth and cold, thought and action. The danger in this, Gene Collier discovered, was a tendency to accommodate every change in the flow of forces. "All well and good," said Gene out loud one evening after the light began to fail, "I'll go with most things, but not everything. There has to be something you got to be willing to fight all the way for." He put his book aside, jumped directly up from a sitting position, and did fifty jumping-jacks.

His meetings with Gao Ma-ting became briefer; the subject of repatriation caused Collier to withdraw, to slump in his chair and become totally unresponsive. Gao's questions went unanswered, his statement of the options that would be open to Collier apparently went unheard.

There came a morning, still bleak and with an irregular

singing wind blowing down from the mountains and across his fields, a normally chill morning that was abnormal in some barely perceptible way. Imperceptible to another man, perhaps; but to Gene Collier the warmth beneath the chill, the breeze behind the wind were easily discernible. It was coming.

On a similar cold, dark morning one week later, a sharp metallic rap startled Gene Collier, startled him not because he had been asleep but because he lay there expecting it. After a winter spent as a bookish porcupine, Collier was pushed down the dark hallway by a guard he had never seen before toward the rear entrance of the prison. Tibideaux was waiting. "Your-tool" and "my-tool" supported him under his arms like crutches, and he let himself sag weakly when he saw Collier approach. "Like I was saying, I don't think I completely recovered from last summer."

The two men did not shake hands and they didn't say anything very personal. Captain Gao did not appear. The guard swung the door open and closed it after them. The tools on their shoulders, they walked unescorted slowly toward their fields, their breaths turned to mist alternately in the crisp air. With the exception of not having to clear the rocks from the land, the process was precisely that of the previous season.

There was one difference: American planes and helicopters passed over them almost daily. Tibideaux waved and seemed cheered by their apparent interest. Collier always stooped when they approached; his stomach remained in knots long after they had passed. The planting, to which Collier found himself drawn for the duration of the winter, was even more satisfying than the previous year, perhaps because he knew exactly what the challenges were going to be. He even hoped to clear another plot and experiment with some new crops, but there simply was not enough time; no sooner had the preparation and planting been done—late owing to a persistent frost—when Gao insisted on spending more time during the afternoons talking with Gene about the end of the war and the choice he would soon be forced to make. It was time Gene could have used more constructively in the fields; the continuing discussion with Gao was upsetting.

Three weeks before the Armistice was signed, Gao told Gene he could begin his journey home, if he chose, by early August.

"I'll need at least three months to bring in the late crops."

"We will deal with your decision last," Gao said.

One week later Tibideaux was not at the rear door. "My-tool" was tipped against the wall at a preposterous angle, and Collier took this as Tibideaux's final joke. Collier watered his fields alone.

During sleepless nights, Collier heard a great deal of activity about the prison—trucks and distant voices. He heard fewer guards, fewer footsteps, fewer doors closing.

"This situation is insane, Collier," Gene was told by Gao Ma-ting. "We cannot continue to keep this prison running merely to enable you to improve your agricultural techniques." Gao smiled at his own joke. Gene thought only of rotting spinach. "It is a paradox, you know. The war is over. I cannot wait to return home, and you will not make a decision."

"What do you think I should do?"

"I? I can not say."

"I mean what would you do if you were me?"

"I am Gao Ma-ting. I am fortunate, I know what I must do."

"When are you leaving?"

"Within one week."

"This might sound crazy, which you already think I am anyway, but what's your home like, the town I mean?"

"It is very old, and the people are very poor. There is so much work to be done, it will take a lifetime. Maybe two or three. But you can see the Great Wall on most days, and the evenings are very silent, the birds . . . oh, you cannot tell about Yang-Xien." Gao looked away, embarrassed once again by having spent words foolishly. This happened to him too often with Collier; ultimately it was a small price to be paid for his meddling with the essence of other men's lives.

Porcupine-man was being forced to move one way or the other. Pain or isolation. Maybe both. Collier felt an internal vibration down in his testicles. As it rose, it took the form of a growl. Had it come out, it would have been a scream. It didn't. It was blocked in his chest by a wall of tensed muscles.

During the weeks that remained, the porcupine-man imagined himself staying where he was, alone in an abandoned camp with his books, his crock, "your-tool," reading in the winter frost, planting and harvesting in the spring and summer. That would be the porcupine solution, but he did not mention it to Gao. He realized, finally, that when home is not Home, it is not only a disappointment to the creature who would nest there, it is repellent. It was a slow and painful realization for Collier. The scream did not come out, but it was agonizing nevertheless.

The final meeting of Collier and Gao took place in the library. For a long time Gene said nothing. Gao Ma-ting focused his eyes on a point above and beyond Collier's left shoulder. When Gene finally spoke, he heard himself say, "Tell me again, what would my name be in Chinese?"

PART III

SHENSI

15

Figurehead

There is a quality sometimes evident in people who have survived a threatening physical situation in life—a serious automobile accident or a delicate operation—that often changes the essence of their personalities. They are left with a passive wisdom, an elemental tolerance, a fluid understanding; yet none of those things exactly. It is, rather, the unique residue of what they have carried back with them from Hell. It helps them to put life in such a perspective that worldly extremes shrink considerably and all human activity seems to cluster about a very tiny core. Having touched the ultimate limits of "To be" and "Not to be," they see most other distinctions as essentially insignificant.

Not all people who have been to Hell and back carry with them this special residue, but this phenomenon does not yield to conventional explanations and comprehension. Like a distant breeze that cannot be seen, whose existence is perceived by its effects—the rustling of leaves or the raising of dust—this extraordinary quality is evident in certain people.

Gene Collier had not been to Hell exactly; nevertheless, he had been transformed in a substantial way. His was not precisely the deep peace of the sojourner from Hell; however, the characteristic that most clearly marked Collier's altered personality was not too distantly related.

Gene's choice of going to China might have been a wish to leap into the abyss. It wasn't. It was a desire to flow in whatever direction seemed most unfamiliar, perhaps even an unconscious wish to go a great deal out of his way in order to glide home from a very unlikely place. Of course, Bai's theory that home was a repellent concept for Collier also had to be considered, but it would be just as well to accept his displacement with his same willingness to take the world, no matter how strange or foreign, as it was offered without analysis. On the deck of a small sea-tossed freighter in the Yellow Sea on an overcast morning in late August, Collier was moving toward home in a most unlikely direction.

The sun shone weakly through a constant haze while the small ship cut large waves as it bucked eastward. It was apparent to the crew that it was going to be considerably longer than the scheduled voyage of two days. The sea was rough from the moment they had left Sinuiju, and it promised to remain so all the way to Tang-Ku. Gene Collier, of course, could make no comparative judgment. Every member of the crew that he saw was irritable, some were downright mean; none of this touched him, none of it mattered particularly. Collier rarely saw the young soldier who had been designated his guard, but Gene remained under constant surveillance.

To reproduce exactly what Gene Collier "saw" is not an easy matter, for some of the residue of his nineteen months as a prisoner of war (or criminal of war, if you happen to prefer it that way) in Pyongyang was the fact that he saw the world in a soft focus. He heard sound with greater than usual resonance. Words, even in Chinese, became sound patterns and values. His ability to distinguish constituent odors in everything he smelled became unusually sharp, even though everything was subsumed by the salt essence of the sea. In short, his senses were not dulled, and he did not relapse into the unfeeling, buzzing condition that had overcome him in Pusan and Koje-do. He was experiencing, rather, a transformation of his senses; they were still reliable messengers from the external world, but now they carried very different parcels.

Collier stood at the bow of the ship, his arms twined around the hemp of the railing, his large bony fists locked around them as the ultimate stability. His body took the brunt of the bucking movement. Sometimes, as the hull fell over the precipice of a receding wave, he leaned so far forward as to appear to be the ship's figurehead. An ever-constant spray forced his eyes into slits. There were moments when he had to suck the spray into his mouth in order to breathe. This man was obviously no longer a captive or even a reluctant guest. Instead of choosing a more comfortable position on one of the lower rear decks or staying below until the ship had reached its destination, Gene Collier drove headlong toward China.

Dressed in a yellow oilcloth slicker, a sweater, quilted trousers, and his U.S. Army boots, Collier maintained this forward position for twelve or thirteen hours on that first day. Since no food had been offered to him and there was nothing to read, there was no practical alternative. A stroll around the crashing deck was impossible. The hammocks were much too small and unstable to accommodate him comfortably for any length of time. So Collier stayed forward.

The overwhelming power of the sea, the unpredictability of the violent motion, the variety and harmony of sounds that comprised a constant roar, the extremes of violent and subtle coloration of sea and foam and sky; these could not be dismissed by the man who rode the ship and his senses across the Yellow Sea.

The experience had a specific message for Collier. It was

carried by Collier's senses to various parts of his body. Understanding arrived at various times at Collier's liver, testicles, spinal cord, kneecaps, and the coccyx, that little skeletal vestige of animal tail. It was simple. The message said: We are all foreigners in the world. None of us is welcome—only tolerated. Everyone will be asked to leave.

At midmorning of the third day, about the time he discovered a dark strip on the horizon, Collier sensed that the force of the waves had abated. By diminishing degrees of violence, each too slight to be very revealing, the sea permitted Gene Collier's approach to the land mass he had chosen, an approach to a new isolation. He had a distinct sense of choice; he was moving toward what he wanted and away from what he did not want only because wanting something implied not wanting something else. That was why living in the world was not easy, even for people who have received a strong sample of the alternative. "Hell," Collier said in a normal speaking voice, "we're all foreigners anyway."

The harbor of Tang-Ku was crammed with small, gray freighters with smaller, colorful junks and houseboats clustered about. The summer sun was shining strongly, but a crisp breeze blew from the land, snapping pennants and carrying shouts, laughs, and metallic sounds from the docks out to the approaching Collier. The city was, like most old seaports, functionally unattractive and grimy. Collier had never before been in a seaport; he had mixed feelings: On the one hand, it was all new, thrilling; on the other, he assumed all of China would look like this. How could Mrs. Philpotts have gushed over any place that looked like this?

The ship glided past other ships. There were ritual waves from some sailors on those ships and a few shouts. Some shouts were returned by crewmembers on his ship, all of whom were occupied in various strenuous activities. A red-bearded man on a large tanker they were passing hollered to Collier something in Swedish or Norwegian. Collier

threw out his hands indicating noncomprehension. Red-
beard then hollered, "Where from?"

"Kor-ee-aaa," Collier shouted through cupped hands;
the voice was not his own.

Nearing the dock, Collier picked out Bai's face almost
immediately. Bai could not have missed Collier. Coming
directly toward the deck, the ship and the man in yellow at
the bow seemed one and the same.

The events of the following week were almost exactly as
Gao Ma-ting had told Collier they would be. Bai was, indeed, there to meet him, and, surprisingly, he behaved in
a friendly, straightforward manner. He made no ironic allu-
sions about the war, about himself, about Pyongyang,
about Collier's decision; in fact, Bai seemed to be a very
different person on the mainland. He was dressed differently, in a trim brown suit, gray shirt, and blue tie; but the
change that most impressed Collier was that Bai appeared
much smaller and very wrinkled.

"You are to be with us in Peking, as you know, Mr.
Collier, for four, perhaps five days before we ship you off
to Yang-Xien and Captain Gao. I have an automobile waiting. Since we are already somewhat behind schedule, I
suggest that we proceed; there are some very busy days
planned." He said "schedule" like an Englishman.

"Swell." Gene's thoughts were of his rubbery landlegs.

Bai's fingers touched Gene's wrist, and as Collier looked
down, Bai moved his hand in the direction of a shiny black
automobile.

There was construction proceeding almost along the entire length of the road from Tang-Ku to Peking, but Bai's
driver drove at an uncommonly high speed the whole way.
Although Collier's perception of the land would have been
slightly out of focus even at a slower pace, it appeared now
as a variety of sweeping green and brown blurs.

Bai said, "You have brought some cool weather with you.

Peking has been sweltering in the Tiger Heat throughout the summer."

Collier smiled; he didn't know how to respond. Then, after a few minutes, he heard his voice say, "I'm really in China!" But he couldn't know if these words had been spoken or merely imagined.

The "busy days" to which Bai had referred were also blurs, and as such they were not, for Collier, busy at all. They flew past him as had the sea foam and the fields of grain along the road to Peking. For Bai they were hectic.

Because Bai had agreed to ship Collier off to Gao in Shensi when he was through with him, he thought it less troubling for all parties not to have Gene meet any of the other American expatriates, even though they were also in Peking. This particular man was already marked for ship-ment; no good could come from a meeting with the others. But Gene did meet literally hundreds of local and national officials and heroes, having his picture taken with each one, not once but numerous times. He was interviewed in Eng-lish and in Chinese (through interpreters) as many as six times in the course of a single day; in each instance, his words were recorded. Once he was filmed behind a table as he responded to questions in English from Bai. One of the bulbs kept blowing out, and the filming seemed, even to Collier whose senses were flowing, to take an inordi-nately long time.

He was photographed eating Peking duck, which, under the confused conditions, he hardly got to taste. He was shot against the wall of the Summer Palace and in ten different factories. He sipped *mao tai* and was toasted by General Po I-chi at the Peking Military Institute. He was toured and dined and observed and examined. Questioned and tu-tored. Fussed over and forgotten. Never was he alone for a single moment; not even at night when he shared a room with a fairly pleasant soldier who smiled too much. The same young man was within coughing distance whenever

Collier stepped up to a urinal or over one of those strange, low straddle-toilets.

The effect of the busy week on Gene Collier was complex. On one level, he floated on the rush of events so that their direction, meaning, or ultimate purpose made no difference, even though on another level Collier had intimations of some perceptions and memories of remarkable clarity. Early one glorious morning, for example, as he was being escorted along Xien-Men Street toward the Old Imperial City, Collier stopped near a small park and saw a few dozen old men doing the graceful morning calisthenics known as *tai chi chuan*. They stood in a loose, diamond formation, but each man was leaning differently, each exploring the nature and extent of the particular space he occupied with slow sweeping arms and pendular movement of shoulders, neck, and head. Many of the men were as old as a man could ever get to be. Collier's eyes made contact with those of a tall fellow at the left point; after some seconds, the frozen moment was broken off by his sudden, gap-toothed smile. Collier recalled that moment, the still-shot of that exceptional face totally.

He also clearly remembered the exact wine-red of the palace walls; the shape of the willows by the Wu-Men Gate; the graceful curve of the tiled roofs in the Old City; the rush of humanity in the streets in the afternoon, so many carrying heavy objects strapped to their backs or their sides; the remarkable quiet produced by so many bicyclists and pedestrians; the innocence implicit in the tilt of a girl's head; the swiftness of a shopkeeper's fingers on the abacus; the familiar smell of pine needles that was prominent in the numerous parks around the city, and which became the base upon which most other city smells were piled.

Generally, however, it was as though Gene Collier still rode the bow of a struggling ship, and most color, form, movement, texture, and sound remained only impressions and blended rhythms. Instead of the ship there was his political itinerary; he moved in an ocean of people, their faces were the foam, their curious glances a fine, biting spray.

Much of the time, most of what he saw and heard remained on that first level; it was not so much remembered as stored. That is, in a general way Collier knew what had occurred, but he could not be certain what was specifically filed away. His memory of his life prior to arriving in Peking was uneven and unnerving. He could, for example, remember Mrs. Phoebe Philpotts in a blue blouse with a large bow at the collar, a gray dirndl skirt, and high-heeled shoes that accentuated her tight muscular calves. But he could not for the life of him remember—and he remained awake most of one crisp night trying—the name of the President of the United States.

He had learned to speak a few words in the Peking dialect. *"Xie-xie nin"* was "thank you," and *"zai-jian"* was "goodbye." Bai repeated those words for Collier often, but it was difficult for him to capture their texture even when the sounds were correct. For speaking Chinese, or so it seemed to Collier, altered the normal position of the jaw and, in fact, changed the entire set of the face. Collier had not enough experience in the world to know that this was the case with every language: People tend to look the language they speak. Furthermore, national gestures related directly back to the particular formation of sound with tongue, teeth, and lips. It seemed to Collier that this strange language, with the demands it made on the neck and jaws, freed the hands in a remarkable way. He noticed many people talking energetically while they performed unrelated activities with their hands—wrapping packages, sweeping the floor, pointing to a bird.

By the week's end Collier noticed that the Chinese words he had learned, especially when they came without conscious thought, sounded as though they came from someone else. He had the most fleeting intimation of the man he was going to be. This man, oddly enough, felt more isolated toward the end of his week in Peking, after he began to recognize certain common human denominators, than he had at the beginning when he was literally a man apart. He also sensed for the first time that a new language was the truest mark of a new life.

Bai appeared in Collier's room looking at once smug and contrite. He was smug because he had accomplished everything he had desired with Collier; he was pleased with himself and with the praise of others, some of which had already exceeded his hopes. He was contrite and apologized deeply to Collier because there had been some confusion over the travel arrangements; Collier would now leave Peking and arrive in Yang-Xien two or three days later than originally planned. "We are trying to get word to Captain Gao about the change," Bai said as a look of concern flashed across his face. Collier, floating on the surface of his new life in Peking, felt frightened for about as long as it took Bai's concern to dissipate. The contrition that Bai registered with a pinched brow and tightened, narrow lips seemed as artificial as the pleasantries he exchanged with Collier's watchful roommate.

Two unplanned days were spent mostly in the streets and markets and parks of Peking. They were unrestricted only in the sense that the omnipresent young soldier was unable to dissuade or coerce Collier from certain activities. Collier drifted into a fish market during a midmorning lull. The place was, by the way, the only place he had been in Peking in which a pine, or a closely related nutty odor, was not present. Fish—dead and alive—ruled absolutely. Collier was attracted for some moments by a cartload of squirming eels, continually knotting and undoing themselves. When he turned away from the cart, he found himself facing upwards of fifty people watching him as though his face was a demonstration tv in a store window; they seemed intrigued and confused by what they were watching, particu-

larly around the eyes. Collier looked slowly and deliberately back over his shoulder again at the large tray of eels;
when he turned forward finally, the faces were exactly as he
had left them. A short-haired child in the front row pointed
directly at the tip of Collier's nose; the kid's eyes and mouth
formed perfect "O's." Against the insistent urging of his
roommate tugging at the cuff of his sleeve, Collier, with a
very stupid smile on his face, took a cautious step forward,
the first of a series. The silent crowd parted swiftly and
neatly, closing just as quickly behind him as he came forward; for the fifty yards to the street this was his manner of
leaving the fish market. His attendant dispersed the crowds
well enough to allow Collier's wanderings to continue.
Gene could not know if the emotion registered by those
faces was fear or merely wonder, or both at the same time.
It didn't matter.

Wherever one looked in Peking, one's eyes brought in
numerous people, mostly dressed in white. But on closer
examination there seemed to be an equal number with dark
skirts and trousers as with light ones. A great many wore
variously shaped white caps. Younger people tended to
wear short pants. Collier's eye occasionally picked out the
face of a girl or two in a crowd. Her hair in pigtails, sometimes piled on her head and tied with bright ribbons, her
face always suggesting abundant energy and hope. When
on two or three occasions, a girl caught Collier's innocent,
admiring gaze, she looked away quickly in mild fright.

The eye cannot move freely around the high-walled inner city or the lower walled southern city and not see the
wine-red and pale green combinations that provide Peking
with its dominant color motif. And during a bright summer
afternoon it is impossible to fail to hear a strange, faint
whirring underneath all the other sounds. Since his arrival
Collier had carried the soft sound as an associative impression of Peking; during a relaxed hour on a park bench he
discovered its source. A great many of the pigeons had

small whistles tied to their legs. And as they flew across the midday sun and circled above the Old Imperial City, their very flight was a bird-song. Collier listened for hours, enjoying the coda best of all, the time when the whistling diminished in pitch and intensity as a bird prepared to land. There was always a coda to be heard amidst the symphony's other movements. He admired the pigeons of Peking and, also, the whistle-makers.

Collier was awakened in the middle of the night by his roommate. The young man was fully dressed in his uniform, and so Collier perceived that it was time to move on. His comb, soap, towel, razor and blades, and a new brown sweater had been placed in a small canvas traveling bag. The soldier's agitated eyes told Collier that time was an important consideration; he dressed quickly and ran his fingers through his hair as he left with his roommate.

Cool evening. Few lights in the streets. Absolutely no other people or sounds. The automobile waited with its motor running quietly as Collier and his guide settled in the ample rear seat. The driver was not the speedster who had driven Bai and his guest from Tang-Ku. At the point where the new commercial city to the east of the old core of Peking began, the car turned sharply northward, so that on his left Collier could see the high walls once again lined with fine old trees and dotted with rounded moon-shaped gates. On the right he could see the smoke and stacks and utility poles of another China.

Their destination was the railway station, which turned out to be not so much a station as numerous open-air platforms. Collier was pleased to see, even in his half-awake condition, clusters of people at the heads of various platforms in the universal postures of travelers caught at ungodly hours in bus and train stations the world over. Baby slept on mother's shoulder; mother propped herself against husband's back; husband sat on bundles and bags, chin tucked on chest, hand on wife's forehead. A loud-speaker brought messages of very poor quality. After each announcement, it was clear to Collier that the natives understood only slightly more than he did—just enough, perhaps, to be more troubled and confused. Although there was an announcement every five or ten minutes, no trains arrived or departed.

Gene Collier had seen the sun come up many times before in his life: out hunting with his father, on guard duty at Koje-do, during the early spring in Pyongyang. Each time he was surprised at just how cold, how dead the world can get only minutes before it is saved once again. In his legs, especially, he felt the frigid hopelessness of the pre-dawn hour. No sooner had an orange sun skimmed the horizon and bubbled up over it than an old train rattled softly toward the farthest platform.

The train was an old European model, with numerous compartments linked by a passageway along the far side. It rattled even as it stood in the station. Collier, having never seen such a train before, assumed it was of Chinese design; he wanted to think the best of it. People carrying bundles and children emerged from shadows throughout the station and streamed toward the train. The loudspeaker squawked continually. The soldier nodded and pointed toward the train; Collier followed his brisk pace. Along the length of it compartment doors were swinging open and closing, packages and children were placed in the compartments, groups of tired people said farewell with fond looks and shy touches of cheek upon cheek.

Collier's escort led him past the human activity to the forward-most compartment, a distance few of the other travelers wanted to cover carrying their burdens. As soon as the two men were seated opposite each other, the train gave a loud and shattering lurch forward, pinning Collier to the wall and throwing his companion to the floor on his knees. Surprisingly, the train, whose arrival had been awaited for hours by over a hundred passengers, did not stay more than five minutes at the platform. Within a few seconds another lurch—not quite as disruptive as the first —shook the train, then another, a diminishing series of them finally resulted in acceptable movement.

The antique train moved slowly out of the station and then swung to the west, rolling slowly past the high red-walled Old City, past golden parapets and white-bridged moats. The sun had risen fully behind the train and its rays came through the polished window of Collier's compartment at such an extremely oblique angle that the light was separated into a rainbow spectrum. Picking up speed, the train passed the western city, where much new construction was visible. The homes clustered around communal court-yards. Tiled roofs. Faces in the windows.

As Collier saw fields of grain, farmers out cutting with scythes and sickles, dark thatches on the houses, he realized that the city had been left behind. The train attained its normal traveling speed in the countryside, and as it did, the passengers were aware of its double motion: forward and side-to-side.

The sun raced westward with the train, and since its angle through the window became less acute after an hour or so, it appeared to be gaining.

There were numerous stops at stations, barely marked as such, for long periods of time. No one boarded the train, and small numbers of people, struggling with their bundles and children, got off. Cars were frequently uncoupled until, when the train finally wound its way through the foothills of rounded mountains, Collier was able to see the train's rear close behind him out the window.

Tiredness came on him during this long, winding stretch and he saw through the glass melting browns and tans, ochers and reds as soft focus again became a sweeping blur. There was not another stop for over two hours. Collier

swayed with the train and was rocked into a light, squint-
eyed, disassociative sleep. He slept through two more long
stops and awoke abruptly exactly as his companion stood
up over him, reaching out toward his face. Gene Collier
shouted a sound like the "huh-hah" of his ditch-digging
days and pulled himself rigidly against the straw backing of
his seat. The train was slowing and the soldier opened the
door and got down even before it finally came to a squeak-
ing, wheezing halt.

When Collier disembarked and turned around, the soldier was talking to a tall thin man dressed in a faded blue
jacket and trousers. As Collier approached, he slowly
recognized Gao's face and more quickly concluded that he
was troubled, perhaps even angry. He was both, but he
smiled and extended his hand to Collier. They shook hands
firmly; each hoped feeling had been transmitted. Gao said,
"Welcome."

Collier, looking beyond Gao's shoulder at the rather substantial walled town, said, "Yang-Xien is much larger than
I thought."

"We are many hours from Yang-Xien." And the look of
annoyance again came to Gao's face. It was not the composed face Collier had first seen in Korea. Collier's military
companion then, as though taking his cue from the hiss of
steam coming from the locomotive, snapped to attention,
extracted a brown packet from his breast pocket, handed it
to Gao, and turned abruptly back toward the train.

Gao, for his part, accepted the packet, gave a clean, ritu-
alistic nod, and began to step with his hand on Collier's arm
toward the walls of the city. "I must tell you that I am—"
He stopped. "Words in English are not yet familiar to me.
. . . I am upset. I have been here for two days waiting for
your arrival. Days I could not miss in Yang-Xien."

"But they were supposed to contact you."

"Of course. Yes."

A distance of four or five hundred yards over a slightly
pitched sandy plain led from the railroad tracks, which

ended suddenly about ten yards before the locomotive, to the pillared gate of the town.

Gao and Collier stood with their backs to the west. High in the western sky some huge white clouds had turned color. They were iron-gray and above the men in mere seconds; weather usually came through Shensi as the Mongols had, swiftly and forcefully. The first large drop fell in the sand near Gao's feet, unnoticed. Another struck Collier's forehead and ran quickly over his face. This Gao noticed. His face froze. "Run," he said.

The first few steps for Collier constituted a loose shuffle. He noticed Gao sprinting well ahead of him toward the gate. "A race?" he thought. And he began to dig in with his toes. He thrilled at the sense of acceleration he felt. First, he noticed Gao no longer pulling away from him; then he saw the ground between them diminish. Then he saw nothing clearly. Driving rain. A wind that pushed against him like an offensive lineman. Flashes of lightning. Thunder like the tearing of the earth. Midnight darkness. Gao's faint voice: "This way . . . this way." Collier's legs weakened. He fell and slid forward on the hard earth that felt as though it had been given a thick coat of grease. "This way."

Almost as quickly as it had arrived, the storm blew past. Gao, wet but not soaked through, appeared at the gate and helped the besmudged Collier into the muddied town, through a low alleyway, and inside a tiled house in which the rich smell of grain predominated. As the darkness gave way to the flickering light of the hearth's fire, Collier saw a white-turbaned and toothless woman stepping out of the corner. Gao addressed her softly, and after the long verbal exchange he presented her with a handful of coins. Collier took off his clothes and wrapped himself in a thin linen cloth. The old woman disappeared with his garments and returned with them rinsed and twisted. She stretched and lifted them high above the hearth, where they hung until dry.

There were some low chairs and a table behind the

hearth. Here Gao and Collier sat, and Gao began to explain the difference between being troubled and being angry. He was angry because two precious days of his presence in Yang-Xien had been lost. He was troubled by the problems he had encountered in the village since he had returned from Pyongyang; he proceeded to tell Collier in the greatest detail exactly what they all were for the next four hours. Only the woman reappearing with two bowls of rice, cabbage, and beans broke the stream of specific woes that had troubled Gao's existence.

No sooner had Gao folded the last piece of cabbage into his mouth than he began in mid-sentence to relate more of his troubles. ". . . because they have been raised on despair and distrust. We have chased out many of the undesirables and divided the land equally—twelve *mou* for everyone willing to work it. This alone is a great achievement. But now each stays on his own land fearful that his neighbor will steal his crops. Already there have been thefts and beatings. It is as though we have exchanged the oppression of the landlord for the tyranny of personal greed." Gao Mating stopped speaking, although it was perfectly clear to Collier that he was continuing the monologue mentally. In time even that ended and Gene felt he should say something. "You can't expect too much right off." Gao glared at Collier.

In Peking Collier had slept in Western beds. On this first night in Shensi, he was introduced to the *kang*, a door that sometimes also served as a bed. The old woman and a boy lay two *kangs* across the dampened hearth.

In the late summer of 1953, mules were the common means of transportation in Shensi Province as they had been for the previous millennium. The mules of the north were small and moth-eaten creatures with brown eyes and an expression so tender that it belied their ability to carry hundreds of pounds over dusty roads. Gene Collier, stooped and extremely uncomfortable on a woven woolen saddle cloth that was no cushion at all, struggled unsuccessfully to find a position that would be tolerable. Seen from a distance, his mule appeared to be carrying a loosely tied sack of potatoes back to Yang-Xien. For the first hour or so conversation was a reasonable diversion; for the next seven hours only the challenge of his endurance being tested prompted Collier on.

As the mules came over the crest of a moderate rise, Gao Ma-ting finally said the only words that could have broken Collier's preoccupation with the step by step torture of the sweet-faced animal. "There is Yang-Xien." A walled village no more than two hundred feet in length and depth. Whatever it would become in the life of Gene Collier, it was at least nearby; that in itself was a positive sign. Collier said nothing. Gao repeated, "Yang-Xien."

"Yeah."

The road, like the terraced gardens beyond the village, followed the contour of the land. Unfortunately for Collier this meant a suspension of the painful gratification of dismounting for a while longer. The road took them well to the north before bending back on itself to the village gate.

When they reached the northernmost point of their approach and began the final swing around the last mound, Gao stopped and simply pointed in a direction Collier would never thought to have looked—slightly behind them and off to the right. "Great Wall," was all Gao said.

Collier turned and saw on a hillock not a wall but a towered parapet and the vague path where the Wall had been. That path cut across to another hill where another tower stood. In Shensi the Wall had not been rebuilt as it had in Hopeh. The nearer tower formed an impressive white outline against the lavender sky. It widened considerably at the base, not only by design but owing to the stones and rubble that had fallen or been dragged there. To Collier's eye it seemed to be the giant stub of an often-lit candle.

During those few moments Collier dwelled on the candle, not on his own extreme discomfort. When Gao kicked his mule into motion again, Collier's torment was reactivated. This time, however, the end lay directly before him; it drew closer with each new twinge of pain.

16

Er fanshen hen hao

The whole is, of course, generally greater than the sum of its parts; but the whole at one time may be different from the whole at another time, even when the parts remain exactly the same. Collier's face was a perfect example. An examination of the face in the *Pleasants High Yearbook of 1949* would have revealed the same parts as the face that was at rest on the *kang* in the small house in Yang-Xien that he shared with Gao Ma-ting. The parts were exactly the same. Same large ears that bent slightly forward. Same thin lips turned downward at the corners. Same jut of jaw and beak-like nose. Eyes set wide apart and, when open, revealing the same dark, watery quality. Yet now this was the face of a totally different man. The whole had been transformed by what those same eyes saw, what the ears heard, and lips uttered. The simple boy who believed that Mrs. Philpotts had something of value for him but who did not know what it was or even how to find out, had been schooled further by events and the world. Although he certainly comprehended more than he ever had, Collier was still far from worldly wise. The basic internal change seemed to be that for the first time in his life, Gene was capable of asking the right questions when new and difficult situations presented themselves, and a great many such situations awaited him in Yang-Xien.

During his first week in the village, Collier ate, slept, and was walked through and around the square at midday, on Gao's instructions, by a boy known as "Cai-cai." The boy was the village idiot, so Collier was viewed by the rest of the villagers primarily as an aberration that had happened to materialize. The assumption was that he would disappear as suddenly as he arrived. Since no one had ever taken Cai-cai seriously, there was no need for anyone to feel threatened by the tall, stooped man who followed him about the village each afternoon. In this simple manner the people of Yang-Xien began to accept, on the first level of physical acceptance, the presence of an unfamiliar form.

Gao Ma-ting had come home to serious trouble that kept him very busy the week of his return. A number of family feuds had broken out. There were beatings, burnings, and threats of even greater reprisals. This, too, helped to further the villagers' tolerance of Collier. His presence was insignificant compared to the excitement that was being generated by the local violence.

Lack of physical activity made Collier extremely weary. It was reasonable for him to want to know what the trouble in the village was all about; it was unreasonable for Gao Ma-ting not to volunteer the information. Nevertheless, Collier had to ask for answers he felt he had to be aware of if he was going to stay in Yang-Xien. "Unless," said Gene, "you're telling me to keep out of your hair by being silent." The phrase meant nothing to Gao. They were seated at a table near the hearth; Gao's eyes flared in anger momentarily, but were almost immediately quenched by reason.

"Cai-cai," he called. The boy appeared and silently

cleared the table of bowls and utensils. He returned with paper, ink, and a Chinese writing pen. "Here is Yang-Xien," said Gao, drawing a sure rectangle along the borders of the paper. "The gate is here." Two slash marks. "And the square with the tower and the well in the center. So." A small circle and a rectangle.

"There were approximately one hundred twenty-five persons in Yang-Xien in 1948. Now there are exactly ninety-one. Excluding you and I and Cai-cai and Ming-sa the housekeeper." Gao drew a small "x" inside the gate, which Collier correctly understood to represent the house they themselves inhabited. Then, moving in a clockwise direction, Gao divided the space between the village square and the outer walls into eight parts, with the two areas in the far corners being the largest segments. In each part, beginning with the area next to the "x," he wrote, in English letters, the sound of the family names: "Nin-Gai-Bu-Fan-Duan-Tian-Xia-Men."

"These are the other family names in Yang-Xien. When I was a boy my father taught me how they formed a sentence if you go around clockwise from our house. *Nin* means 'you.' *Gai* means 'should.' *Bu*, 'not.' You-Should-Not-Eat-Short-Sweet-Shrimp. The last word, *Men,* means 'gate.' So you can learn the names of all the families if you remember 'You-Should-Not-Eat-Short-Sweet-Shrimp-near the Gate.' "

Gene repeated the names as Gao's brush pointed them out: "Nin-Gai-Bu-Fan-Duan-Tian-Xia-Men: You-Should-Not-Eat-Short-Sweet-Shrimp-near the Gate."

"Fine. The Fan are gone. They owned all the farmland that has ever been workable here. You saw it as we entered the village. Of course that farming area will be usable once again if I can ever find a solution to this problem." Gao began to rub his eyes with the weariness of despair.

"The problem."

"Yes. Well. Long before I arrived the Party sent two

cadres here to reorganize the village. In 1948 and 1949.
They did that indeed. One was greedy for money; the other
for women. After they took the land from the Fan family,
they did not pay them as they should have; in fact, they stole
some money from Mr. Fan and, according to all reports,
acted reprehensibly. There were some improprieties concerning the Tian family also." Gao looked away shamefully.

"Then, after Fan had been forced to leave, they divided
the land in seven parts and gave each family a share. That,
at least, was as it should have been, but there was no preparation for ownership. And after reports of their activities
got back to the Shensi District, the two fled. The others
then stripped the house of Fan; the Bu and Duan families
moved some of the children and old people into the house.
The Tian are still a problem. For years they have sold tools,
ground the grain, and shipped handicrafts to markets.
They own most of the oxen. They have always exploited the
others; they have a stranglehold on the ones who work the
land. I feel that they are even worse than the Fan, who were
the landlords. Sometimes it takes a peasant years to pay for
the very tools he needs to survive." Gao had begun to raise
his voice. Collier placed his hand on Gao's wrist.

"Well, here is the situation. Each family has had men
camped on its own land during the entire harvest. They eat
their meals out there, fires burn through the night. Tools
are stolen; they fight over boundaries constantly. And
through it all, the Tian hold control over them as they
always have." Gao stopped and seemed to realize that by
merely stating the problem to someone who did not understand it certain things were becoming clearer to him. Also,
he had begun to calm down.

"All the land should be jointly owned. That way, fewer
hands would be required to tend it. Others could be building irrigation—making more land usable for farming. We
could make tools in the village for many tasks. A school
perhaps for the illiterate ones and the children. The village

should function as a single, well-organized unit. A council of all the families could run it. We could ship our products. . . ."

"Have you ever had a meeting of all the families to talk things out?"

Gao continued his discussion of the land undeterred: ". . . the profits will belong to no single family; at the same time they will belong to every family. As with the fields." Here Gao interrupted himself. "I have called a great many meetings, but never have I threatened, never have I presented myself to them as a soldier, always as another villager who wishes to lead the turnover. It is true, however, that the Eighth Route Army still remains the symbol of both liberation and authority." Some very solid ideas had already formed in Gao's mind. "I will present them with all the possiblities that cooperation would afford and exactly how to achieve them." Gao felt himself gathering strength.

He began a dialogue with himself in English, much to Collier's amusement:

"I must be very concrete, so they will know exactly what their days would be like the new way."

"Yes, yes. Nothing vague."

"Of course, I must not lie to them. I must tell them it would take a great deal of work."

"But these people are not afraid of hard work."

"I will offer the Tians money for their tools and animals."

"But this is a problem because when the Party has sent money here in the past, it has been . . . misused."

"And if they will not sell?"

"We will have to take it away from them." The uncharacteristic words came naturally and without thought.

Gao Ma-ting smiled. "That is the most 'American' thing I have ever heard myself say, Collier. No, if I am successful, the Tians will accept the money."

"The promise of the money," said Gene.

Gao directed a mock *kou-tou* to Collier. "I know precisely how I wish to proceed." Gao had now been transformed into a man who appeared unable to fail.

"You, Collier, are a wonderful catalyst."

Gene, who did not know the word, *kou-tou*ed in response.

The following day Collier's walk through the village had an entirely different quality. There was a distinct power in being able to name a thing, a power that primitive people have always known and valued. Collier circled the village, testing the memory device, and discovered not only recognition but that force of knowledge. As he peered over the low wall into the court of the You (Nin) family, the stranger felt as though he had already begun to define them, had begun to understand them, even though he saw no Yous in the yard, only three piglets running in circles for exercise. A strong odor of night soil carried rather pleasant associations.

The scene among their neighbors, the Shoulds (Gai), was exactly the same (pigs not people.) From the window of the Bu house next door an old man in a woolen skullcap stared at Collier with such resolve that Gene had to break off his own gaze; and Collier assumed the entire Bu clan would be his sworn enemies. Had he not known the family name, he probably would merely have commented to Gao that he had encountered a queer old man.

The former dwelling of the Fan was a madhouse: chickens and pigs and children; three women with brooms made of twigs, an old man digging on his hands and knees in the corner, a young man on the roof; animal and human chatter and motion of such intensity that the head and shoulders of Eugene Collier, Jr., of Hundley, West Virginia, went by completely unnoticed. There was enough activity of interest here for Collier's eye to occupy him for quite a while, but Cai-cai, who obviously had his orders, tugged at Collier's pocket with the persistence of a horsefly.

There was no human or animal activity that could be seen

from the path around the square in any of the other houses or yards. But the yard of the Tian family was of a different quality from the others: very much larger, a stone path from gate to doorway, a pile of neatly set firewood, a border of orange and yellow and brown mums, which reminded Collier of the presence of flowers everywhere in Peking, a fact that his eye had realized then but his brain recorded only now.

Cai-cai had disappeared. Collier accepted this discovery with mixed feelings: On the one hand, he was no longer the ward of an idiot; on the other, he was alone in this Chinese village. His legs took him to the well, into which he dropped a pebble and believed he saw a white flash before he heard a splash. Then to the tower that was the center of Yang-Xien. The tall splintered door at its base swung open at his touch and crashed with surprising force against the wall. Eyes from every house in the Nin-Gai-Bu-Fan-Duan-Tian-Xia-Men rotation watched him enter the dusty, cob-webbed entranceway and saw his head, during his slow ascent, pass the small openings that had once been windows. That ascent was slowed by the fact that a plank-step had given way under his weight at the outset; this made him extremely cautious, for should it have happened again near the top, the entire staircase could collapse beneath him. *Staircase* is something of a euphemism; the ascent was accomplished over a series of rickety ladders placed across the width of the tower accordion-fashion, so the climber zig-zagged his way toward the top. Where the tower narrowed, the ladders rose more steeply, until Collier reached a small platform at the top.

Sunlight poured in from the top but was filtered so thickly by dust and webs that Collier had the sensation of moving through a warm snowstorm. The "crick" of wood and the scurrying of unseen creatures continued during the entire ascent. When he arrived at the top and had tested the platform, Collier had his choice of four openings to see from. He began with the west and saw a plain so hard and barren and of such a pale shade of red that he associated it with the aridity of Georgia clay. Toward the south the plain softened and rolled slightly. The color darkened and clumps of pink and yellow and brown vegetation formed islands of life. The terrain and his position helped to create a fantasy that placed Private Collier in Fort Apache as a lookout; behind every clump and boulder was a movie Indian. A flight of small swifts which flew directly past the tower and out of sight to the west brought him back to reality.

Looking out from an opening eastward, Collier saw knolls and hills, perfectly terraced and lush with growth. And a group of men, whose gruff voices and abrupt movements surrounded a solitary, quiet figure. Gao, of course. Collier's face smiled.

To the north the lavender mountains seemed to rise like strongly yeasted bread. And the remnants of the Great Wall, reduced to a trail and some towers struggling against the undefeated force of gravity. Two things of importance during Collier's ascent and panoramic examination: His eyes saw not a single tree; and for a few short moments he was the highest man on the entire Shensi Plain.

As he passed one of the small windows facing west on his slow descent, he saw a small figure—Cai-cai on the run— leading Gao Ma-ting toward the village. Like a truant about to be caught, Collier tried and succeeded in getting back to Gao's house before he could be caught wandering freely about. He had just assumed a casual sitting position in the corner when he heard Gao speaking to the old woman in the yard as he stormed through. "No one, absolutely no one is to climb the tower." Spittle flew from Gao's mouth violently. The tone of voice was exactly that of an exasperated father toward a disobedient child, and it touched something so basic in Collier he rose suddenly and looked for all the world as though he was about to throw a punch.

Gao Ma-ting sensed his level of desperation and stopped in midbreath.

Gao said, "I am needed in the fields. We will talk when I return this evening. Keep watch on Cai-cai." The eyes almost flashed a smile.

Collier said, "Damn your ass." The words and the drawled rhythm brought him momentarily back to his home, his boyhood.

He spent the afternoon with Cai-cai throwing a penknife into concentric circles marked in the earth. After he discovered that he was engaged in a competition with the boy, his aim improved and he became much more consistent. Still, Cai-cai won every contest and grew more serious with each victory.

In the darkness that permeated the area around the hearth Ming-sa, an old woman who could remember a very different time, but who chose not to remember, began to prepare the evening meal. It was present-day fact, and not memory, that fashioned an unchanging, bemused stoicism on her broad, dark face. She could have remembered a great deal of a former life, had she wished to. She could have remembered the collapse of a loess cave that was her first home and the flooding that took the lives of many of her family. She could have remembered hunger as a condition of living and sisters being sold to the Catholic priests in Peking to work as serving girls. She could have recalled the young man who was her husband, who first taught himself to read and then became an ardent nationalist— how gentle he became to her and how he was brought home lifeless from a political protest at the provincial capital. She could have recounted things about a life in China that Collier, for whom China was, at best, pigeons with whistles; at worst, Bai's politics applied to people, could never have imagined, and would have rejected if he had been told. Ming-sa chose not to waken such dreadful dogs.

In watching her hands prepare the cakes and vegetables

for the evening meal, Collier became aware of her fingers. Each of those stubby fingers moved independently; as, for example, when the three middle ones tapped down a different portion of the surface of a small cake while thumb and pinky pulled in the edges all around. Ming-sa could have as easily been playing the piano; each finger performing a different function in order to produce a fine harmony.

When Gao ducked through the door a few hours later, his face registered a peculiar combination of pleasure, disappointment, and anger. "They will send representatives to a meeting only if you will be there. You have no objection, I hope."

"No, no. Why? I mean why would they want me to be there?"

"It seems as though you have made more of an impression in Yang-Xien than we have been willing to admit. They have never seen anyone quite like you."

"But what will I do?"

"Just sit there. They will not stare at you directly, but they will examine you very, very carefully."

There was no reason for Gao to be annoyed at Collier, but since he refused to accept the anger he felt toward the people whose lives he wished to transform, people who failed to understand what was in their own best interest, he let it flow unchecked toward Collier. With a certain pleasure he said, "They call you the 'Frenchman.'"

"Why?"

"Well, the old man Bu once saw a Frenchman in Tientsin and he walked as you do, with the same loose gait. So he has named you Fa-Guo-ren; that is, 'French-Country-Man.' It is not likely that we will be able to change it, for the Duan and Xia also have called you 'Frenchman.' It is not going to be easy to have them call you Kao-Li-ye." Gao smiled so that it looked as if his face had cracked open; it was a graceless triumph.

In fact, it was no triumph at all, for its intended victim was not vulnerable. "No kidding. So they call me Frenchman. Isn't that something?"

"We are to meet in the large room of the Fan house at sundown. There will be a truce in the field until morning. Three from each family. The Tian woman and her two eldest sons have also agreed to come. She will cause the most trouble."

In time the strident undertone in Gao's voice softened, melted, and disappeared. During the same time Gene Collier's old football sense of tactics activated itself. "What will the set-up be for the meeting tonight?"

"Set-up?"

"In the room of the meeting. Will we sit around a table, on the floor—what?"

"Ah, hah. Of course. I see what you are suggesting."

Gao and Cai-cai left almost immediately to "set up" the meeting room. This was done in several stages: The chickens and children had to be cleared out of the large room; a table, chairs, and benches had to be rounded up and placed most effectively for Gao's purposes. Cai-cai cracked Gao's shins with a low bench he moved long after he was first told where to place it. Finally, the work completed, Cai-cai was ordered to remain on guard at the door (no one was to enter until Ming-sa came with some food) while Gao himself returned home to prepare for the crucial meeting.

Instead of spending the time discussing the evening over dinner with Collier, Gao Ma-ting chose to spend the time dressing and, more importantly, watching himself dressing in a small wall mirror. He practiced authoritative facial expressions which reflected a range from benevolent despotism to violent retribution. He wore the uniform in which Collier had first seen him, the boots, belt, and holster polished much more impressively now than before. The red-starred cap and red-barred collar tabs implied a past filled with valor and sacrifice.

Collier ate his dinner, watching Gao fidget across the

room, and he anticipated a disaster. He said, "I used to play football." A sentence which meant nothing to Gao. "Sometimes in front of thousands of people. And before the game in the locker room I could see guys who wanted to play the best game of their lives, maybe because their girl friends or their folks were going to be at the game." Gao was listening only because he had exhausted all his faces and had tried the revolver in every possible position. "I mean they wanted to do good very badly. And they usually did bad. Exactly because they tried too hard at doing good."

"How did you play?"

"No one ever came to watch me. I just played because, well, that's what I was there for. They say I was pretty damned good. . . ."

Collier had taken a large ball of rice on his chopsticks and negotiated it into his mouth. He was chewing as he added, " . . . and I think I know why it happens. The guy, the guy who's driving so hard for a goal just doesn't see the possibilities that come up like the guy who's more relaxed. As long as just the things you're looking for happen, you're okay, but that hardly ever happens in football." He added, "Gao, if you don't sit down and talk to me and just goddamn relax, you're going to blow that meeting tonight sure as shooting."

Gao sat down across from Gene and drew in a deep breath, held it, and let the exhaled air find its own way out. Then he held a hand up horizontally at eye level; the pinky and thumb quivered like flower petals. "Of course there is the bell tower."

"What?"

"Well, I've been thinking about that tower. A bell could be the unifying thing in this town. And it wouldn't take that much work, really. When you are reorganizing a town, a bell in the tower could be used to send messages out to the field. Save time and effort. But it would be a symbol that the town was together. Symbols are important in this kind of thing. You could mount it?"

Gene smiled and nodded.

Gao, now reaffirmed and pleased with all of his decisions, paid Gene a compliment of sorts: "Mr. Bai had always doubted that you had ever gone to university, I was certain he had been wrong. Your knowledge in these matters justifies my position."

Gene dropped a small ball of rice on the way to his mouth. "Thank you," he said.

Point of view is first a physical phenomenon; it is what you see, or think you see, from where you stand. This was the case with Gene Collier in the meeting room of the former Fan residence. The room was an "L" shape with the arm and leg of the "L" approximately equal in length. Two tables had been placed end to end to form a diagonal across the right angle formed by the juncture of walls. Behind this table sat Gao Ma-ting, imposing in his uniform, and his strange guest. Theoretically, Gao was to address twenty-one people—three representatives from each of seven families—but he did not expect perfect attendance, even though he had assurances from the patriarchs and matriarchs that they, or their representatives, would attend. Twelve or fifteen would have been a remarkable success. After Gao had placed his chair at the midpoint of the speakers' tables and in front of Collier's and had placed his pages of notes in the proper order at his left hand, he gave the sign to Cai-cai to open the door.

The entire population of Yang-Xien entered like water through the crack at the top of an earthen dam, first in a trickle and then in a rush, until the pressure decreased and there was no more high water to rush through. Perhaps some of the children and very old people had been left home, but Gao would have been hard-pressed to conjure a face that was not before him.

They quieted immediately upon entering and seeing Gao in uniform. Although a great number were looking toward

Collier, they did not look at him directly. Mostly, they slid their eyes over the earthen walls, perhaps dwelling a moment longer when the stranger happened to come between them and the flatness of surface that interested them. After all, he was now called Fa Guo-ren, and there had been no such name in Yang-Xien ever before.

Suddenly the perspective of exceptional faces focused for Collier. Suddenly he realized, "Jesus Christ, it's China. CHINA!" He had been to Peking, the Imperial Palace, the countryside of Hopeh, Shansi, and Shensi, a good portion of the last province bareback on a mule; he had eaten native food in the native manner and even learned a few words; he had visited museums and seen vestiges of the Great Wall, which symbolized twenty-two centuries of continuous history. He had done all these things and only known he was in China because his brain gave him that particular information when he requested it. Now he felt China through the soles of his boots; his bony ass was against a Chinese chair. Chinese air, smells, faces: "Jesus Christ, it's China. CHINA!"

Although he did not wish to stare, Collier's eyes dwelt on certain things; they were not easily convinced to move on. A woman's face framed by a skullcap and a high white collar, a fringe of black, silky bangs almost touching her arched eyebrows, and an expression which held the delicately poised tension of fear and hopefulness. A cheeky young girl with her hair parted in the center and tied at her neck, whose bright eyes stared defiantly from beneath wisps of hair that would not lie flat. The Frenchman's eyes rested on an old man's toothless face that rested upon two fists, which were, in turn, piled on bony knees; the overall effect was of a rock poised on boulders on a cliff. Another old man had elf ears and a white mustache like a pair of parentheses that started at the corners of his mouth and curved downward toward his chin; it gave him the appearance of a grinning troll. Next to this tiny face was a huge

one that broadened as it moved from an uneven crewcut to
a flat, wide jaw studded with piano-key-like teeth. A mother
with her head wrapped in a bandana held up a bundle of
quilts that, upon closer examination, wrapped a fat-faced
baby. Another young man's skin was darker than Tibideaux's. No two faces were the same in form or expression,
hue or texture.

When Gao rose and began to speak in modulated tones,
Collier dropped his eyes and stared at his hands folded in
his lap. For many minutes he listened. What was actually
happening and Collier's perception of what was happening
were two very different things, but he guessed that matters
did not get off to a good start. Then a small, gray-haired
woman stood and spoke loudly over Gao's voice until he
stopped. She continued speaking, turning to the crowd
with upraised palms, for many minutes. Her eyes flashed
wildly. The effort she made in reaching her high pitches
gave her plea the tone of a harangue. "Madame Tian," Gao
whispered to Collier. Wisely he let her continue unchecked
until she had managed to anger nearly everyone present.

Gao stood and said, "*Yi fanshen hao—Er fanshen hen hao.*"
Then, because he now had a tangible adversary—Madame
Tian—and some strong words to react to, he began systematically to compare two ways of living. Collier was quite
certain that Gao, through shifts of emphasis and body gestures, was saying, "On the one hand . . ." and "but on the
other . . ." When Gao described the future that was possible, he seemed to single out individuals in the crowd and
tell them what sort of new day they could awaken to. Gao
Ma-ting had recaptured for the first time since he had left
Korea the methodical rhythm of speech that had made him
appear to be a special man in Collier's eyes. His was the
voice of sweet reason. This, at least, was how Gene perceived it. Collier noted, too, the orator's trick of a repeated
phrase every few minutes: "*Yi fanshen hao—Er fanshen hen
hao.*"

Now there were questions. Gene guessed that they were concrete in nature and had to do with money and food and hours. He imagined that Gao responded concretely. Of course, nothing of the sort may have been happening.

Now only the children and old men remained interested in the Frenchman, but there were enough of both to keep Gene from relaxing. He realized that he was bathed in a film of oily sweat.

Gao talked on and on. More questions. Madame Tian rose and was hushed by the others. She hissed as she sat back down. Some children had been allowed to fall asleep in mothers' laps; others had been led off by older sisters. It had gotten very late.

The crowd had reduced itself to three representatives from each family, so when the meeting was over for most of the populace of Yang-Xien it actually began for those who mattered. Collier did not move, believing that the simplest movement—a yawn, cracking knuckles—would be a source of offense to these people Gao had to win over. He perceived that things had begun to go badly, for two squat, barrel-chested men seated on opposite ends of a long bench had each delivered long, excited speeches. There was an unmistakable presence of incipient violence in the room.

Gao walked around the table and up to one of the angry men. Collier felt an electric charge of adrenalin shoot into his shoulder blades and a pang of nausea followed almost immediately. Gao unbuttoned his holster, drew out his thin, blue-black revolver, and placed it on the bench in front of the fuming man. Gao spoke quietly and deliberately. He gestured toward the gun as though he were a host offering a dish of dried fruits. He said other words. Collier's heartbeat resonated in his ears. Then Gao Ma-ting's entire body softened. He reached for the man's shoulder, and the man leaned forward ever so slightly to make it just that much more accessible.

"*Yi fanshen hao—Er fanshen hen hao,*" Gao said once again. He seemed calmer and even more reasonable than he had hours earlier. As he spoke now, he ticked off points on his fingers. Clearly, if endurance was to be the critical factor in Chinese debate, Gao Ma-ting would not be found wanting.

The sky had lightened into what the people of Shensi called false dawn, an hour or so before the sun's direct rays bent over the eastern mountains. The "L"-shaped room had emptied, except for Cai-cai asleep against the wall near the door. Gao gathered up his papers, and Collier tried to stand on legs that had begun to turn to stone.

"Well, how did you do?"

"*We* did quite well. Tomorrow you will have to help me direct the harvest."

There were restrictions, new problems to be surmounted, difficult promises to be kept, details of all sorts, of course; Collier didn't want to know about them. Never had a *kang* seemed as welcome as it did this morning.

Gao had been transformed; rather, Gao had rediscovered and tapped the core of leadership in himself, and the villagers had spent the evening trying to determine of what quality and how deeply the vein actually ran. His claim had been staked out just in time.

Collier remembered the phrase and pronounced it correctly almost without thinking: "*Yi fanshen hao—Er fanshen hen hao.*"

"Yes. Very good. That is what did it. These people need a slogan. 'One turnover is good—two turnovers is very good.'" There was no need to explain further, but Gao was not yet talked out. "You see, to get rid of the landlord was good. It will be better now to share everything and become totally independent. For you see if—"

"Gao. Gao. For heaven's sake. I'm convinced."

And Gao Ma-ting smiled the smile Collier had remembered, deepened and given a self-deprecating flavor by a sudden flush on his cheeks and dropped eyelids. The two men decided to leave Cai-cai asleep in his awkward but functional position.

Gene Collier slept on a *kang* laid over the still-warm hearth. Gao, seated at the table by a half-shielded lantern, began to make a list of tasks that would have to be done in Yang-Xien. There was no particular order; in fact, he purposely thought randomly. He could establish priorities later. "Place old Nin in charge of all the pigs in village— build central sty near outside gate." "Reinforce tower steps and install bell." This was an excellent idea. "Centralize all handicrafts." That was a winter activity. "Establish school and literacy program." (My God, how many years ahead am I thinking!)

Then in quick order: "Establish responsibilities; appropriate tools; appropriate animals; bring in all crops; divide them and distribute fairly; prepare the rest for market; ship to Santung and Yenan; payment for Tian. . . ." His pen trailed off. In the morning chill Gao Ma-ting felt the sudden swell of fear that he was not up to the chief task, that he was neither good nor wise enough to make the second turnover a success. Panic had almost overcome him. He went outside to urinate.

Collier, sleeping lightly, heard Gao stir as he rose from the table. Collier rolled over and murmured, "Right, Coach."

Gao understood each word, but not the meaning of the expression. He assumed it was an idiom.

The porcupine-man, now that he was in China and knew that he was in China, began to dream regularly of another time and very different people.

17

The Blind Ones

Winter came suddenly and it lingered. A raw wind blew constantly from the east for six months although there were no excessive accumulations of snow. It was the coldest and the warmest winter most people in Yang-Xien ever remembered. Every cold winter was said to be the coldest ever; this year, however, there was more fuel in the village than ever before. A wheezing truck had meandered up from Yenan with an unexpected shipment: seed for spring planting, some cloth, two bales of cotton padding, a heating stove for the village hall (the "L" room), some pieces of rough-hewn timber, and a pile of coal the likes of which no eyes in Yang-Xien had ever seen before. Although Gao Ma-ting's program had been progressing nicely (he had managed to ruffle only a few feelings, and most of those belonged to the Tian), this delivery from a city the villagers had never seen, from an organization they had no reason to trust, gave Gao and the Party to a lesser extent the credibility and trust that would allow him a slightly wider margin for error in the future.

The coal was piled in a huge mound before the tower in the center of the square. Cai-cai guarded it; no, that is not quite correct: Cai-cai was the proprietor. Each morning he swept away whatever snow had blown onto the pile with a broken-handled broom; this act of love gave him sufficient authority in the minds of those who previously had seen him only as an idiot to ration out the coal. He did this by filling every bag himself. He apportioned amounts in the manner of a kindly father, able to meet the varying needs of different children without antagonizing any of them. Not a single piece of coal was stolen because Cai-cai was known to take a turn around the square at unlikely times of the day and night. At any rate, there was obviously enough for everyone.

During some of the harsher days of winter, Collier and Gao walked the farmland, paced it off, drew rough maps, and made plans. The seeds that had been delivered and those the families already possessed made it possible, given sufficient will and manpower, to prepare and seed a great many *mou* of new lands. But the unused land that required less preparation was on higher ground and would be harder to work, while the poorer land was closer and reasonably flat. In addition, all new land had to be divided and apportioned equally to each family. The success of the changes Gao had already initiated was due to the fact that there were still tracts of measured and marked land that belonged to each family rather than to a communal entity. "From where we have come," Gao said too often for Collier's satisfaction, "it is necessary to go through a period of private ownership. Even as we approach the stage of full cooperation, it is important to retain the idea of independence."

"Never saw anything you could eat grow out of an idea," was what Collier said now as he paced away from Gao down the south slope of a potential farm.

The work on the tower steps went slowly. There wasn't

enough wood to rebuild them totally, so a discriminating patch job—which, of course, was a good deal harder than constructing a new set of steps—was begun by Collier and the Xia, younger and elder. These two methodical men were known to the villagers as the Moon and the Sun, the son's slightly misshapen pale face appearing to be a sliver of the father's radiant fullness. Collier led the assault with what passed for a crowbar, followed up by the Moon, who took the piece to be replaced down to the Sun, who cut a new piece to the proper size with a tool that was part saw, part knife, part ax. Then the Moon fastened the new piece into place by striking in nails with an ancient mallet. The important construction decisions were left to Collier. It was obvious that the old door was going to have to be rebuilt completely, so Collier, in a rare moment of youthful exuberance, backed off from it a few paces, approximated his old three-point football stance, and rushed forward to block the door. The blow from his forearm and shoulder took the door cleanly off its hinges and it broke in two against the far wall. The eyes of Sun and Moon widened, narrowed again, and slid sideways to glance at each other. The old door would have at least blocked some of the freezing wind that then whistled through the tower. Conditions were very difficult but, given the social forces operative, no one dared complain, and the work was done. Collier had the splintered remains of the door carried back to Gao's house. A new door was constructed out of lumber found behind the old Fan house.

The bell was installed late one afternoon, and when old man Xia was invited to christen it, he pulled on the clapper with such force that his son and Collier were deafened for many minutes. But the villagers all came out of their houses and old Xia leaned out of the tower and doffed his pale-blue cap. From that day—and the exact date, unfortunately, is unrecorded (one of Gao's rare clerical oversights)—the bell was rung every sunrise and sunset by Cai-cai. It is still a mystery as to how he managed to keep so accurate a schedule.

Because the "L" room which was the Village Hall was now heated by an efficient coal stove, it was easy for Gao to get excellent attendance at the numerous meetings even without Collier as a curiosity. It was in this room that one of Gao Ma-ting's most important personal qualities emerged, and this was patience. Gao came to realize that even the men of Yang-Xien merely wished to be heard; they did not necessarily want to oppose any particular action. Gao let each man speak at length; usually the meetings lasted well past midnight. The last words and, more important, the final actions were his.

Not all of his programs were successful. Old Nin, whose pigs had been the finest in Yang-Xien, had difficulty running a piggery for the entire village. Only after his own pigs had been properly tended and fed would he take care of the others and, as it turned out, he had insufficient time for them. But Gao's second strongest point was an ability to turn adversity into advantage. He went to Madame Tian and begged her to allow her youngest son to show Nin how to establish a well-organized pig operation. She, of course, complained about the money that was still owed her and the poor quality of the land she had received for some of her oxen, but eventually she relented. A young Tian was soon involved in the Yang-Xien pig cooperative.

One of Gao's crowning organizational achievements that first winter was the establishment of a clothing factory in the "L" room. Each morning and afternoon, fifteen of the village women met and divided the tasks of cutting, sewing, and finishing padded jackets and trousers. Of course, they indulged in laughter and harmless gossip, pastimes that had never been so well used as an incitement to more productive activities. The operation was a success: The women worked efficiently, there was no waste, a cheerful, communal attitude prevailed at all times, and the numerous garments which they crafted were well made. The largest jacket and trousers, especially made for Fa Guo-ren, were delivered to Gao's house one evening by a giggling girl who volunteered no word of explanation or instruction; the clothes, of course, spoke eloquently for themselves.

There were enough garments by midwinter to allow most of the adults in Yang-Xien a second outfit; the women, however, refused to accept any of the clothing they had made. Gao, assuming their refusal was because they had never before possessed more than one set of clothes, went to the factory to tease the ladies out of their ignorant coyness. He was met by blushes and titters. There was no spokeswoman, so Gao stood in their midst and, while turning, he delivered a short, forceful speech about the need to learn new ways, to *fanshen* (turn over) an old set of clothes for a new set.

The eldest daughter of Nin emerged as the group's representative; that is, three or four other girls pushed her forward. She explained haltingly that they wanted the clothing exchanged for other things, things the village did not have. "The more clothes, the more things we will receive." Behind her the women nodded to show that the decision was unanimous.

Gao Ma-ting was moved by their unity and economic consciousness; he had read in Party pamphlets that such acts were not to be expected until years in the future. He applauded their motives but said that next year would be time enough to begin the bartering of clothing. "You have suffered much. You deserve some new clothing."

Miss Nin again stepped forward and spoke so softly that Gao only heard the second half of what she said: " . . . furthermore, the new jackets are not as warm as those we have already."

"Of course they are. Look," picking up a jacket from a table and turning it inside out, "look at how well it's padded."

"No. The clothing we wear already has fleas." Her face flushed red; the others giggled at so straightforward an explanation.

Gao had forgotten in his three winters out of Yang-Xien. His fellow villagers welcomed fleas and lice in the padding of their winter jackets, since the bites and scratching necessary produced the desired effect of stimulating the wearer's circulation. He agreed to barter or sell all the clothes; then he retreated out of the "L" room, spun around and walked directly to his desk, where in a bold hand he added "Program of Personal Hygiene" to his list of tasks for the future.

The major failure of Gao's first winter was that he never began a very crucial program. Yang-Xien was a village of the *xia-tzu*, or "blind ones," as illiterates were called in northern China. A few men could write their names and read a handful of characters, but the average villager was totally illiterate. Besides Gao only Madame Tian and her children were fully literate, and she, after her retreat on the pig issue, seemed to be the likely one to run a school for the "blind." She refused abruptly and absolutely. Apparently there were some distinctions Madame Tian would not allow to fall away—the educated as opposed to the noneducated was the chief among them.

When that wonderful shipment from Yenan arrived, it did not contain the character and picture pamphlets Gao had requested. He had decided to set up a school and teach all the classes himself, but the absence of the books made the project too difficult to undertake. He felt overworked as it was with his organizational tasks, and the opportunity to blame Madame Tian or the higher-ups in Yenan was very attractive. Definitely next year, said Gao to himself.

Collier was also overworked, but he did not feel put upon because he did not work against a schedule; time in Yang-Xien was never a conscious consideration for him. His life was a woven thread of tasks. As things worked out, after the tower repairs he was in charge of use and maintenance of the village's tools. With the assistance of the Sun and the Moon, he made a long, flat cart, the largest and most sturdy one ever built in the village. They also constructed numerous small barrows for use in the fields. He drew plans for various primitive irrigation systems. He experimented with making bricks out of mud and straw, and he made a Ping-Pong table from odd pieces of wood and the remains of the tower door. It was not until early summer, however, that a ball and paddles could be obtained in trade from Yenan.

Gao, whose lists of tasks had become a great joke in the village, gave two projects first priority for spring: the preparation of the new farmland and the establishment of a regular, weekly delivery service to and from Yenan, over fifty miles away. But he realized that there were other important tasks and, if properly organized, there would be enough of a work force in Yang-Xien to accomplish a good many of them. He had a master plan, one which had been waiting for its time to come. Gao released it at a meeting of family representatives. There would be five Work Brigades: Farming, Transporting, Animals, Repairs, New Building, each with a strong, knowledgeable leader and all responsible to a single overseer (who else?) for the entire operation.

The council meeting ran once again almost until the sunrise bell, but when it was over there were five brigades and five leaders. Lists of the members of the various brigades had been worked out after much discussion, argument, and the sort of trading off that goes on among professional U.S. baseball teams. The leaders had to round up their brigades quickly in order to get an early start on planning for the spring activities. During the week each leader spent many hours with Gao, being given what he called the "Large Vision," an unnecessary "pep" talk, and a list of specific goals with a time schedule for each. Each brigade was then assigned an identification color by Gao: Red—Farming, Yellow—Transporting, Blue—Animals,

Green—Repairs, Black—New Building. The next morning there was a bulletin board constructed quickly by Collier on the wall of the "L" room; each color was painted in on the week's schedule so every member would know when his brigade was meeting. There was a meeting scheduled for some group or other every evening of the week—Red, Yellow, Blue, Green, Black; Brown—all the brigade leaders and Gao; Orange—the original council members and Gao. In order to convene a meeting, Cai-cai rang the tower bell with a slow clanging so nagging in its persistence that the brigade members hurried along so that it would stop sooner. The bulletin board with its painted chart drew villagers as though it were a source of heat. A group was always clustered about it, pointing and jabbering and very often arguing about the merits of being *Hong* (Red) or *Hei* (Black).

Gao had transformed winters in Yang-Xien once and for all. Whereas this had formerly been a time to withdraw and conserve heat and energy, the villagers now were alive with anticipation, with the friendly competition of differing allegiances, and with a strange new sense of daring. All of it translated into a undercurrent of totally new feeling in the village. The feeling was hope.

When Gao and Collier sat across the table from one another in the evening, they did not share very much; even the quality of their weariness was different. There was a deep irony in their separateness that neither of them realized; they were both porcupine-men to a strong degree. That is what they liked about each other, and what they had intuited about each other almost immediately; the irony was, of course, that the very same force which attracted in an overall way began to repel them in day-to-day proximity. It was the sharpness of quill rather than the need for warmth that had now become predominant.

Gao Ma-ting's isolation was primarily a measure of his insecurity, although no one in Yang-Xien would have believed that, had they even understood the concept. Gao was like the climber who climbs the mountain not only because it exists but because he must prove that he exists along with it. And although he had progressed a good distance toward the summit in a short time and had overcome a great many obstacles already, he was in some respects less certain of himself than he was when he began. If the summit was ever attained, the experience would probably raise new, totally unexpected doubts rather than put an end to Gao's anxiety. For such a man, the stark shadows of yet higher peaks would always loom in the distance. With every advance, Gao Ma-ting's deepest uncertainty grew, but so did his ability to overcome it and to continue functioning. He was, after all, taking a whole village up the mountainside along with him, literally raising the elemental existence of Yang-Xien to a higher plane.

Gao's isolation did not concern Collier at all. Ever since he had become a regular working member of the community, Gene was like a powerful underwater swimmer who plunged, twisted, circled, and rose again in a foreign element that freed his imagination as walking or running in the air never could. There was a fluid, dreamlike quality to his existence, but this was a lucid dream in which work and gentle physical language, strange vocal sounds, and averted eyes held wonderful meanings.

True to his porcupine nature, each man withdrew to a new point of balance, one that was more satisfying for Gene than for Gao Ma-ting. Of course the nature of their activities had something to do with their respective happiness. Although Gao had urged him to head either the New Building or the Repair brigade, Collier chose to be a simple farm laborer. They did not argue over the choice: Gao was too involved in planning another assault up the mountain; Collier was tumbling happily below the surface of the water at

the time. "The Moon would be very good in Rebuilding,"
was all Collier said.

"Of course."

Spring came with a continuous drizzle. The village was
fortunate. Often in the past the rains were so severe that
serious flooding made planting impossible until midsum-
mer, if at all. Gao realized that there were many ways in
which he had been fortunate: no disease, enough food and
fuel, a relatively dry and early spring. He hoped there
would come a time when luck would become a minor consideration. This thought, however, came during the flush of
his success in organizing the Yang-Xien Work Brigades.

The Chinese earth smelled different from anything in
Collier's experience, an odor at once musky and sweet. It
may seem odd, but Gene thought it smelled both young
and old. The addition of the night soil seemed to tip the
balance decidedly on the side of youth.

Cai-cai's first bell of the morning was not selective: It
awakened the entire village along with the Farm Brigade
for whom it was intended. Gene rose painfully for the first
few days because his body was not used to the hard digging
and shoveling it was required to do. Gao arose on the
second call, about forty minutes later, when most of the
others arose. Bells now rang in Yang-Xien a dozen times a
day; never measuring the hours, but tasks and assignments.
Cai-cai was uniquely suited to perform this function, for
there was not another mind in the village so uncluttered
and devoted to order, unless of course it was Gao's.

Collier's tool was a long-handled American spade,
stamped along the stem with the brand name and place of
manufacture: "ACE SPADE—Toledo, Ohio." Gene had ex-
propriated the spade from the jumble of tools that had
belonged to Madame Tian, the ones he had reclaimed and
reconditioned during the winter. The tool was perfectly

balanced, its handle conformed exactly to his wide, flat palms and long fingers; and when he drove it into the earth with the force of his boot, it bit crisply, the long handle bending just enough to snap a large chunk of earth loose cleanly when he put his back and arms into the action. "Your-tool" had been a friend to him in Korea; the Ace Spade was a part of him here.

It was clear from the outset that Gao was correct about the working capacity of Chinese peasants. The full component of the Farm Brigade arrived at the field early. Men Tai-chen was the brigade leader, a healthy, bright-eyed man who commanded as much affection as respect. He had organized his people very effectively and marked the land to be prepared with splashes of vegetable dye so that everyone knew his or her task and area from the very first day. There were over fifty men, women, and older children functioning in complete silence as members of picking, raking, digging, and barrow squads in the morning mist. Men Tai-chen, known most commonly as Bu Bing (Never Sick), drew Collier aside and walked him around the perimeter of the field indicating the location of a system of drainage ditches. Gene had drawn the plans for the ditches and turned them over to Gao two months earlier. Every ten or twelve feet Bu Bing pointed to a spot and Collier dug a fairly deep hole; in this fashion a rough, dotted outline for the drainage system was marked off. Bu Bing did not stay with Collier very long once he was convinced that Collier understood how to implement the plan he had fashioned himself. Bu Bing was off to the field where he raked stones and talked quietly to the barrow carters who came to take the stones where they would be used later to line the ditches.

Six bells rung rapidly by Cai-cai announced the fact that food was leaving the village for the field. Almost immediately two women emerged from the newly built gate behind the Village Hall shouldering a hamper strung from a pole that dipped perilously close to the ground. During the ten or twelve minutes that it took for them to arrive in the fields, the workers began to call to each other, make jokes, and chant an impromptu slogan, very much in the manner of students in a strictly disciplined class after the teacher has been called away. Their labor, however, didn't diminish a whit.

The hamper held steamed rolls exuding great aromatic puffs of millet flour and air, and a huge pot of tea. The Farm Brigade formed a circle on the damp earth and they ate and drank and chattered. The small old man next to Collier was the elf-eared fellow with mustaches like a pair of white parentheses; he talked freely with Gene, totally pleased by the fact that he was never interrupted by a reply.

These food carriers arrived at midmorning every day. And "every day" meant seven days each week until the fields were planted and the ditches were well on their way to completion. The next problems to be solved were those of heat, drought, and the transportation of water from the village well. The Farm Brigade members alternated the chore of wheeling pots of water out to the field on the small barrows. Collier continued to work daily on the irrigation system. He believed that through the installation of a series of small sluice gates, water, especially rain water, could be collected at the highest tier and shunted selectively to any area of the field Bu Bing wished. The loss through seepage was small owing to the layer of small stones along the bottom of the entire system. (Gao during one of his unnecessary "pep" talks often cited the shift of stones from the field, where they were harmful, to the ditch, where they were beneficial, as symbols of the wonders of *er fanshen.*) Collier's irrigation system worked. His achievement was recognized at the weekly Farm Brigade meeting.

There was evidence all about Collier of the passage of time in the form of growth: of pigs, crops, children, friendships. Like all other creatures, Collier existed in time; but unlike most human creatures, his consciousness did nothing with the evidence of change about him other than take note of it. The process of doing things well, from planning to completion, was the measure of all things to him. He had grown a square beard; he had changed to the padded blue clothes of winter, but he saw these as things that simply occurred; they were never signs that he was getting older, that another year had passed, that his former self was being left behind somewhere.

Soon there were fifteen brigades, and it appeared that Gao would run out of colors before he ran out of tasks to organize. Villagers enjoyed his penchant for organization because the man's activities brought excitement to Yang-Xien. Also, the first harvest had been a great success and the trade with Yenan outstripped even Gao's expectations.

During an intensive one-week campaign called "Away With Dirt," the Sanitation Brigade eliminated the sources of household pestilence and established a standard for sanitation that was maintained thereafter. The Communication Brigade, consisting of Gao himself and Cai-cai, was now in nightly radio contact with Headquarters at Yenan; the necessary equipment had been purchased with excess profits. Other changes: more food generally and more pork and chicken in everyone's diet; three small factories—tool, barrow, barrel; regular political education sessions; a second well and water storage facilities; weekly Ping-Pong tournaments. And perhaps most significant of all was the initiation of a human cultural phenomenon previously unknown in Yang-Xien—topical conversation. Of course people in the village had always talked, but never before had they something always to talk about at length, never before had they had a future to discuss. Collier, however, was less conversational than ever, perhaps because he was negating time while the villagers were just discovering it. He spoke mostly in clipped responses and short requests. His vocabulary in Chinese had grown to more than three hundred functional words and phrases; naturally he had trouble with the tones, the high tone in particular, as did most Westerners. He couldn't climb up and strike it as cleanly as he should have, so unless the context was absolutely clear his high-toned *mā* (mother) might be mistaken for a dip-toned *mǎ* (horse). Fortunately, Collier's eyebrows went up even when his tones did not, and the villagers soon came to understand the intent.

Not everyone in Yang-Xien was pleased with the changes Gao had wrought. The older members of the Tian family and some curmudgeons offered just the sort of opposition that was absolutely necessary if *yang* was to proceed to bend gracefully to *yin*.

Gao Ma-ting had become increasingly insecure. And effective.

Cai-cai's existence was a thing of beauty.

Eugene Collier's life was good.

Things were proceeding nicely in Yang-Xien. A school for the "blind ones" still hadn't been started, although Gao had received teaching pamphlets from Yenan.

With the first light snow of winter came a most unexpected personage. Fan Tai-cheng, youngest daughter of the wayward landlords of Yang-Xien, returned. Her presence raised some troubling questions, most immediately concerning whether she would be allowed to stay and where, since her old home had been officially converted to the seat of the village council.

Madame Tian seized the opportunity to make new trouble. She welcomed Miss Fan to her home, although she had secretly resented the girl's wealth and grace in the old days. Everyone assumed that the girl had come back to reclaim her family's property or at least to insist on some form of repayment. Everyone was excited with the prospect of what would be done, and they talked about it well into the night.

Everyone but Collier and Cai-cai, who rang the tower bells, cranked the generator for the evening radio report to Yenan, and locked the Village Hall after the last brigade meeting broke up and the last Ping-Pong game had been played.

18

Two Stars

The village had acquired a number of things that had been sorely lacking before, namely, common direction, energy, productivity, a sense of hope and daring, and a leader who had a flair for organization. Nevertheless, the village continued to lack a certain spiritual essence generally known as a soul.

Madame Tian, in her desire to upset the onward and upward movement of the village that had shunted her aside, was to be severly disappointed once again. The girl, Fan Tai-cheng, who she had hoped would delay progress if not obliterate it completely, proved to be precisely the soul that the new Yang-Xien lacked.

Fan Tai-cheng stood calmly before a special meeting of the Village Council and explained her reasons for returning to her village and for doing so at precisely this time. She had small feet and hands and had the most charmingly delicate face, piercing eyes and a confident low voice. She was beautiful in a self-possessed way that none of the men in the room had ever seen before, but her physical attributes went unnoticed, for she was a Fan, and therefore a challenge. The men had not so quickly forgotten the deference which a member of that family commanded. They could not trust her because her presence made them distrust themselves and all that had occurred in Yang-Xien in such a short time.

"About what you are doing in this village, word has spread. The transformations you have made are such that it would make any citizen of Yang-Xien proud to claim her heritage. . . ."

No one but Gao was really listening, and he believed the girl's words to be merely introductory in the polite tradition of the gentry. He firmly expected this portion to end, to be punctuated by a "however, I have come to claim. . . ." This preface was merely an annoyance; there would be no turning back in Yang-Xien. He wondered how great a mess the girl would try to make.

" . . . have been for the past three years at the Revolutionary University in Peking." Miss Fan's face broke into a smile as she began to recount the length, breadth, and texture of her revolutionary education. "It seemed to me, then, that I had been offered the rare opportunity to come home to my village, where my family had for so long been an oppressor of the people, and begin to correct some of the wrong they have done. When I heard that there were no medical services here, I was most gratified"—her face became serious and earnest—"because that has been my training. I have presumed to bring certain equipment with me." There was still much to be discussed of course, but Gao Ma-ting recognized the very same motive in the girl that had sustained him in Korea and led him to reject activity on higher political levels in Peking. She, too, was devoted to her village, her home. A doctor and a teacher! This was not sheer coincidence, he thought; it was the result of excellent planning.

Gao left most of the questioning to the other men, who

asked about things Miss Fan had already discussed in her statement; but they had not listened very closely to her words. She again displayed the purity of her motives and the happy conjunction of her skills and the village's needs. But since she was a Fan and they were peasants, the same questions were asked three more times, until Gao stepped in. "You are welcome, Fan Tai-cheng. We must now determine where our medical center is to be located."

Gao assured Fan Tai-cheng that a small room, formerly her household nursery but now used for storage, would be cleaned out by a soon-to-be-formed Medical Brigade of which Miss Fan would be the leader. The Sanitation Brigade also would come under her professional supervision. She would require shelves and an examination table to be made; if she drew a simple sketch of her needs, the Building Brigade would give it a high order of priority. Then he said, "I wonder, however, Comrade Fan, if you would be willing also to initiate a program to teach the reading and writing of the characters to our illiterates. We do have teaching guide pamphlets for the purpose, and there is a great need to bring our fellow villagers out of the darkness."

"I shall organize classes as soon as possible."

"You see, I had planned to conduct such a program myself, but I am needed for so many other things at present that—" Gao's eyes closed slowly and his hands opened in a gesture of helplessness.

"Of course. I understand."

There were fifteen other people in the "L" room, but the tone of the exchange between Gao Ma-ting and Fan Tai-cheng was that of two very close friends who, after a long period of separation, somehow manage to pick up the thread of an old intimacy almost immediately upon meeting again, even though she was little more than a child when he knew her previously.

It became clear to Gao in the next few days that Miss Fan knew a great deal about the workings of Yang-Xien. She understood the existence and function of all the brigades, of short- and long-term goals, of the problems Gao had faced and of his solutions. Her factual knowledge so astounded him that Gao decided to ask her about it, which he did on a visit to her medical center (ostensibly to see if the work had been done and to inquire about her future needs). When he entered the room, she was wearing a white smock and had her back to him, extending her small frame on tip-toe in order to place some rolls of gauze on the highest shelf. Her ankles were so delicately formed that Gao opted to let her efforts continue so that he could watch them rather than offer a helping hand. Cai-cai broke the silence pushing through from behind Gao. His foot struck a corner of the table and Fan Tai-cheng spun around quickly, a smile on her face. Seeing Gao, her original smile became another smile, a deeper, more serious one.

Cai-cai was sent away to perform a task, and when Gao soon exhausted all other means of trying to discover Miss Fan's source of information, he asked directly: "How do you know what has been happening here so well? You have not been here, to my knowledge, since I have returned."

"I was on the network."

"Network?"

"Of course. All the local reports are radioed back to Headquarters in Peking."

"But I thought Yenan—"

"Every night Yenan calls Peking, as do Tientsin, Sian, and Tatung. I was often at Headquarters to take reports, or my friend did it, and I always inquired about my village. You have established a very fine record here."

Gao blushed, "Well, er, yes, perhaps, but there is still much to be done." Fortunately at this exact moment Cai-cai rushed in to signify that Gao's presence was required at the piggery.

From the outset, Fan Tai-cheng made herself indispensable. The Sanitation Brigade whitewashed every kitchen

in the village. She set two broken bones and healed a painful infection in old Nin's mouth. She delivered a baby with
consummate ease. But it was her bright, cheerful face, her
flinty goodness, that made her loved and quickly established her as the essence of the new Yang-Xien. Of course
Gao was the organizer who made changes possible, but
"Doctor" Fan became the symbol of the *er fanshen*.

In the version of history that had become fashionable in
Yang-Xien it was generally accepted that the Fan family had
been driven out in either 1948, '49, or '50 by the revolutionary wrath of the united villagers. This was not the case.
There was, of course, the irritation caused by those two
thieves who paraded as Party cadres, but this did not cause
the Fan family to be driven out of Yang-Xien. It was, rather,
their ability to see the future clearly and to realize that
whatever hopes they had were southern hopes. And so, like
a great many of the rich landowning families in northern
China in the spring of 1949, the Fan dug up their wealth
(most of the landlords' traditional wealth was in gold, sil-
ver, and porcelain buried in casks), packed carefully, and
moved southward.

Fan Tai-cheng refused to go. She did not fully understand why herself; perhaps it was the face of her father,
which indicated to her that they would never again return
to Yang-Xien. Perhaps it was the fact that there was an
alternative: Her sister, Ling-chen, was with her husband's
family in Peking with her baby while he served in the army
in Manchuria. They had offered Tai-cheng a place should
she wish to remain with her sister. Perhaps it was a spark
struck from the excitement of the times that had ignited
Fan Tai-cheng's will; perhaps she was innately rebellious.
However it was, the eighteen-year-old girl rejected her father's expressed wishes repeatedly and so was eventually
sent to her sister in Peking. Then there followed work in a
hospital (in every capacity except surgeon), and studies at
the university when it reopened. Throughout these extraordinary years she was totally absorbed in the life of the

great city, until the moment when she was summoned home by a voice over which she had no control and which was heard only by her better self.

Now she was back in her old nursery room setting up shelves of medical supplies, meager now but soon, with Gao's help, to be quite sufficient. She stopped, leaned against the wall, and put her hands on her cheeks. Fan Tai-cheng was a happy woman.

Those who thought about such matters as romance, that is, all the women and a few of the old men, knew very quickly that it was an inevitable thing, a match between this beautiful, unselfish young woman and the village overseer. They thought that it was not good that this doctor should have had such freedom in her life, even if she had been fortunate enough to make the proper choices. Nor was it good for Gao to spend so many days without a woman; it was time for Ming-sa to step aside and let a younger woman move into the small house by the gate.

The women began referring to Gao and Fan as the "Two Stars," after an old love story in which two stars manage to shine through on a cloudy night in order to discover one another. So were they known to the romancers even though there was not a great deal of evidence to support the comparison. The two were almost never alone, and when they were, it was usually for a very short time.

Once before a meeting of the Sanitation Brigade they found themselves in the "L" room before any of the others arrived. Cai-cai was a trifle late with the meeting bell; in itself a very, very unusual mistake. "I do not want to interfere, of course, but I would like to make a request," said Gao.

"Yes."

"When you begin to teach your reading classes, er, would you begin with the learning of dates. In that way we can establish a sense of finishing projects at a certain specific time."

"I will." Cai-cai's bell rang out crisply at this precise moment, as if to punctuate a new era in the village.

Within a month everyone was able to read the date on top of the bulletin board, and the future had been formally introduced to Yang-Xien.

Collier and Gao had not lived together for almost three weeks. The parting was functional and amicable. Gene had begun to spend a great deal of time in the shed where he also had become moderately proficient in forging and tempering new blades for work tools out of useless scraps of old ones. And since the hearth glowed perpetually, it was foolish to waste the heat at night. Ming-sa still brought his food, but often Collier forgot to eat it. He enjoyed his privacy and the smell of his new abode, especially the dirt floor that had been worn smooth and hard as clay by years of being a floor; it smelled exactly like old leather. He was disturbed by thoughts of Gao, but not by anything Gao had ever done; rather, by what he had forgotten to do: Gao had not laughed for months, or smiled in weeks. Collier smiled almost continually, even more than Cai-cai, not a broad or foolish smile; rather, a slight curl of the lips and a pleasant narrowing of eye that indicated the harmony of the inner man and his outer activity.

Fan Tai-cheng had known of the American who was called the Frenchman before she had arrived. She saw him almost daily from the low window of the medical center. He was aware of her only as a presence, not through any specific knowledge, until Gao supplied him with a terse, political biography of her. Collier was forging the head for a digging tool while Gao relayed the information; sparks were flying wildly, making Gao very uncomfortable. Collier finally said, by way of displaying his lack of interest, "I need a pair of goggles, if you can get them," between smashes against the great, flat stone that served as an anvil. Gao wrote something in a small yellow notebook and said, "We cannot get everything we want, you know." Collier glared at him before his next smash. And Gao was off.

Now Gao was subject to ridicule for other reasons than his lists. He had a wristwatch that he looked at as though it were the trigger of an involuntary nervous tic, and he announced exactly how long he would be able to stay when he arrived anywhere, other than at official meetings. The villagers recognized Gao's extraordinary capacity for work and his talent for planning; nevertheless, the dominant reaction to his name when he was not present was respectful laughter. Collier was an exception; he thought Gao should have avoided some of the pitfalls of authority more successfully than he had and he was disappointed in him.

The information he had received about Fan Tai-cheng, after being translated from political to personal terms, impressed Collier considerably. He drew the few facts he had and some reasonable surmises into a tight ball and recognized in her a clear and admirable motivation: She loved her home more than her family, more than anything else in the world.

Collier, who had learned that silence was not merely the absence of sound and was usually preferable to it, wanted to talk when he met her. He stroked his beard thoughtfully. He did not know what he wanted to say to this woman, but knew that he did not have words for it, whatever it may be. She was with Gao; they had come to the shed with a large metal pot that she wanted to use for sterilizing instruments, if Collier could patch the hole in the bottom. There wasn't much to be said; even Gao pointed and gestured rather than make a specific verbal request.

"Tonight," Collier said to her through Gao.

Gao relayed the fact that the pot would be ready that evening and indicated that he would escort her back to the medical center, even though a glance at his wristwatch indicated that he could hardly spare the time.

Miss Fan would not be rushed. She said slowly and self-consciously to Collier, "You-ah are-ah not-ah French-ah. You-ah should-ah be-ah called-ah Mei Guo-ren, not-ah Fa Guo-ren." Then she was gone, whisked away by her companion. Gene discovered much later that she had been speaking English, speaking it fuzzily with the charm of an innocent drunk, adding the suffix "ah" as a way of separating words and drawing in soft breaths. Then it occurred to him that "Mei Guo-ren" must mean "American."

They tried to speak again that evening when Fan Tai-cheng returned to claim her pot. But they understood none of the words. Did she really say "running dogs"? Was Collier's tone clear enough so she knew he meant "soup" and not "sugar" when he pointed to the pot and said, *"tang"*? She seemed to smile beneath her smile.

In the spring, when Doctor Fan was vaccinating all the villagers during the "Destroy Disease" campaign, she came to the shed with a syringe and a wad of cotton to inject Collier, who was busily fitting large wheels on the barrows that would bear the brunt of the "Transform the Earth" program. They spoke in English slowly and with difficulty; however they communicated better than they had before, now that they wished to speak to each other beyond their abilities to succeed, and such was the content of their pathetic gestures and utterances. Once they understood this fact, all other understanding was possible.

If on a cloudy evening a person happens to notice only two stars in the heavens and assumes they are the only ones up there, that person had better look much harder, for in time other stars will certainly become visible. The stars, of course, seem fixed; the clouds always move. And people's eyes are even less reliable than their hearts. The romancers in Yang-Xien would have been shocked to discover that there was a third star, every bit as bright as either of the others, and much closer than anybody had suspected.

After the pressures of planting had passed—and once again Yang-Xien was blessed with excellent weather—the village received word of its first marriage since the People's Revolution. When the village overseer and Doctor Fan finally allowed word of their impending marriage to be uttered, Gene Collier realized how deeply attracted he had been to Fan. The force of that attraction, now that it had no fit object, became a repellent, isolating pressure. The porcupine-man again withdrew from what he had begun to love.

19

Yangtze Swimmer

The Yangtze Kiang runs from the Plateau of Tibet to the East China Sea for a distance as long as the United States. And it has split China as cleanly as the curved line dividing *yin* from *yang*, often behaving in a destructive manner more akin to original sin than the resolution of contradictions. Its random and raging floods have snuffed the lives of millions of helpless people. During periods of drought, it produces different destructive results by completely disappearing. In old China it was the symbol of power uncontrolled, of untamed, arbitrary, and perfidious force. It was also the common inspiration for a particular kind of romantic artist who produced long, narrow paintings of exaggerated mountain gorges dotted with mandarins, holy shrines, and ethereal oxen, all maintained by sufferance of the river below.

Throughout the 1950s the Yangtze remained relatively well behaved. The government had planned and proceeded with preliminary work on a vast power complex that would eventually tame some of the river's excesses and

channel her tantrums constructively. There were four major bridges and a number of narrow cart and foot spans
linking the shores; and a myriad of boats, from rafts to
modern, engine-powered ships, crossed her constantly.
The greatest movement on the river, however, is up and
down along its shores, from Chungking to Hankow, Nan-
king to Shanghai.

Its color reflects its passage eastward to the sea. The
Yangtze is red-tinged through the mountains of Yünnan
Province, light blue through Szechwan, and runs an unnatural brown east of Chungking until it is filtered by the
abrupt turns of the high ground in Hupeh where it is transformed into a deep blue. That rich purity of color is distorted by the wastes of the large cities east of Wuchang; but
when it arrives simultaneously at Shanghai and the sea it
remains essentially blue, heightened in tone by all the colors it has been along its journey. At a point about two miles
into the East China Sea, the Yangtze Kiang disappears.

It was not known, when Mao Tse-tung announced his
intention to swim the Yangtze in 1957, exactly where the
attempt would be made. In fact, there was great doubt that
the Chairman was serious; after all, he was sixty-four years
of age and there did not appear to be any political reason
for him to undertake a task such as this. When he
reaffirmed his intention to the Politburo and further told
them the place would be slightly to the east of Hankow,
where the great river had never before been crossed, the
members were horrified. The State Council urged the
Premier, Chou En-lai, to dissuade the Chairman from so
unreasonable and dangerous an act. Rather than debate
with the man he had known for the better part of a lifetime,
Chou merely asked why this thing would have to be done,
and why would it have to be done by Mao at this time?

Mao, characteristically, answered sequentially on levels
ranging downward from the political and general to the
personal and specific; from long-term goals down to im-

mediate gratifications. Then, before Chou could interrupt, Mao enumerated the risks, which he minimized. "The place has been selected carefully," he said, his eyes flashing playfully. "It must be a place where no one has crossed before. That is the psychological purpose; we will soon have to ask our people to do things they have never done before. The currents in the river are very strong; this is a task that can be accomplished best by guerrilla means. Besides, my friend, all over I see slogans that remind me of my own words, 'Dare to think and dare to do.' It is time for me to dare again, is it not?"

"I will tell them that you cannot be dissuaded."

"And you will be saying a truth."

The day was warm and clear, perfect for a swim. Mao wore a faded striped robe and rubber sandals on his feet. The throng restrained itself: It understood the swimmer's need for concentration. Two young swimmers preceded the Chairman into the water and began swimming slowly for the far shore. Mao moved to the water's edge, took off his robe and sandals, and walked in up to his knees. Inside the old man standing there in a pair of shapeless gray shorts one could discern another man—a tall, vigorous young man who had organized a city of caves in Yenan and dared to wage the battle against impossible odds that finally transformed life and consciousness in China forever. The young man was bundled in a layer of old, protective fat.

Mao followed the young swimmers, but did far less swimming than they did; the "guerrilla" means he employed were sailboat-tacking maneuvers that enabled him to zigzag across rather easily with the help of the eddying currents. On his return he swam a bit more, pulling himself upstream and catching the prevailing current, which brought him back and across easily. No sooner had he emerged and disappeared in a great flowered towel than the Yangtze Kiang was full of swimmers.

Mao Tse-tung joked often during the fall of that year about China's squadrons of river swimmers. He told the Polish ambassador that reports of plans to use a swimming force to take Taiwan were absolutely untrue. He later told a reporter from America that he wanted to swim the Potomac and the Mississippi before he got too old and added that "Washington would be glad to let me swim the Mississippi at the mouth, where it is fifty miles wide."

To understand Mao Tse-tung is to understand that his motive in swimming the Yangtze was political. The following year the nation would be asked to reorganize itself into communes, years before most experts thought it would be ready and while the system of small cooperatives had just begun to bear fruit. To understand Mao Tse-tung is also to understand that his motive was personal. He wrote this poem immediately afterward:

> I care not that the wind blows and the waves beat,
> It is better than idly strolling in a courtyard;
> Today I am free!
> It was on a river that the Master said:
> "Thus is the whole of nature flowing!"*

To understand Mao tse-tung is to understand that one must first be commanded by the river in order to appear to command it.

*Edgar Snow, *Red China Today* (New York: Random House, 1971), p. 176.

20

The Greatest Leap

The Great Leap Forward was not an applicable designation for the changes that occurred in Yang-Xien in 1959. This year did bring, of course, an incredible number of advances: the planting of almost two thousand pine seedlings on the plain to the west of the village; the end of illiteracy and a regular school for all the children. They differed from earlier signs of progress, the digging of the irrigation ditches, the second well, and the trade with Yenan only in range and scope, however, for Yang-Xien had begun leaping much earlier and had not stopped from the day Gao Ma-ting brought the stranger to the first council meeting. In fact, Yang-Xien had physically begun to overleap itself: There were almost as many homes outside the original walls of the village as inside. No longer did a visitor coming from the east see a tight walled fortress on the Shensi Plain; no, now he discerned a great deal of contoured farmland surrounding a village that reached out like an extended hand. The fingers of that hand were the new houses built by the old families in order to make room for their expanded needs. Not only had they broken through the walls enclosing the village; they had, in their extensive sharing, demolished the invisible walls of custom that had kept them separated from one another. Only Madame Tian remained aloof. Even her children participated in a great many of the cooperative activities. She, however, was ill much of the time and seemed to prefer infirmity to any relief that might be brought by Doctor Fan. Madame Tian tried not to refer to that woman at all; when she did, it was always as "Devil's Wife."

Madame Tian was not the only person in Yang-Xien who had looked upon the "wedding" of Fan Tai-cheng and Gao Ma-ting with a measure of disapproval; for a number of old women and men the idea of a contractual ceremony performed after consultation with Party officials in Yenan lacked the proper sense of dignity and mystery. It was the first marriage in Yang-Xien in which a priest did not preside and make the guests tearful and frightened. It was the first marriage in Yang-Xien in which there was no celebration, no guests; a great disappointment to many of the younger people who had hoped to attend.

The two were married in the "L" room before a meeting of the Fertilizer Brigade began. In the room were a few children and old women. Only two of the lanterns had been lit, so the room was unevenly dark; a flickering candle brightened suddenly and just as suddenly diminished.

They stood before Bu Bing, vice-chairman of the Legal Committee, who was seated at a table preparing a scroll for their signatures. He dipped a Chinese writing brush into the ink and quickly splashed a row of characters down the left margin of the page. These he repeated on two sheets of graph paper. When it was time for the petitioners to sign three times, Fan Tai-cheng drew what appeared to be a pagoda, a pond, and a bird on each; Gao printed a series of vertical boxes. The eyes of Ming-sa, peering in at the doorway, were misty with memories of her dead husband;

those of Cai-cai, who was hiding in the darkness under the table, saw only the shuffling of feet and the twitching of Gao's heel.

When Bu Bing rose, he shook hands with each of the newlyweds. They, in turn, faced one another and smiled very slightly. Gao's words of thanks were simply, *"xie-xie."* Cai-cai dashed for the bell tower to ring the combination marriage chimes and announcement of the weekly meeting of the Fertilizer Brigade.

Gao went to Collier's shed the following morning, stood before him for a long moment, and smiled. The smile was the embodiment of all that was fine in Gao Ma-ting; it was the smile that Collier had not seen for over a year. It said, "Wish me good luck." At the very end it became a laughing smile. Gao extended his right hand; Collier pulled off his glove and locked his hand firmly into Gao's.

The irrigation and drainage systems were severely tested in the spring of 1958; the rainstorms the old-timers claimed to have remembered as children materialized with a violence that frightened them even while affirming their memory. The entire village became a bog. But very little of the good earth in the fields was lost in the alluvial wash that took so much soil from the surrounding hillsides. The shed was the site of a great deal of preplanting activity. Here the new chemical fertilizer was mixed and stored, and here the seeds were divided and the tools sharpened, oiled, and laid out for use. The shed was so crowded and so pungently odoriferous that Collier spent his nights on a *kang* where Cai-cai slept until the waters began to recede in late May.

Owing to impassable roads, most work slowed to token levels. Although the rains delayed most of the chores and the people were generally anxious and often edgy, they were not depressed, and this was a measure of the psychological transformation that had taken place in Yang-Xien.

Nor did any of the old family feuds reemerge. Gao was magnificent; marriage in no way diminished his energies. Exuding nothing so much as the Mad Hatter's officious impatience, he arranged meeting after meeting and never for a moment did he cease his list-making. Rain was not a mountain climber's primary concern. For additional comic relief, the villagers peered through their windows each time Cai-cai struggled out to the bell tower; half the time he ended up on his backside in the mud after a losing but elaborately active struggle to maintain his balance.

The Leap which China was attempting had been accomplished in Yang-Xien by a series of difficult little hops. Because of its isolation, it continued to be excluded from the new commune status that would have hurt its progress meaningfully. Other towns and villages, some of which had not even moved toward internal cooperation, were forced into large administrative entities too vague and abstract to promote human sharing.

The spring rains produced a slight irritation on Collier's withdrawn life. It manifested itself in a strange way. He began quietly to sing and whistle mountain songs of his youth, particularly one that was distantly related to "The Wabash Cannonball."

There was another irritating symptom that came in the form of a recurrent set of thoughts, and these were prompted by a visit to the home of the Men family, where he saw great-grandmother Men, the oldest weaver in the village, seated in the darkness at a tapestry loom that ran the length of the entire wall. Those gnarled hands speedily running the shuttle over and under such closely spaced threads allowed him to see the extraordinary, tenuous quality of each of the threads that formed the tapestry. He was astounded at the sheer unlikeliness of the threads in the loom as well as the tapestry of his own life. The events that had shaped his activities and the people he happened to share them with were similarly interwoven. Then he became distrustful of any process that relied so heavily on chance. Even when working with white hot metal at the forge, he would select an event—his capture in Korea—and think of all the things that might have happened to prevent his being in that particular place at that particular moment. In fact, it seemed to him, finally, that had any previous situation been altered, had there been no Jersey Red or Fatty Conklin or Phoebe Philpotts, then all the things that followed would probably not have followed at all. This chain of thought always led back to prime causes and suppositions: had he not come from West Virginia; had his folks been rich; had he. . . . Usually he whistled a low whistle while on these excursions to other lives. The day before the sun finally appeared over the Shensi Plain, Gene Collier recalled being surrounded by dwarfs in the hotel in Tacoma, Washington, and he thought, "Had I been born like that, I'd sure want to know what the hell had caused it, and I'd never get a good enough answer." The next day the villagers of Yang-Xien began to move slowly to the fields; there was no longer time for private thoughts.

The year was the most productive of any in the history of the village: There were more animals slaughtered and shipped, more grain and vegetables grown, more tools and barrels and clothing manufactured, more people (118) living in greater prosperity than ever before. When one morning in October Cai-cai climbed the tower to ring the bell for the final full harvest day, his eyes saw something in the east that they had never seen before—a tall metal tower. Electricity was on its way. Cai-cai called to Gao, who came on the run while buttoning his jacket; the overseer didn't know what in the world to expect, perhaps another invasion. At the sight of the tower, Gao Ma-ting had an emotional twinge. It may have been a sense of triumph or sentiment or, perhaps, the sadness of a climber near the summit; whatever it was, it was a mixed, complex feeling. "Power," he said to Cai-cai, but the idiot didn't believe he had an explanation.

The mixed feelings of Gao were as nothing compared to those of Gene Collier during the spring and early summer of 1960. He learned that Yang-Xien was about to become the easternmost point in a kitelike configuration that would enclose more than thirty thousand *mou* of arid land on which eleven thousand people would live. Yang-Xien would be the administrative fulcrum of this vast geographic and productive entity.

Gao Ma-ting, still maintaining a prominent position in Yang-Xien, would become directly responsible to a committee of men and women from Yenan who would arrive in Yang-Xien when the electricity came in the fall.

Collier had a long talk with Gao, during which he sought to understand the specific nature of the changes that were coming to Yang-Xien. To his mild surprise, Collier found that Gao approved of them completely and sincerely; "fullheartedly" was how Gao himself characterized his acceptance. It was all very simple in his mind: Change must come; the problem was always to direct it toward beneficent and productive ends. Collier, Gao said, would have a great many important roles in the development of the commune. "What we have done in this village must be done now for others and on a larger scale. The same but, of course, not quite the same. It will be a great challenge. If *yi fanshen* was good and *er fanshen* even better, then *san fanshen* will be the best of all." Gao Ma-ting spoke what he truly believed, but he did not fully convince his former prisoner.

Gene Collier, while walking back from the house of Gao, stopped at the old well. The sky still held the colors left by the sun that had just fallen below the horizon. There was enough of a chill to vaporize the breath even though the spring schedule had been on the village bulletin board for a month. He sat down on the edge of the well wall and looked first up at the darkening sky in the east and then back over his shoulder into the well. The demands of the new commune would send him far beyond the Great Wall much of the time.

In his short life Gene Collier had made some incredible leaps and had been tossed in remarkable directions; he had chosen to alter a course for no apparent reason a number of times; he had strange new courses selected for him. He had been at various times pedestrian, romantic, unpredictable, self-punishing; but never before had his actions been the result of sheer panic. As he sat in the deepening gloom, there was panic within him and a raging, distorted fear not directed at anyone or anything, and more frightening for that very reason. The panic might have been mistaken for hysteria, but the man still had sufficient control over his reactions. He was like an experienced underwater swimmer who is trapped momentarily below the surface.

Collier's dominant feeling was rage; rage with himself for his inability to approach Fan Tai-cheng, rage with whatever force paralyzed him when he wished to move toward something he wanted to love. Other villagers could not tell, so restrained was the rage within Gene Collier. Perhaps if he were not so well controlled, he might have done something wild, uncalculated, even destructive, and it would have been exorcised, or at least dissipated for a while. For weeks Gene Collier functioned normally while the man within gasped unsuccessfully for air that was no longer available to him in Yang-Xien.

Mr. Bai's theory of Home—"He knows the value of home too well, and he is frightened by it"—would appear to have been finally corroborated in Collier's behavior. And now that the time had come for Collier to make a deeper commitment to this village and its people, he found himself incapable of such an act of faith.

Gene Collier told Gao of his decision to leave Yang-Xien and China. When he left Gao's house well after midnight, he was worried only about the specific effects of his decision, but his rage, fear, and panic already had begun to subside. The inner man, faced now with the serious problems of extricating himself from a very painful situation, breathed uneasily. But he breathed again.

Gao had told him that nothing could be assured; this was a political decision that had to be made on the highest levels, but Gao would work very actively on his behalf. When Gao told his wife about Collier's decision to leave, she sucked in her breath and her face looked as though it had just been slapped, but she requested no explanation.

Collier left the village in early September of 1960 on the predawn truck shipment to Yenan. All the villagers knew he was leaving but they did not know precisely when. They remained pleasant to the end. He was in the fields repairing two sluice gates the day before his departure. He left Yang-Xien as he had come; perhaps he had been a phantasm after all.

Only Gao saw him off, and the man Collier met in Korea eight and a half years before looked at him sympathetically, as though he were sending a dangerous relative to the asylum. All of Collier's clothes had been manufactured in Yang-Xien. The driver of the truck was the middle son of Madame Tian and the shipment consisted of many bushels of soy beans and unground millet. Very soon after the truck had passed through the main gate and turned toward the west, Collier heard the first bells of the morning in the distance.

PART IV

HOME

21

Last Campaigns

Gene Collier returned to America in a very different fashion from any he had ever experienced before. Unfortunately, he was too confused, too numbed by the shock that his most recent displacement had caused his psyche. When he was left by two expressionless Chinese officials at the Canadian consulate in Hong Kong, Collier most closely resembled an amnesiac who has been rescued from a short but debilitating life as a derelict. It was only a matter of minutes, however, before his benefactor came forward and began the rehabilitation process with just the sort of physical transformation that Gene Collier could respond to. Mr. Sweet, a small, tweedy, pipe-smoking man, introduced himself with a firm handshake and these words: "I'm the feller who's gonna take you home, son."

Then there was a short ride in an official-looking car, a clean hotel room, a hot bath, a shave, a long sleep, and few words—all arranged quietly by the blue-eyed, ruddy-faced Mr. Sweet. After dinner had been sent up to the room and Collier rediscovered his appetite, Mr. Sweet presented Collier with a good suit of clothes that fit perfectly and announced that they would be leaving in a few hours. "Promise not to ask you any questions 'til we arrive back in the good ole U.S. of A."

Mr. Sweet was indeed the perfect traveling companion; not only didn't he force conversation, he didn't even steal glances at Collier. Gene traveled first-class for the only time in his life, and his appreciation was so deep that he regretted the announcement of the plane's arrival in San Francisco.

Mr. Sweet possessed a wallet full of identification cards and certificates that enabled them to circumvent every obstacle. They even were directed through a side door of the Custom's Office by an official into a waiting limousine, in which they sped along a sweeping expanse of highway very close to the shore toward the span of the great bridge, the bay, the city of San Francisco. Mr. Sweet got out of the limousine first and held the door open for Collier. They walked up the marble steps together. Then it occurred, the event that brought Collier suddenly face to face with America in 1960. As he moved toward one of the many doors, it sprang open. By itself, as if anticipating Collier's wish, the building opened itself to its visitor. It was a "Welcome Home" he did not expect; in fact, he froze before the portal, unable to walk through with confidence. Mr. Sweet, who always spoke with clenched lips even when his pipe was not in his mouth, recognized the problem, said, "Rrrrmmmmmmm," and demonstrated the mechanism's safety by walking through unharmed. Collier followed, but more speedily and with a distrustful glance backward. The door which opened and closed itself was such a remarkable thing that it occupied Collier's thoughts for days.

It would have been extremely difficult for someone to have deduced that Mr. Sweet was a C.I.A. agent. He hardly ever seemed to be anything but merely present. Collier's first days in the United States were spent in a room with Mr.

Sweet, being interrogated, if that word is quite apt. Mr. Sweet would say a word, teeth clenched, such as "Prison-mmmmmmmm." And then, after a few biting puffs, say, "Mmmmmmm, 'bout how long?" And Collier would fill the void with everything he could remember.

" 'Bout this thing?" And Mr. Sweet produced a copy of the petition Collier signed in Pyongyang.

"Well, you know. They kind of had us there and it was easier all around to just cooperate."

"Mmmmmmmmm-torture?"

"Well, sort of . . ."

"Sort of?"

And Collier constructed an elaborate lie.

Frank Sweet spent five and one half days questioning Eugene Collier, Jr. His object was to make a number of determinations, the chief one being the extent to which Collier was a threat to the national security. Early on, he established Collier's personal innocence and soon after that his political harmlessness. Then he had to determine the extent to which the turncoat could be useful. This took considerably longer, but Mr. Sweet decided that Collier would simply be ineffectual in this area. He learned nothing new of a specific "intelligence" nature about Chinese national defense or even daily village life, even though Collier told almost everything he remembered. The information did, of course, have corroborative value. So Mr. Sweet bit, puffed, and mumbled, and Collier poured out words for five and one half days. The only things he did not mention were the whistling pigeons of Peking and the success of his irrigation systems.

When Mr. Sweet announced that Collier was free to leave, and then asked him where he wished to go, Gene discovered he had no alternative. "Back home to West Virginia, I guess," was what he heard himself say.

"Mmmmmmm. Somethin' might be done."

Everything was done. Shave. Haircut. Clothing. Travel

instructions. Plane tickets. Some of the money Collier was entitled to from the Army; more would be sent to him later. A ride out to the airport. A handshake from Mr. Sweet and the mumbled words, "Mmmmmmm prob'ly be in touch 'n a while."

Collier was an object of curiosity on the planes and in the terminals waiting for flights to arrive. He was so obviously vulnerable that the eyes of others sought him out as naturally as air rushes to fill a vacuum. To make matters worse, he did not read a newspaper or a book; he did not attempt to occupy himself in any way. He merely sat and stared and looked vulnerable.

Collier followed other passengers down walkways when flight numbers were called. He walked as though some internal part of him had been broken. Stewardesses singled him out for special consideration, not out of tenderness but because their trained eyes warned them of possible trouble. But the same protector who looks over innocents and drunks brought Gene Collier eventually to the Ohio County Airport in Wheeling, West Virginia. It was nearly midnight.

The most obvious irregularity of the plane's arrival was lost on Collier for a while; the airport was crowded with many thousands of people held back by a line formed by hundreds of burly policemen. Only by hearing the words of other passengers, the stewardesses, and the pilot on the plane's intercom did he begin to piece the information together: "Kennedy," "election," "arriving in Wheeling any moment." The explanation finally meant nothing to Gene Collier.

In the terminal the mob caught him and held him in its milling, throbbing movement. There was dance music coming from the building. A college kid thrust a pint of whiskey in his face, and as he swallowed the burning liquid, he became momentarily ill. The mob pushed him through the opened doors into the chill air against the chest of a state policeman, a soft-eyed bull of a man who pushed away Collier and the people behind him. "Kennedy" placards were lined up along a railing on the side of the police line. A small knot of people, the bands on their straw hats proclaiming "Nixon," were bunched around some of the other policemen.

As Collier was pulled back into the terminal building against his will, he heard an announcement: "Attention, please. The Kennedy party has been delayed leaving Washington. It is now expected to arrive one oh five ay em. We repeat, the Kennedy party. . . ." That phrase utterly confounded Collier.

The crowd thinned out very slightly in the next hour. The pushing and drinking continued. An area was cleared and young people began to dance to the music that pervaded the building, strange primitive dancing. Every available sleeping space was occupied by a sleeper in every conceivable position. Sometimes a single space was taken by two or three sleepers.

Collier drifted with the changing currents and looked closely at faces, which reacted rather strongly to the expressions he showed to them. The girls were all rather young and skinny, often speckled with pimples. Collier roasted under the burning, pitiless light of unrestrained neon.

At around 12:45 some people outside began to shout. "A light . . . in the sky . . . blinking light in the sky." A roar. The mob became a beast. Mad rush of bodies through the exits toward the landing area. Constant shouting. Confusion. Then Collier, taller than the people around him, saw the flickering light in the sky. "There," he said. The beast pushed against the state police, but the cage held.

All eyes followed the flickering light as it circled in the sky above the field and began to drop very slowly to the ground. Finally the plane rolled to a spot too far away. The beast pushed with new energy against the cage. The wheels eventually came to a halt. A ramp was rolled up and the door flung open. Then a stream of disheveled men emerged, most of them cranky, some of them flashing victory signs; one bald-headed man pointed up in the sky to the east.

"Shit, that's just the press plane," the guy next to Collier said. And he was right. But in the sky to the east Collier saw another winking light, and he shouted for people to look. The whole drama was played over again. The second plane, however, rolled to a halt much closer to the beast. Bright lights were turned on the open doorway. A head and shoulders appeared and then ducked back. Then a long pause with a shimmering white quality. John F. Kennedy appeared: tanned, confident. The beast, with one great lunge, knocked the police askew. Collier found himself running the fifty yards to the plane. He saw a woman fall in front of him but never saw her again.

The beast gathered itself up and stopped, panting at the foot of the ramp. Two burly men appeared behind Kennedy, swept around him and became his blockers down the steps and through the crowd. People lunged to grab him. Someone hooked a lapel and received a karate chop from one of the blockers. Kennedy's interference swept him safely under the plane and out of Collier's sight. And then, only moments before the frustrated beast could turn destructive in its confusion, Kennedy appeared again, sitting on the backrest in the rear of a tan convertible that materialized miraculously from behind the plane's tail section. He was still flanked by his blockers, but they were sitting on the rear seat, lower than he was. The automobile came around through the crowd, which parted reluctantly before it. Hands reached for Kennedy but they were brushed aside by his blockers.

He passed near Collier, whose thought was, how could a guy wear only a suit and not even show that he was cold. Collier, dressed similarly, was shivering.

Then Kennedy was gone and the beast was suddenly

there without a purpose. Almost immediately it transformed itself from beast to people, and shortly after that the people went in their various directions back to their own lives.

Collier, too, had been a part of the beast; and now he, by finding a taxicab that would take him to the bus station, sought his way back to Hundley, back to what once had been his life.

22

The Black Water

It had been ten years since Eugene Collier, Jr., of Hundley, West Virginia, traveled by bus, and the last time it had also been on a long, winding passage through the Appalachians. That last bus trip took him all the way to Augusta, Georgia, the beginning of a very great circle route.

Buses had changed a great deal during the decade; the one Gene Collier rode in now was a brand-new multitiered, electronic bubble. It glided rather than rolled; amber, green, and red lights glowed constantly and there was a faint but constant buzzing in the deodorized darkness. The vehicle had a hermetic, sanitary quality, like a laboratory or an operating room, and the only sensation of movement Collier felt was against the seat of his pants and in the pivoting of his head as the bus turned.

On that previous trip he had been engaged much of the time by the people outside and the land; farms, towns, mines, forests, the mountains themselves; shacks, cafés, gas stations, railroad depots, and junk yards; the school kids, cops, truckers, businessmen, old-timers. On that journey he had watched it all go rolling by, and he had seen his own face, the image of a man-child, part know-it-all, part damned fool, superimposed on the mountains, valleys, streams, horses, mules, people, and birds that were caught in the eye's mind. Through his present darkened window he saw very little. The moon, coming to fullness, was a lighter shade of blue in the glass; there was no color distinction between sky and mountains. This time the glass reflected the muted amber, green, and red lights and the shoulders, head, and cap of the calm and efficient bus driver, instead of his own face.

Most of the other passengers were soldiers, and most of them were young black men. A gray-haired lady across the aisle read under a spotlight; hers was the only naked light, and it made the darkness in which Collier sat seem safer by comparison. This was no human environment; and as such, it was ideal for Collier, for he was clothed in perfect isolation. An entire world of mechanical doors, anesthetic airplanes, and sanitary buses could not come soon enough for him.

Every thirty or forty minutes the bus would stop, the driver's voice from an overhead speaker would say, "New Martinsville" or "Pine Grove," and a person no one else could make out came down the darkened aisle and slipped off. After a while the names began to become familiar to Collier ("Middlebourne" and "Ashley" and "West Union"), towns where the Stork had played football on rocky fields, where he had made tackles and blocks that could be heard across the field by the big-boned men in the stands. Many a time there was a palpable hush when the Stork came in high for a tackle and nearly separated the runner's head from his shoulders as he knocked the ball from his hands. Specific plays flashed through Gene's mind: a ball that popped up in the air that he grabbed and ran with down the sideline just before it hit the ground; how he stepped out, trying to make his strides come out even with the ten-yard markers; how springy the path of grass was under his cleats, and how he whooped the whole seventy yards with a voice that didn't belong to him.

He must have dozed, although his sleeping thoughts were the same as his waking ones: a hodgepodge of football and travel impressions.

The sun came to the mountaintops first, overleaping the familiar river-valley road on which the vehicle glided. The tinted glass still left much indistinct, but Collier's eye was struck by something not quite right with the mountains; it was as though he were looking at one of those "What's-wrong-with-this-picture?" puzzles. But there couldn't be anything "wrong" with the mountains.

The bus slowed and the driver's voice said, "Highlands Square," and the area was bathed in sunlight. From a billboard huge eyes looked directly into his; they were familiar eyes. The gigantic face managed to look forceful and tender at the same time. The hairless head was at once efficient and vulnerable. The words were in red, white and blue on a gray background: (Red) WHEN THE GOING GETS TOUGH THE TOUGH GET GOING! (White) TRUST HIM—HE'S A WINNER AND YOU WILL BE TOO. (Blue) VOTE FOR THE MAN WHO ALWAYS HAS A PLAN . . . BEN A. CROWDER FOR GOVERNOR—VOTE! As the bus moved on toward Pleasants, that strong, enigmatic face on billboards dotted more of the landscape. Collier didn't know what he thought about coming back to this situation until he realized that he was chuckling. "If you can laugh at something that scary," he told himself, "I guess you'll be all right."

Riding again in the shadows of the valley, he was disturbed by the "What's-wrong-with-this-picture?" quality of the mountains; but now that he had something to laugh about, the disturbance became very minor, indeed. He dozed again.

It was the bus driver's own voice, not the electronic facsimile that woke him. "Hey, feller," said the perfect face after it had turned backward, "you gettin' off or not? This is Pleasants." And Collier rose, passing the gray-haired lady, still reading under the spotlight, and a black soldier who was asleep in his seat like a folded marionette. The sunlight at the door of the bus stunned him momentarily. "Pleasants," said the bus driver again, and Collier stepped off.

Into sunlight so bright that it blinded him for a while. He felt someone brush past him; he heard a woman's high-pitched voice and sounds of the bus pulling away behind him. Then he covered his eyes, Indian fashion, and began to make out a few details. He scanned the south side of Main Street and saw nothing but waves of yellow and red and brown and black earth, waves of earth where Popeye's Billiard Parlor, Mom's Malt Shop, the Town Hall, the park, Mr. King's Notions Store, the gas station, where the whole south side of Main Street used to be. He turned around and saw the north side. Everything seemed about as he remembered it, but it had all become faded and very brittle. The street was caked with dried mud and a heavy film of dust rested on everything. No cars, no people.

Bob's Café looked open, and someone was tending the grill. Gene Collier walked across the street, in through the screen door, and took a seat at the end of the counter. A fat woman dressed in a soiled black waitress uniform with the sleeves slit so her arms could fit through attended the grill. She said, with her back to Collier, "Take a while to heat up. Coffee's ready."

"Fine."

"Toast?"

"Fine."

Someone came up and sat down next to Collier. Gene noticed the large brown spots of age on the hands and the spit-shine on cracked, ox-blooded cordovans. "I saw you get off, young feller." The old man was bald, straight-backed, and dressed in a shiny blue suit. Gene figured that he must have cut himself shaving just a short while before because a moist dab of tissue on his chin had absorbed enough blood to be ready to pass the excess off in the form of a trickle. Collier couldn't take his eyes off the spot. "You're Stork Collier," the old man said, but Gene understood it to be a question.

"Uh huh."

"Well, we met quite a while ago, but I don't expect you'd remember." Gene leaned away a trifle in order to get a slightly fuller perspective, but still that bloody spot intruded. "Ed Lambert," the old man said, "used to write sports for the *Speculator*. Millie, this here young feller was the best damned lineman ever to come out of these hills." Millie did not turn around. She didn't even check him out in the greasy mirror.

The two men at the counter shook hands. "Stoppin' off on your way up to see your father?" Before Gene could respond, Ed Lambert said, "Sure did pay a lot of union dues while he was workin', so it's fair to expect they'll treat them all right when they have to go up there."

The confusion in Gene's eyes seemed to Ed Lambert like the beginning of anger, so he added, "But I hear they take real good care of the patients." Then he rambled: "Ain't no one's fault. After your mother died and your sisters moved on out, it wasn't long before your father couldn't make it on his own anymore. I only hope to God I got a place as good to go to when I can't look after myself anymore."

Gene's mind pieced together the information quickly— mother dead, sisters moved on, father in a rest home. "How long'll it take me to get up there?" he asked absently.

Lambert's eyes registered mild surprise, but he said, "Oh, it's about an hour to Barringtown, right, Millie?" No reaction from the woman.

"What time does the bus come through?"

Millie said, "Noon or thereabouts. Same bus you come in on, going back the other way."

Gene tried to imagine what the meeting with his father would be like, but he had trouble even reconstructing his face as it used to be.

The old man was talking: ". . . after that I lost track of you. Knew you got hurt down there playin' for Crowder. Wasn't he a hell of a coach, ole Ben?" Collier's mind continued racing. "But where you been?"

"Oh, around. Army."

"Played any football?"

"No, not really."

Millie came with the toast and coffee.

"How d'you like the way the town's changed," the old man said, and he drummed his knuckles on the edge of the counter. Gene saw Millie's back stiffen.

"What's happened here?"

"You happen to be talkin' to just about the only man in this town who can really answer that question. Fact is, I'm writin' a book about it."

"Mud slides," Millie said, "mud slides and floods. Half the town's already been washed away. That mountain's goin' to just come down right on top of us, and if it don't, the black water'll wash us all away."

"Erosion," corrected Ed Lambert. And he proceeded to talk his book to Gene Collier, explaining technical terms— "spoil bank," "unstable rock," "overburden"—in very great detail.

"Stuff's killin' us," Millie said, "an' this ole fool wants to make sure he's got all the names spelled right. They tore out the trees, so now everythin' just rolls down here, mud slides, the black water, the whole damned mountain."

"Can't you make them stop?"

"They have stopped," Millie said. "They stripped that whole damned mountain and moved on after another one. More coffee?"

Ed Lambert then finished telling about his book. He would try to make it an objective study of a complex tech-

nological, economic, and social problem. Millie brought
them both some coffee in order to shut Lambert up.

"How could I get a taxi to take me out to Hundley?"
Collier said.

"Ain't none," Lambert answered between sips.

"Well, is there someone who'll take me out? I'd like to
get a look at the old place before I move on. I'll pay."

"There ain't no Hundley. Not for two years," Lambert
said.

"Black water," said Millie while scrambling up two eggs
for herself.

"Water just built up behind the ridge line until one day
it broke through and washed the place out. Everyone was
evacuated in plenty of time," Lambert explained.

"The black water," Millie said, and the eggs sizzled on
the hot butter.

"Would there be any way for me to get out there just to
look around, see what it's like?"

"Well, I'd be glad to take you out as far as the old mine
road. Yessir, Millie, this here young man was about the best
high school lineman I ever saw come out of these hills. Only
one who could touch him was Earl Plumb—he was a great
one too; got killed in Normandy back in '44."

Again Gene Collier's mind began to race with questions
and he suddenly had trouble swallowing his toast.

A clock whose hands said "Coca" and "Cola" showed
that it wasn't yet seven-thirty. "If you'd drop me off," he
said to Ed Lambert, "close as you can get, I'd be able to
walk back in time to catch that noon bus."

"Seems so."

Gene took a half-dollar piece out of his pocket and
placed it on the counter between the two cups of coffee. A
mail truck rolled by on the street outside, producing a deep
echoing sound in the rear of Bob's Café. But Gene was
unable to hurry Ed Lambert. Finally Collier stood and announced his intention to walk, and Lambert said, "Hold on,

hold on, young feller, nothin's goin' to go away up there."

"Hah," said Millie.

Lambert drove a '58 Plymouth with great tail fins that Collier, on first glance, thought might be an amphibious car. As he approached it, he noticed that its rear threw pointed shadows fifteen feet across Main Street. No one on the street, no other cars.

Lambert swung south off Main Street onto Mine Road #1, which for about five hundred yards was the chuck-holed obstacle course Collier remembered. Lambert nego-tiated it proudly, at least as well as the school-bus drivers had ten years before. Off to the left and right, not ten yards from the road, were, as far as the eye could see, those rigid waves of earth, much larger now than they had first ap-peared, and though they varied in color from yellow to black, something about the texture indicated the same life-lessness. Up ahead, in the form of a huge, gray, contoured birthday cake, was Mount Hundley; the rest of her was below in the form of waves of dead earth. On the level nearest the top of the mountain Collier could see some firs, left seemingly as a final insult. They appeared to be the only trees anywhere.

Lambert stopped. "Can't go much farther. Bad for the car."

"Yes. Sure."

"Say, you wouldn't mind if I round up some of the boys, some of the fellers who used to remember the ole Stork, would you?"

"Well, you see, I'll be leavin'."

"No trouble."

They left it at that. Collier slammed the door and threw Ed Lambert a "thanks" with a combination wave and sa-lute. Lambert backed up before he found enough room where he could turn around.

Within fifty yards Mine Road #1 began to rise and fall with the same regularity as the rest of the land, and a few yards after that it was composed of the same dead earth. Collier walked over the waves of land. Almost immediately he realized that he would not be able to find the site of his house, for not only had it been buried and moved, there wasn't a single reference point that had not been shifted or obliterated. He had hoped to find a place where he could remember the mountain looking a certain way, but they had changed the mountain. He walked on.

As he descended a particularly steep decline, his eyes caught a tree, a scrub fir, growing out of the earth at a strange angle. It was poised perfectly between tipping over from its own weight and still being able to maintain its root system and continue to grow. Collier angled over to it. The earth at the base of the tree was cracked, in some places so deeply that Collier could see a number of the tree's roots. He began to kick some of the reddened surface earth into the cracks. Suddenly he looked up, certain he would see a bird, but there was none.

He shook the trunk of the tree, no thicker than a small woman's thigh, and it seemed to be almost firm enough to root. It must have been tossed around quite a bit before it found this spot.

Ed Lambert's words came to him then: "Ain't no one's fault." His father's face began to come together in his mind.

Gene Collier placed his hands around the tree and suddenly, violently shook it with all his might. Then he backed off from it on the downhill side, crouched, and charged at it; when he hit it with his shoulder, chest, and arm tucked against his body, he heard a "Huh" being forced from his lips. He also felt the tree yield slightly. Again he charged it. Again the "Huh." And again it yielded.

There, near where he remembered living as a boy, the man sent his body hurtling against the small tree, and by degrees he began to budge it out of the earth. But the tree did not yield easily. The man began to tire. Nowhere was it written how many thrusts and how many "Huhs" expelled from his throat would be required in order to rip out that particular tree.

Collier, out of balance with anger and fear, began to fall to his knees after each blow, but he always struggled up and charged once again, sometimes feebly and sometimes with new strength. His face looked like that of a crazy man.

Only once did he rest. It was after a strong charge. He fell to his knees, his arms around the tree.